KAYLA'S TRICK

THE TOUR SERIES - BOOK 6

JEAN GRAINGER

CHAPTER 1

*A*na groaned in her sleep as Conor lay awake beside her in the dark. The wind and lashing rain that had been relentless all night was beating the windows, but he was warm and cosy beside his wife. The wild storm had been forecast, but it sounded even more violent than the predictions had suggested. He hoped the hotel was bearing up. The old buildings had suffered a little during the last storm; the ocean had overtopped the sea wall that bounded the castle on the south side and flooded one of the stables and a greenhouse. Poor Artur had been so upset, as all his lovely seedlings were washed away in salt water, but the insurance had paid out and now all was well again.

The baby was due in ten days' time, but it couldn't come a moment too soon. Conor was so excited to have a new addition to the family, but more than that, he longed for an end to Ana's pain.

Her back was giving her so much trouble, worse than when she was carrying the twins, and though she didn't complain, he could see how hard this pregnancy was. The oncologist had warned them that a pregnancy after cancer and its treatment wasn't without complications, and she was right. Ana had been nauseous since the start, and it wasn't just in the morning either – it went on all day. Everyone

1

assured him it would stop after the first trimester, but it didn't. Ana was so excited about this baby – they both were – but sometimes as he watched her struggle to cope, he wondered if it had been a mistake. He would never voice such opinions to Ana though; she was determined to deliver the healthiest, happiest baby in the world.

Moving was hard with her big bump now, and she settled into a more comfortable position, throwing her arm across his chest. Even in sleep she was restless.

He stroked her hair and she seemed to relax. His heart went out to his poor girl – as if she'd not had enough to deal with having had the twins and then breast cancer. They were both astounded and delighted to discover she was expecting another baby, but it had been a very difficult nine months.

Joe and Artie did their best around the house to be helpful, though at ten years old, their efforts often resulted in more mess than anything else. At least Ana's mother was on hand. But he was really looking forward to the baby being delivered safely and Ana back to her old self. Both the doctor and the physiotherapist seemed sure she would be fine once the pressure of carrying the baby was taken off.

He tried to visualise his son or daughter. He and Ana had decided they wouldn't find out the gender of the baby; the twins wanted it to be a surprise, and they didn't trust themselves not to let something slip if they knew. Conor didn't mind; the idea that he would have another child was wonderment enough.

He checked his watch in the darkness. It was almost four a.m. It was no good; he wasn't going to fall back to sleep. Gently, so as not to wake Ana, he got up. He figured he'd go downstairs, have a coffee and catch up on some work. It was late November, and they had a big Christmas event planned at the hotel.

BUSINESS WAS BOOMING. They'd even had to turn down a big offer from a film company that wanted to make some TV show in the castle as it would have been too disruptive. So many hotels would jump at business like that in the off season, but the five-star resort was full to capacity most nights of the year. It was exciting and gratifying but also such a huge responsibility. There was hardly a family in the area that didn't have someone working for him, and he knew how much the locality needed Castle Dysert to continue to be successful. It was great but margins were tight, and so it was a constant struggle to stay in the black despite the bookings.

Several tour groups had booked in from the USA as well as many families who decided that slaving over a turkey was a thing of the past. A more affluent Ireland meant some people could go to a five-star castle instead of cooking.

Castle Dysert was going to look amazing. Olga had found an interior design firm in Galway, and the owner had all sorts of ideas. From what he'd seen so far, the transformation of the hotel into a winter wonderland was going to be nothing short of breathtaking. It had cost a fortune, but the brochure produced using advanced photo technology that showed the hotel decorated had done the trick and they were booked out.

It struck him as kind of sad that people would want to spend Christmas in a hotel. He would never want to be anywhere at Christmas except at home with Ana and the boys, his parents-in-law, Artur and Danika, and his own father, Jamsie. The new baby would be here this Christmas, and already the twins had asked Santa for something for their new sibling to be left under the tree. But he was glad that Castle Dysert was providing the most luxurious Christmas anyone could imagine for those without a family.

He'd spent the last week interviewing Santa Clauses, a hilarious task, and was confident he'd settled on someone as close to the big man as it was possible to find in West Clare. For many Irish hotels, the winter was a time of barely scraping by, but his second in command, an earnest but dedicated young Icelandic woman called Olga Jakob-dóttir, refused to accept that people wouldn't want to enjoy Castle Dysert all year long. She quite rightly pointed out that nobody came to Ireland for the weather anyway, and so the fact that it was cold and dark during the winter months was a positive when you had a luxury castle with roaring fires, comfy bars and restaurants and, when it was dry, a beautiful ocean shore to walk by. She convinced him to run all sorts of programmes, and she had been right. They were a triumph. There had been a murder mystery weekend with a medieval theme over the Halloween break, and they ran a cookery retreat – though Chef nearly had a stroke at having guests in his kitchen – a hill-walking and storytelling festival and all manner of outdoor things. So all in all, the winter programme was a great success.

Costs were higher of course. Heating alone was astronomical, and preservation orders on the centuries-old castle meant it was hard to insulate retroactively. Insurance too was crippling; the courts gave out ridiculously high judgements, and the result was many of his fellow hospitality colleagues found themselves facing ruin in the face of huge compensation claims. Theirs was a staff-heavy business too, and he prided himself on paying his employees properly, so the wages were higher than any other hotel in Ireland. But it was worth it. The 7,000 five-star ratings on Trip Advisor spoke volumes. People very rarely failed to mention how welcoming and professional the staff of Castle Dysert were. It felt good to be able to keep everyone on all year in what was normally a seasonal business, and he heard more than once how people who might otherwise have emigrated had now settled in the area because of the guaranteed work. While Castle Dysert was doing well, staying on top was a bit like shoving a rock uphill, but they were faring better than most.

He crept downstairs, past the boys' room and the room where his father was sleeping. Jamsie had come down to help out with the boys in the last weeks of the pregnancy. He and Ana were the best of friends, and she loved having him around. The boys adored their granda. They had Artur and Danika as well, and Conor often marvelled at how lucky his boys were to grow up surrounded by so much love. It was in such contrast to his own lonely childhood.

He went into the big warm kitchen and made a cup of coffee and opened his laptop. He'd received an email from Liz, his sister. He'd never even known he had a sister – well, a half-sister – until Jamsie turned up after a four-decade absence. Jamsie had finally admitted he'd left his family because he'd got a girl from their town pregnant, and Liz was the result. Jamsie and the young woman soon parted ways, but Jamsie insisted on staying in his daughter's life. This was something Conor found a bitter pill to swallow at first, that his father was adamant not to lose his daughter but seemingly could walk away from his sons effortlessly, but they'd had it out. Jamsie knew he'd messed up. He was embarrassed and felt that he could do nothing for his sons anyway, so it was best to let them alone. It was a rubbish excuse and Jamsie knew it, but he'd regretted his decision all of his life and was doing his best to make up for it now.

At first Conor had had no interest in meeting his sister, but she reached out and on a whim he invited her and her fiancée over to visit. Liz was a vivacious, confident woman, who last year married Damien from Belfast. She and Conor hit it off immediately, both good-naturedly teasing their father Jamsie about his love of flash cars. From the first day they met, it was easy between them and they both knew Jamsie was both relieved and happy to see their blossoming friendship.

On that first visit, they talked a lot – about Conor's mother and his brother, Gerry, who had died, about Liz's mother – and they felt a connection neither of them had anticipated. Now they kept in touch regularly, and Ana and the boys loved her and Damien.

He opened the email.

Hi Conor,

Greetings from a stinking-hot South Africa. Damien and I are both fine, though this volunteering business is not for the faint-hearted. We've set up a vaccination station and are administering as many vaccines as possible. Damien spent all of yesterday training nurse's aides to do injections, so we are getting through lots of people, but the queues are out the door. It would break your heart. Medicin sans Frontières are doing such tremendous work here – it would make you want to up sticks and come out here full time, to be honest. We just might. My mother will have a canary, of course, but that's just an added bonus!

Anyway, just checking in. I'm assuming I'm not an auntie again yet. Dad texts me a few times a day with the updates, and he's even using words like cervix and engaged. Your Ana is certainly making a modern man of him.

Give her and the boys a massive hug from us, and we're waiting for the good news.

Lots of love,

Liz and Damien

Xxx

Conor smiled. He was so proud of her. She and Damien were both doctors. They had no children, and it was hardly likely at this stage; she said she didn't want any. They volunteered every year for a few weeks to alleviate suffering in some of the most poverty-stricken places on earth. He wouldn't be one bit surprised if she gave up their life in London and their fancy practice for a life in South Africa.

He hit 'reply'.

Hi Liz,

Great to hear from you and glad to hear you and Damien are doing well. Yes, all waiting here for the little O'Shea to make an appearance. Poor Ana is really in trouble with her back, and she is ready for this all to be over.

I can just imagine you living out there, and if it's what you want, then you should just do it. None of us are getting out of here alive, as they say. The boys had to do a project in school on someone they admire and they did it on you and Damien, so you are now adorning the walls of St Edmund's National School. If that isn't the big time, I don't know what is!

I'll hopefully speak to you soon, once our son or daughter joins us.

Love, Conor x

A loud crashing noise outside startled him, and he got up to see the boys' goalpost hurl across the garden and hit the garage door. Lightning lit up the sky as the thunder rumbled ominously almost at the same time. The storm was directly overhead. He was in pyjama bottoms and a t-shirt and debated whether to leave the goalpost where it was until morning or go out into the torrential rain and retrieve it.

The stillness of the kitchen was shattered by his ringtone, his phone vibrating loudly on the table beside his laptop. Anxious not to wake Ana, he reached out and grabbed the handset, answering the call.

'Conor, where are you?' It was his wife.

'I'm just downstairs, love, are you –'

'Baby is coming!' she gasped.

'OK, don't move!' He hung up and bounded upstairs, taking the steps two at a time.

He knocked on Jamsie's door and went in to wake him. 'Ana's in labour. We need to go.'

Jamsie sat up. 'No problem. Good luck, son. Give her my love and don't worry about a thing – I'll manage everything here.'

'Call the hospital and tell them we're coming, will you? And text Katherine – tell her I won't be in.'

'Right away.' Jamsie smiled and waved Conor out. 'Off you go.'

'Thanks.'

Ana was standing in their bedroom, her hands gripping the brass rail at the end of their king-sized bed. He could see she was in the middle of a contraction. Wordlessly, she moved to him, resting her hands on his shoulders. He rubbed her back gently as the pain subsided.

'I woke, and my waters, and then pains,' she managed.

'OK, how far apart are they?' He looked at his watch.

'I don't know,' she said, wincing as she moved. It was hard to know if it was her back or a contraction, but he decided just to get her into the car. Pulling off his pyjamas and grabbing a pair of jeans and a sweatshirt, he dressed in record time, shoving his feet, sockless, into runners.

He helped her into dry pyjamas and kissed her nose, giving her a wink. 'OK, darling, let's get you to hospital, eh?' He put his arm around her and helped her downstairs.

'My bag.' She gasped.

'It's already in the car. I put it there two days ago.'

Conor carried her out, throwing his coat over her to try to keep her dry. The wind was so strong that it was hard to remain upright, but the car was parked close to the door and he managed to get her on the passenger seat without her getting soaked. He was drenched himself but didn't care.

He jumped in and took off down the main road. The wipers were working overtime and the visibility was very poor as the relentless rain flooded the road before them. Several times Conor had to take a chance and drive through a flood, each time praying the car didn't stall. Beside him, Ana gasped and gripped the seatbelt.

The dips and twists on the narrow country roads did nothing to help Conor's efforts at speed. Ana gripped the door handle, or Conor's arm, depending whichever way the car had to turn, as he drove. A tree had come down in the storm, and Conor exhaled in frustration, terrified for a moment that he'd have to turn back, but thankfully there was enough room to skirt around it. Normally hearing the branches scrape the side of his car would have made him wince, now he couldn't care less. The screeching wind buffered the heavy vehicle, and the rain pelted relentlessly down, the din making conversation impossible, even if Ana could manage it.

'Almost there darling,' he soothed as another contraction gripped her.

Finally, mercifully, the lights of the hospital came into view. He realised his knuckles were white he was gripping the steering wheel so tightly.

He stopped at the set down, then parked as close to the door as he could.

He gently lifted Ana out, and again covered her with his coat.

'It's OK, pet. I've got you.' He held her close, ran for the hospital and carried her into the reception area.

'Conor.' Her eyes were bright with tears. 'Don't leave me.'

'Of course I won't, darling.'

'Welcome, Ana. We're all ready for you.' A smiling midwife appeared, and her soothing tones relaxed Conor. Ana was in the right place, and these people knew what to do. She was put in a wheelchair and she gripped his hand.

The porter asked Conor to move his car to the car park, explaining where he could find Ana once that was done.

'Two minutes, I promise.' He let go of Ana's hand just as another contraction took over her body. He marvelled, not for the first time, at the strength of women.

'Go – hurry!' Ana said through gritted teeth.

He dumped the car in the first space he came to. He had a feeling it was going to be quick this time.

As he ran back to the hospital, his stomach was in knots, his mind a maelstrom of emotions: the excitement of meeting his child, combined with the fear all men face at watching their children enter the world, and mostly the feelings of awe at what his wife was capable of.

Thankfully the hospital was quiet, and he was directed to the delivery suite immediately. He was shown where to wash his hands and then was led into the little room. The obstetrician was examining Ana as he entered, and she greeted him warmly.

'It's showtime, all right, no messing about with Ana.' Elaine Kinsella was a young gynaecologist, and Conor and Ana had liked her straight-talking ways enormously.

'So, Ana.' She took off her gloves and spoke directly to her. 'You are almost nine centimetres dilated, so I reckon we are almost good to go. How are you feeling?'

Ana had said that she didn't want to have drugs if possible, but Conor wasn't sure that was such a great idea. Childbirth looked excruciating. But she was adamant. She'd been practising hypno-birthing and had discussed it with Elaine last week, who was very much in favour of it. Minimum intervention, let nature do its work was Ana's philosophy, and Elaine agreed completely. As per his wife's request, the lights were low, a hypno-birth track was playing softly in the background, and the only people in the room were Ana, Conor and Elaine. Ana had put plenty of high-energy snacks in her bag, balls she made herself with dates and cacao and seeds, all covered in dark chocolate, as well as bottles of home-made kombucha. To Conor, the drink was the most vile concoction imaginable, but Ana loved it. It was apparently very good for you, but he'd take her word for that.

He watched in awestruck amazement as Ana set about giving birth to their child. She listened to the soundtrack, and she seemed entirely focused on the task at hand. She was calm and determined and met each surge mindfully. She spoke in Ukrainian to the baby, telling it how welcome it was, how much they were looking forward to meeting it. Conor had learned enough of her language over the years to understand her most of the time, though speaking it was still very difficult for him.

She walked around the room, wearing one of his old t-shirts – she said it made her feel safe and loved – resting against him when she needed to. He gently massaged her back as she straddled a chair, which seemed to give her some relief, and when the surges were intense, she gripped his shoulders with such strength, he knew he'd be bruised tomorrow, not that he cared. He wanted so desperately to support her, to be everything she needed him to be.

The time passed quietly, both of them focused on the job at hand. He gave her snacks and drinks and cooled her down with a wet flannel when she perspired. In between surges, they even laughed a bit. They'd attended classes before the birth, and he had clear instructions about what Ana wanted and what his role was. It felt good to know what to do and to be a part of it.

Elaine examined Ana once more and declared that it was time to push.

After a very short time – at least it seemed so to Conor – Ana gave birth while kneeling on the bed, her arms resting on his chest. The baby's cry was the loudest sound in the room as he and his wife clung to each other, tears running down both their faces.

Elaine announced, 'Well, congratulations, Ana and Conor, you have a lovely little girl.'

Conor settled Ana into a more comfortable position. The shirt she wore clung to her, wet with perspiration. He propped her up on some pillows and gave her a drink.

Without wrapping her in anything, Elaine placed the baby on Ana's chest under her t-shirt, and Conor gazed at his wife and daughter in astonished adoration.

The little baby rested calmly over Ana's heart as her mother kissed her head. Conor couldn't take his eyes off her perfect little face.

'We'll do all the weighing and checks in a little while, but for now

I'll leave you to get acquainted with this little lady,' Elaine whispered, then quietly left them.

Ana cuddled the baby close as Conor wrapped his arms around both of them. Never before, even with the twins, he thought, did he feel such an overwhelming sense of love and the need to protect.

'She's so beautiful.' Conor couldn't take his eyes off her.

'Isn't she? I hoped for a girl, but I honestly thought she was a boy. I can't believe we have a little girl.' The wonder on Ana's face was like a light inside.

The baby opened her eyes, which were a dark, almost navy blue. She had a mop of dark hair, not blond like her brothers.

'Hello, sweetheart, welcome to the world,' Conor whispered. Her little fist was up beside her face, and when Conor put his pinkie finger on her hand, she opened her fist and wrapped her tiny fingers around his.

'This is your daddy, and he's the best daddy anyone could have,' Ana whispered.

Conor felt that his cheeks were wet once more and realised he was crying again. 'What will we call her?' he asked.

'I think we should call her Lily, after your mother.' Ana stroked her daughter's cheek.

Conor swallowed the lump in his throat. Ana had never met his mam, but he spoke of her often. Ana had found an old photo he had of his mother and him, taken when he was about five, and got it fixed up by some old photo expert; now it was in a frame on their coffee table. The boys called her Granny Lily and referred to her often. His mam's face swam before his eyes; she actually looked like his daughter – dark hair, dark-blue eyes. She'd had a gentle, quiet disposition and a heart of gold. How delighted she would be with grandchildren.

'Hello, Lily O'Shea. You are so welcome. Wait till your madcap brothers see you – they'll be thrilled to bits.' He caressed his daughter's tiny head.

The porter arrived and wheeled Ana and Lily, bed and all, back to Ana's private room, and Elaine and Conor followed. The sun had come up, and though the weather was overcast and grey, the storm seemed to have abated.

Elaine took Lily off to weigh her, measure her and check her over. Conor kissed Ana and then helped her shower and change into clean pyjamas. She was sore and very tired but so elated that their baby was here and healthy, and nothing could bring her down. As they were in the bathroom, the staff came in and prepared the room. Conor helped Ana back to the bed with clean sheets; tea and toast were waiting for her on the tray.

As she sipped her tea and munched the hot buttered toast ravenously, Conor thought to himself that he'd never loved her more.

'Here we go. She's perfect,' Elaine said as she walked into the room and returned the baby to her mother's arms. Lily was dressed in a white sleepsuit and wrapped in a fluffy blanket, and she began happily feeding at Ana's breast.

The pain that had been on his wife's face for the last nine months miraculously was gone, and it was like his old Ana was back. She looked adorable, with her wet blond hair cut in her signature pixie cut. Her green eyes filled with love as she gazed adoringly at her daughter.

'Isn't she perfect?' she whispered. 'I can't take my eyes off her. We made her. It's incredible.'

'Well, you did all the work.' Conor smiled. 'And yes, she's perfect, and so beautiful, just like her mammy.'

'You better text Jamsie and my parents – they will be worried.' Ana kissed Lily's head once more.

'I will in a minute.' He too was mesmerised by his daughter. But he knew the family would be on tenterhooks, so eventually he dragged himself away though he didn't want his wife or daughter out of his sight.

He stepped outside and switched his phone on. He had two text messages, the first from his father.

Hope all going well, Son. Give Ana our love. Boys fine.

The second was from Katherine.

Call when you can.

His brow furrowed. The message was sent two hours ago, and Katherine would have known by then he had gone in with Ana. It was unlike her to call him knowing that.

He texted Jamsie first.

Lily O'Shea is the most beautiful baby in the world. She's perfect and her mammy is doing great. Talk soon.

Then he rang Katherine.

She answered on the first ring. 'Conor.'

'Hi, Katherine. Ana had a baby girl, and they're both perfect,' he said to his oldest friend.

'Oh, thank God for that, Conor, I'm so happy. But – and I'm so sorry to bother you with this – we have a problem.'

'What's up?' he asked. Nothing could bring him down.

'The sea overtopped the wall and then swept it away. Conor, the castle is flooded. We're in about a foot of water here.'

Conor thought for a moment. He had worried something like this could happen, but even this bad news couldn't dampen his spirits. 'Oh, well, look, don't worry. Get anyone who's on-site already to do their best to save what we can, and I'll be over in a while.'

'Will do. We're lucky we have so many staff in the residence, and I was working late last night so decided to stay rather than drive home in the storm, so we're all here, and Carlos and Olga too. Don't worry.' Conor could hear the concern in her voice though. 'And give Ana our best wishes.'

'I will. See you soon.' Conor ended the call, quickly rang his parents in law to tell them the good news, and went back to Ana. 'Everyone sends love.' He sat beside her and kissed her head.

Ana had finished feeding the baby. 'Will you take her?' she asked him.

'Of course I will, but God, Ana, she's tiny. I can't believe Artie and Joe were ever that small.' Conor was suddenly terrified he'd break her.

Ana grinned. 'You were afraid you would break them too, and now look how you throw them around and always with the wrestling.'

Conor took a deep breath as Ana passed Lily into his arms. Though she was a healthy seven pounds, she felt so fragile and tiny.

He settled her in the crook of his arm and took her over to the window. The sun had come up while they were in the delivery suite.

He bent his head and breathed in the lovely baby scent of her, gently kissing her downy head. She opened her eyes and gazed at him.

'Welcome to the world, my darling girl,' he whispered.

CHAPTER 2

*D*anika and Artur arrived and were enthralled with their new grandchild. Conor pulled Artur aside and filled him in on what Katherine had told him.

'How bad?' Artur asked. His old lined face looked stricken. He and Danika had lived most of their lives in Ukraine, but a few years ago Artur lost his job and the apartment that came with it so Conor arranged to bring them to Ireland. Artur taught himself English, ably assisted by a six-year-old Joe at the time, and began working as a handyman at the hotel. From the outset, Conor could see Artur was an invaluable asset – he could grow anything and fix anything, and he seemed to know how to solve any manner of maintenance issues. Conor had promoted him to maintenance manager, and he took his career very seriously.

'Bad enough, I'd say. The sea wall disintegrated. Katherine said there was a foot of water on the ground floor.'

'Where is it come in?' Artur wondered.

'In the front door, as well as up through the floor, last I heard.'

'We go now. Ana is all right with her mother.'

Conor nodded. Loath as he was to leave them, he thought he'd better go and see the damage. Ana was sleeping and Danika was holding Lily, so they slipped out.

As they pulled out of the hospital car park, Conor pressed the button on the steering wheel that connected his phone.

'Hey, Siri. Call hotel,' he commanded.

'Calling hotel,' the metallic voice responded, and within seconds Katherine answered.

'How are things now?' Conor asked.

'Bad, Conor, though the water is subsiding now as the tide is going out.' Katherine's voice reverberated around the car's interior. 'We are six inches deep here in reception, and the extension is under a foot already. We're moving as much as we can, but the guests and everything... Some of them are even helping. The toilets are flooding in the bar, and there's water coming up through the plugholes in the kitchen and in the ladies' cloakroom.'

'What did the fire brigade say?' Conor asked.

'The engines are at a house fire in Tulla, an hour and a half away at least – there are trees down everywhere after the storm. They said they'd try to send us a pump, but... There's no sign of it yet anyway.'

'Did you wake Olga?'

'Yes, she's here, coordinating everyone.'

'Can you put her onto me? Thanks, Katherine,' Conor said as he navigated the winding coast road. To their left the Atlantic was pounding the shore, the spray covering the car frequently. The run-off from the sodden fields that sloped gently to the sea had nowhere to go, resulting in huge puddles on the narrow roads. Conor had to drive through deeper and deeper floods, each time hoping the water wouldn't get into the engine.

'Hello, Conor,' Olga said. 'I'm trying to get as much as we can up out of the water, but I'm afraid we've a big problem on our hands. I've sent some of the lads to the sheds. They said there were sandbags there, so they're gone down in the golf carts to bring them up. But the water came up through the flagstones, up the toilets and sinks too. We've turned the electricity off for safety.'

'OK. There's nothing we can do now but wait for the tide to go out. Focus on getting carpets, rugs, anything like that, up high…'

'What about breakfast? The kitchen is under water now. Chef came in, but he is wet to above his knees.'

'OK…' Conor thought rapidly. 'Set up a tea and coffee station in the upstairs ballroom. Get the kitchen staff to secure the kitchen as best they can, electrical stuff up out of the water and so on. Ask Chef if he can get a continental breakfast going up there. I'm about ten minutes away.'

'Right. See you soon.' Olga was normally unflappable, but it was clear she was rattled.

Katherine came back on the line. 'More importantly, how are Ana and the baby?' she asked gently, in a tone rarely heard by anyone but her nearest and dearest.

'Ah, she's great, they both are. We're calling her Lily after my mam. Thanks, Katherine. I'm almost there with Artur. It never rains but it pours, eh?' He tried to laugh.

'No water jokes, please. Let's just save our hotel.'

Conor smiled and ended the call. All he wanted was to get back to the hospital to Ana and Lily, but he needed to be at the castle, at least for a while. Olga, Carlos and Katherine did most of the heavy lifting with regards to the day-to-day management, but they needed to see his face now. Everyone looked to him. He was the manager – and the owner now thanks to his father's investment last year to buy the whole business outright – but Katherine's steely efficiency was the backbone of the operation.

She hung up without saying goodbye.

CHAPTER 3

*A*s he stood in rubber boots in an unrecognisable reception area later that morning, Conor tried to remain upbeat. The ground floor was devastated, though the floodwater had subsided. The sea wall that had formed part of the curtain wall of the castle was totally gone. The combination of the intense rain from the storm, a very high tide and waves that were fifteen feet on the face had combined to wreak havoc.

The staff had gathered in the ballroom upstairs for a well-deserved break. Almost everyone who could get to the castle had, and they had been working hard all morning. Conor had ordered a break and sent out for some breakfast rolls from the local shop. Their own kitchen on the ground floor was totally out of commission. At least they'd managed to reaccommodate the guests to other hotels in the county. The clean-up was going to be a Herculean task. More wet weather was forecast, so they might only have a temporary reprieve from the slowly receding floodwater.

'Well?' Katherine stood beside him, having ushered everyone else upstairs.

"Well what?' Conor sighed.

'What do we do now?' she asked quietly.

He plunged his hands into the pockets of his jacket. The ground floor was under a few inches of water still. The antique rugs and furniture had been moved upstairs, the two suits of armour as well, but the carpet in the bar and all the upholstery were ruined. The restaurant, with its beautiful silk wallpaper and polished parquet floor, was probably also beyond saving, and the damage to the electrics… Well, that had yet to be determined.

'I've absolutely no idea, but keep that to yourself, will you?' He smiled and gave her a wink.

'Conor, be serious for once in your life, for goodness' sake. This is a catastrophe! We could lose the hotel.'

Conor turned to face his old friend and confidante. She had stood by him through thick and thin, and though she came across as hard as nails, he knew she saw him as family and Castle Dysert as home. Her upset was manifest as bad temper.

He towered over her as he placed his hands on her thin shoulders. She was close to sixty years old, and she looked it. Her hair was the same as it always was, dark and tied back in a forbidding bun, and he could see the worry in her eyes. Despite the circumstances she was impeccably dressed in her uniform – black skirt and jacket, white blouse, no make-up, no frills. Her only concession to necessity was she too was wearing rubber boots and her winter jacket. The heating had gone wallop as well since the boiler was in the basement, and the castle was so cold they could see their breath. Katherine's husband, Jimmy, an American who'd come to Ireland on holidays a few years ago and had somehow got through her glacial exterior – he was devoted to her and she to him – was upstairs with the others and had been helping all morning.

'I'm as serious as a heart attack, Katherine. I suppose the insurance will pay out, and that we'll have to close until everything is put back as it was, but how long that will take or the extent of the damage…well, I've no idea. I'm waiting on the insurance company to call me back. They'll presumably tell us what to do.'

'So we cancel Christmas?' she asked, aghast.

'Ah now, we're not the Grinch.' He chuckled. 'Christmas will go ahead. My two lads have been waiting to get tickets to see Liverpool play Manchester United since last year, so Santa better deliver. And you and Jimmy will come to us for Christmas dinner as we planned, so Christmas will go ahead.'

'You know what I mean,' she said darkly.

'I do,' he conceded with a nod. 'Yeah, we'll be closed over Christmas. I know we were relying on that revenue to cover the cost of the renovations of the stables, so we are in a bit of a tight squeeze cash-flow wise, but we'll get it sorted somehow. We always do.'

'And the staff?' she asked.

He sighed heavily. That was the worst bit. There was very little work in West Clare in the winter, and in several instances both husbands and wives worked at the hotel so the castle provided the entire income for the families. People loved what the castle had brought to the region – there were over 120 staff now – and Conor hated the idea of letting them down. That said, he couldn't afford to pay them when the hotel was shut.

'That's going to be a problem,' he admitted wearily.

'Carlos is trying to arrange as many tradesmen as we can lay our hands on, and we'll use the men on the staff as labourers. The ladies can stay inside and try to get cracking on cleaning up the damage.' Katherine apparently didn't care if that sounded sexist, and Conor knew it was a good idea.

'Let them finish their breakfast first, and then tell Olga and Carlos to make two crews, I suppose, inside and outside. The main thing is to try to get ready for tonight's high tide and minimise the damage.'

'Fine. And will I hold your calls?'

He nodded. 'Unless it's the insurance people.'

His phone, which he'd put on silent, buzzed in his pocket. He took it out – sixteen missed calls. Ana, his father, a couple of numbers he didn't recognise, his friend Father Eddie...the list went on. Word was out.

'I'll start calling to cancel guests, I suppose,' Katherine said as she made her way back to the reception area. 'The phones are still working, incredibly, and we have printouts with the guests' details as well as computer files, so I can work from those.'

Conor nodded. Katherine insisted on keeping a paper trail of everything as backup to the elaborate online booking system. He was glad of her attention to detail every day, but today he was especially happy that she was such a stickler.

He made his way to his office. A sour smell assailed his nostrils as he opened the door, and his feet squelched across the sodden carpet as he walked to his desk. He sat in his office chair and surveyed the damage as he called Ana's number. She answered right away.

'Conor, are you all right?' He could hear the concern.

'I'm fine, pet, not a bother.' He tried to soothe her. 'How are my girls?'

'We're fine, but one of the nurses here, her brother works in the bar – you know, Brendan? She says the hotel is extensive damage or something? And then there was a big thing on the radio.'

He cursed whoever had rung up the local radio station. Larry the Lips, as the local DJ liked to call himself, was forever looking for gossip to start non-existent controversy in the local area on his morning dial-in.

'Ah, not at all. We had a flood. The ocean wall collapsed – the waves were overtopping it anyway. But it's receding now, and the insurance are on the way, so we'll get it sorted.' Ana had enough to worry about; he didn't need her fretting about this too. 'I'll be back to you there in a short while and we can talk about it then, but honestly it's all going to be fine.'

'And you are sure? Because it sounded very bad...' Ana wasn't convinced.

'I'm sure. Now I'm just on my way back to the hospital, so I'll see you soon.'

His phone buzzed in his hand – another incoming call. This time it was the insurance company.

'Ana, I have to take another call. Talk in a bit.'

'OK. Bye, Conor.'

He pressed 'accept' on the screen of his iPhone and to his frustration heard Vivaldi's 'The Four Seasons'. Then a robotic voice came on the line. 'Thank you for calling BCC Insurance. Your call is important to us. All of our agents are currently helping other customers, but stay on the line and they will get to you as soon as possible. For information about great renewal deals, or to learn about the range of cover we provide, please visit our website, www.bcc.ie.'

He longed to hang up. They'd called *him* back, and still they put him through this moronic sequence. The endless 'press this and that' drove him daft. It was one of the things he insisted on at Castle Dysert – when someone rang, they spoke to a person immediately who directed their call or dealt with the query. He fought the urge to end the call, knowing that it would be the same thing the next time. Considering the eye-watering cost of the premium they paid every year, he'd have thought the customer service would be better.

He waited, surveying the damage through the window and door of his office. The serving part of the bar area was tiled, so it might be salvageable. And at least the very expensive beautiful hardwood outdoor furniture, which normally was on the deck outside the bar, was in storage for the winter months; even the hardiest of guests didn't relish sitting outside in the Irish winter with the Atlantic Ocean pounding powerful grey waves onto the shore just metres away. But pretty much everything else would have to go.

He stood facing the iron-grey ocean, indistinguishable from the sky, and refused to give in to the despair that threatened to engulf him.

The lawn inside the now non-existent curtain wall that separated the castle from the sea was completely submerged, and he knew without going over there that the stables and courtyard would be under water as well. The horses that the hotel kept for guests were in livery for the winter. They didn't get enough exercise at the castle during the off season, so they went to the local riding school where they were used for lessons and adored by all the children. The Castle Dysert horses lived a charmed life.

The part of the stables converted to staff quarters in the early days of the hotel had been revamped as self-catering units for guests. The conversion had cost a fortune, but the accommodations were beautiful and were going to be used for the first time over the Christmas season. He dreaded going down there and seeing the carnage. The painters had only finished two days ago. The staff who lived on-site now inhabited a purpose-built apartment block near the goods entrance and away from the main castle. It was better to use the period buildings for guests, and it suited the staff too; once they were off, it didn't feel like they were still at work.

He continued holding. He could see out to reception where Katherine perched on a high stool she'd brought from the bar, telephoning and apologising, promising to try to find alternatives if the guests themselves couldn't. They would all need to be refunded. He tried not to think about it.

Vivaldi had been replaced inexplicably with Celine Dion and that song from *Titanic*. *How apt*, he thought wryly.

His father had called earlier, and Conor would have to return his call next. He'd rather have a plan, or at least have spoken to the insurance company, before he spoke to Jamsie. Though his father would never say it, or even think it, Conor felt responsible. When Conor had first bought into the hotel, it was in partnership with an American woman, Corlene, but she sold her share to Conor when his father came up with the money. Conor had been astounded that Jamsie had the kind of cash needed to purchase a five-star castle resort, but all those years he was on the missing list, he was making a fortune flipping property in London. He had only been back in Conor's life for a few short years, and while Conor was glad things were good between them and that the boys loved Jamsie, he hated being beholden. He wanted Jamsie to get a good return on his investment. Looking around now, it was impossible to imagine how that could happen.

'Thank you for holding.' A bright sunny female voice interrupted his reverie. 'Loretto speaking. How may I help?'

'Oh, er...I need to speak to the person dealing with Castle Dysert, please. This is Conor O'Shea, the owner.'

The insurance guy they'd dealt with previously had left the company, and Conor had received a letter saying someone else was taking over their account. But his filing cabinet had been moved upstairs, and to try to find that letter in the current mess was too much hassle.

'Just one moment, Mr O'Shea. I'll see who that is.'

Before he had time to reply, he was treated to more Vivaldi. He exhaled slowly, trying to keep his temper.

'Good morning. Thank you for calling BCC. Liam speaking. How may I help?' A chirpy male voice this time.

'My name is Conor O'Shea. I have been holding for some time now, and someone was supposed to be finding out who is dealing with my account. I am the owner of Castle Dysert, in County Clare –' Conor found he was gritting his teeth.

'Just a minute, Conor.' The chirpy voice, with a strong Dublin accent, cut across him. 'I'll just pop you on hold…'

No Vivaldi this time. The clown had cut him off. The incessant beep of a dropped call was all that remained. Conor was seething now. He rarely lost his temper, but this was ridiculous.

He marched upstairs, stopping Carlos on the way. 'Any idea where my filing cabinet was put?' he asked.

'Crèche,' Carlos replied, rushing past him. Carlos Manner was the operations manager. He and Conor had a professional respect for each other, but it ended there.

Conor carried on to the crèche on the second floor and found it. Someone had helpfully moved it out of his office, but not before it had been standing in stinky old sea water. The mess inside was horrible, and unfortunately the insurance details were in the bottom drawer. Thankfully the cabinet was open; Katherine constantly complained that he never locked it.

He pulled out the file dealing with insurance and, peeling the damp pages apart, found the letter. Right. Olivia McGann. And a direct line. He took his phone out and entered the number.

'Good morning. Olivia McGann speaking.'

'Hi, Olivia. My name is Conor O'Shea. I'm calling from Castle Dysert. You are managing our account.'

'Yes, that's correct, Mr O'Shea. Nice to hear from you. How can I help?'

At last. Someone who wasn't going to put him on hold again or transfer him around from one person to the next.

'Well, we're in a bit of trouble…' He went on to briefly explain the situation and was relieved that she seemed to be listening intently.

'Right, I'll get to you later this afternoon. I'll bring our assessor and an engineer with me, and we can have a look and talk then. Would two thirty suit you?'

'Perfectly, thanks.'

Right. That was one major step forward.

He went back downstairs. Katherine was still on the phone. They would have to face the staff and tell them something at least, but he'd wait till he spoke to the assessor. There was no point until he knew what they were facing.

CHAPTER 4

'The damage is in the region of a million Euro. That's the bottom line,' Conor said. 'The hotel will remain closed until the work is complete and the certifications and rubber-stamping done. The insurance will pay out this time, but they said they'll need us to do some work before covering us next year. I'm waiting for them to get back with specifics, but that's where we're at for now.'

Conor was having lunch in the Old Ground Hotel in Ennis with John Gerrity, the county engineer, who also trained the twins' football team. Though Gerrity had no official role when it came to Castle Dysert, Conor trusted his judgement and was anxious to get his take on what to do next. Gerrity was known as a by-the-book, no-nonsense man and was the bane of developers who wanted to make a quick buck. He worked for the council and no T was left uncrossed nor I left undotted under his watch. Despite his taciturn nature, Conor liked him and trusted him. He'd overseen the initial renovation in the castle and had been painstakingly detailed. But if he'd been less insistent, when the castle almost burned to the ground less than a year after it opened, it could have resulted in much more tragedy. Conor didn't like to think about that night. He had run into the burning castle to extract his sons, and the scars from the burns were still on his back. It was Gerrity's insistence on every detail of the fire plan being met that had saved them.

The engineer listened and then put down his cup, addressing Conor directly, his face grave. 'Your biggest problem is not the renovations this time. Those will be covered, so no problem there. Where you are going to run into an issue is that you'll need to repair the wall and install flood defences to protect against it happening again. The insurance won't pay out every year – that's a fact – so you need to protect yourself. This is climate change as we are experiencing it. Some places, it's droughts or fires, hurricanes and all the rest, but for us it's rising tides and frequent catastrophic flooding. There are those who say we always had floods, and that's true, but their severity and frequency are unprecedented. Now the castle is the only building on that little spit of land, so the council can't send much-needed funds your way since all around the county, people's homes are at risk too. We have to prioritise those, as well as schools and hospitals, so I'm sorry to say you're on your own.'

Conor let this news sink in. 'So what do you think I'm looking at?'

Gerrity took a bite of his plain ham sandwich, then chewed thoughtfully and swallowed. But before he spoke, a young pretty waitress approached the table. She beamed at Conor, and he smiled. She flushed deep red.

'Can I get you more coffee, Conor?' she asked.

'Thanks' – he glanced surreptitiously at her name badge – 'Mia.'

'You're very welcome.' She beamed and started to walk away.

'I'd like a top-up too, please.' Gerrity's request stopped her in her tracks, and she turned with the pot.

'Of course.' She smiled but kept her eyes on Conor. Gerrity didn't thank her, and she walked away.

'I could die of thirst while the women from eight to eighty dance attendance on you.'

Conor shook his head. 'Nah, I know her family, that's all. Her mother works in the nursery at the castle.'

Gerrity raised an eyebrow in disbelief. 'I doubt it. Anyway, as I see it, you have two options. One, you can repair the existing wall and raise it around the entire property. But that contains what is normally a five-metre tide, and in storm conditions like we've had this week, you are looking at anything up to eight metres. So you'd need at least that encircling the entire castle on the seaward side. And that's not taking into consideration that it might go even higher in the future.'

'But an eight- or ten-metre wall would obscure the view of the bay.' Conor hated that idea from the off.

'It would, and it would have to be done in compliance with the preservation order on the building, so you'd have a job sourcing that amount of authentic stone into the bargain.'

'And the other option?' Conor asked.

'The other option is to repair the wall to the height it was and invest in temporary flood barriers that can be put up and taken down as needs be.'

'All right. I like the sound of that a lot better,' Conor said, relieved.

'I can see why, but the cost is prohibitive.' John popped the last bite of his sandwich in his mouth.

'As in how prohibitive?' Conor dreaded the answer.

'As a ballpark – and obviously you can't hold me to this, as it's not even my area – I'd hazard somewhere in the region of three million. You'd need to repair the wall and purchase and install the barriers, and then you'd need to redo the water and sewage under the castle and install soakaways and a few other bits and pieces. But I'd say you wouldn't get out of it under three.'

Conor's euphoria was short-lived. There was no way he could ever get his hands on even a fraction of that sum. 'And if we just repaired the wall?' he asked.

'My guess would be the insurance company won't accept that. You'll need to take remedial action to ensure it won't happen again, and the removable flood barriers are the way to do it.'

Conor tried to focus on what John was saying, but the huge sum of three million Euro kept going round and round in his head.

'You'd have to source original stone,' Gerrity explained. 'The council would refuse to allow any materials outside of the preservation order, so again, expensive.'

'I can't afford either option, and I'd hate to surround the castle with a higher wall. It would ruin it. We struggle to get enough light through those medieval windows as it is, but with a wall, the views of the bay would be gone, and the gardens, the shoreline… And those are my only options?'

'Yes.' Gerrity was blunt but honest. 'I'm not an insurance assessor, but those are the only two options, and I'd be amazed if they said different. At least now you're prepared.'

Conor rested his head back on the booth and exhaled. Even the thought of it made him want to lie in a darkened room. 'What would you do if you were me?' he asked eventually.

Without a hint of a smile, Gerrity said, 'I would never have bought that castle in the first place, so I would never be in this position. You won't be able to sell it, because whoever bought it would face the same problems you do now. And if you don't take some action, well, the next time you'll be on your own without insurance.' He stood up and shrugged on his warm overcoat; it was bitterly cold. 'I'll get lunch.'

'Thanks. I'll need to save my pennies.' Conor smiled ruefully.

'You coming?' John Gerrity asked, as Conor was just sitting there.

'I need to send an email, so I'll do it here. Thanks for lunch, John, and the advice.'

'Pity you didn't listen to me before you bought the bloody thing, but we are where we are now. Give me a shout if you need anything. I'm retiring after Christmas, so I'll have time.' Gerrity nodded and left to go back to his permanent pensionable job at the Clare County Council, and for a moment, Conor envied him.

He ordered one last cup of coffee. He was drinking way too much of the stuff these days, but he needed to stay awake.

The staff had taken the news well. They understood he was doing his best, and he tried to reassure them that they'd be back in business as soon as was humanly possible. But with all the tradespeople on holidays for two weeks at Christmas, it was likely to be at least the spring before they were open again. The staff were entitled to social welfare payments – many of them assured him they could get by on that until the hotel reopened – and he'd told them that they would be paid to the end of the month. But the overtime and extra shifts they were hoping to pick up with the hotel full for the holidays weren't going to happen. January and February would be lean months, but he was going to try to get the doors open again for St Patrick's Day in March.

Jamsie had been wonderful, he had to admit. He'd rolled his sleeves up, helping to get the castle dry and secure, and then went home before Conor to take care of the boys.

Ana was home from hospital with Lily, and their house was full of baby stuff; it was amazing that one little baby needed so many things. Despite the worry, he could just spend hours with Lily in his arms. The boys adored her too and took turns holding her. Conor and Ana were surprised; they'd assumed Lily would bore the boys – after all, she didn't do much – but they were as mesmerised by the little girl as their parents were.

He'd have to talk to Jamsie, tell him there wouldn't be a dividend on his investment this year. He knew his father wouldn't mind, but still, he hated being indebted to him.

He liked to see the closeness between his father and his family, something he could never have imagined. Just a few short years ago, it was inconceivable that Conor would even be on speaking terms with his father, let alone love him, but life had a funny way of turning around.

Conor had had to fend for himself all his life. Jamsie O'Shea left the family when Conor was eight and his brother Gerry was five. He'd just walked out one day, no explanation, no message, nothing, and never came back. His mother did her best, but she died when he was sixteen, and from then until he met Ana, Conor was on his own.

His father showed up out of the blue two years ago, full of remorse, and he would have been met with complete rejection were it not for Ana and her gentle coaxing to at least hear his father out. He did, and while he was not ever going to fully understand or forgive his father's desertion, they were now friends. Life was too short for grudges.

What was he going to do about the castle, he wondered. Normally, he'd talk it over with Ana – she had a great way of cutting through the unnecessary to get to the root of the problem – but she had enough to do with Lily. Everyone relied on him. It was hard to think of a family in the area that didn't have someone working at the castle. If it closed down, the locality would never recover. And he'd have to face those people every day of his life, knowing he'd scuppered their futures. He was usually upbeat and positive, but a wave of despair threatened. Three million Euro? It would take a miracle.

His phone beeped. Father Eddie. A text message flashed on the screen.

That your car in the car park of Old Ground? If busy, no prob, but I'm passing?

Conor responded immediately.

Come in, I'll buy you a bun!

Eddie was just who he needed now. His friend had a way of soothing the soul.

Despite dire doctor's warnings that he was prediabetic, the little priest was a devil for sweets and cakes. His long-suffering house-keeper, Martina, had banned anything nice from the presbytery. She was thwarted in her efforts daily though because Father Eddie spent his time helping his parishioners, who returned the favour with tea and cakes.

Moments later, his small bald head covered with a purple and yellow woolly hat knitted by a well-intentioned but not particularly talented parishioner, Eddie appeared around the door. Greeting this one and that, he made his way to the booth where Conor always sat, plonking himself down opposite him. 'Well?' he asked, but then Mia appeared once more. 'Ah, Mia, 'tis yourself. Will you tell your mam those indoor begonias are magnificent on the altar? She's a dinger! If it weren't for her, the place would be drab as anything till the daffs come out, but she's playing a blinder.'

Mia grinned. 'I'm glad, Father. She has us all driven cracked

31

watering them. She nearly murdered Daddy last weekend because she went to Dublin shopping with her sisters and when she came back the soil wasn't exactly right. She might have a place in heaven, but she's a right demon to us, I can tell you.' She laughed. 'What can I get you?'

'Oh now, Mia, honour thy father and thy mother.' He chuckled and gave her a wink. 'Is there any bread and butter pudding? Or maybe I'll have the rhubarb crumble.'

As he perused the menu, Conor noticed Mia looked uncomfortable.

Eddie didn't need to be told. 'She's been in, hasn't she?' He sighed exasperatedly. 'Martina the Hun. I told the bishop years ago I didn't need a housekeeper – it's not the fifties. But she needed a place to go, and you know what a soft touch he is, so he's landed me with this tyrant now going around telling everyone to feed me like a rabbit.'

Conor smiled. 'What about the fresh fruit pavlova? One for me.' He winked at Mia, and she blushed again. 'And a coffee for Father Eddie.'

'Coming right up.' She was glad to be off the hook in delivering the bad news. She was back in a moment with the dessert, which she placed in front of Conor.

'Pavlova is better than nothing, I suppose,' Eddie grumbled.

'There's fruit in it. Tell her it's one of your five a day,' Conor said, sliding it across to his friend as soon as Mia left them.

'There would be no fear of you eating a pudding anyway,' Eddie said, grudgingly tucking in.

'Not my poison. I never had much of a sweet tooth, but I'll have to go easy on the coffee – I'm going to give myself an ulcer or something. But I suppose I could be on the bottle. The way my hotel is going right now, it's a miracle I'm not working my way through the top shelf over there.' He jerked his head to indicate the expensive bottles of whiskey behind the old mahogany bar.

'Well, you never had that weakness either, thanks be to God. 'Tis many's the poor man, and woman too, who's a martyr to the drink, so thank your lucky stars. So first off, congratulations, and I hear Mammy and baba are flying it?' Eddie stirred three spoons of sugar into his coffee.

'They really are. Honestly, Eddie, wait till you see her. She's the most beautiful girl. She's named after my mam and she looks like her too. She's dark-haired with dark-blue eyes, and she's so tiny and perfect. I just stare at her sometimes for hours – she's amazing.'

Eddie smiled. 'Well, yourself and Ana will give that little girl a lovely life, so God bless you all. And speaking of Ana, how is she?'

'She's incredible. The whole birth thing and the pregnancy, no complaining, not a word about the pain – she just wanted her baby. And the fact that Lily is a girl – she told me she was hoping for a girl. I'm in awe of her strength and that's the truth.'

'Well, isn't it true, Conor, that if the having of babies was down to us men, the humans would be extinct in no time! The women are tougher than us by miles. And now that she has that baby in her arms, all fine and healthy, sure she'll forget all of this and be mad to go again.' He chuckled.

'Well, she might be, but I'm well and truly over the hill, and trying to keep up with little ones is a young man's game. So unless she trades me in for a younger model, I'd say we're done.'

'You're safe enough on that score, I'd say. She's stuck with you this long, I'd say you'll go the distance.' Eddie winked and sipped his coffee. 'Now what about that castle?'

Conor ran his hand through his thick silver hair. It was cut short in the back and on the sides, but he wore it slightly longer on top. He'd gone grey in his forties, and his hair had now, as he approached his fifty-sixth birthday, turned completely silver. Ana said she didn't mind, that she liked it, but for the first time in his life, Conor felt old.

'Oh, Eddie, you don't want to know.' He sighed wearily.

'I do actually. Tell me.' Eddie sat back. 'I haven't a bean, so I can't be of any financial help, but two heads are better than one. I don't need to tell you how worried people are. They know you're doing your best and all of that, but they rely on the hotel.'

'I know they do. That's nearly the worst of it. I could always go back on the road, driving tours, and we'd be grand, but so many people need the work.' He sipped his coffee. 'In a nutshell, I'm up the proverbial creek without a paddle.' He relayed John Gerrity's pronouncement.

As he spoke, Eddie sat and listened. Conor assumed it was a learned skill after forty years in the priesthood, but his friend never interrupted or tried to soothe him with platitudes; he just let Conor get it all off his chest. And though, as Eddie pointed out, his friend had no answers, Conor at least felt unburdened a little.

'So there you have it. I'm finished, aren't I?' Conor was despondent.

'I don't know, Conor. And I know you're not one of my flock, but I'll say a prayer for you – the whole parish out there is praying for you anyway. I do know this – you are a resourceful man, you have a great team with Carlos and Katherine and Olga, and Artur of course, you are surrounded by great people dedicated to you and that castle is more than just a job. So my advice would be to tell them, don't keep it from them how dire the situation is. You've nothing to hide, and you never know what someone would come up with.'

Conor was doubtful. 'I don't know. They need their jobs too, and I might be able to –'

'They all have eyes and saw the damage. Maybe they haven't guessed yet about the longer-term implications but they will, so better make them feel like they are part of the solution rather than waiting to hear their fate from on high.' He leaned forward. 'Look, Conor, you never from day one ran that place like a dictator. You give everyone a hearing and you treat them well, and that's why they've such time for you, why they go over and above every single time. From Katherine all the way down to the part-timers and the students working at the weekends. You trust them. You have enough on your plate with Ana and a new baby. They want to help – let them.'

'That's the trouble, Eddie. Unless they have a couple of million Euro hidden under the mattress, they can't help. Nobody can.' Conor felt uncharacteristically bleak.

'The Lord works in mysterious ways, my friend.' Eddie grinned.

'Well, if you're talking to him, you might ask him to work his magic on my hotel, eh?' Conor drained his coffee and stood. 'I'm sorry to rush off, but I want to get home. I don't like to be too far away in case Ana needs me.'

'Of course. Tell her I was asking for her. I'll pop in to see Lily and herself once she's had time to settle.' Eddie stood too and pulled on his coat. 'It's going to be all right, Conor, I just know it.'

'I hope you're right, Eddie, I really do.' Conor felt none of his friend's confidence.

CHAPTER 5

*A*na was in the bath when he came home, and Jamsie was helping the boys with their homework. Danika had made a beef stroganoff and baked potatoes for their dinner, and she'd baked a tart as well with the rhubarb Artur grew in their little garden. She froze all kinds of fruit and vegetables and used them throughout the year. She was now walking with little Lily fast asleep on her shoulder.

Lionel, the white fluffy Samoyed, named after the lads' favourite soccer player, Lionel Messi, was stretched in front of the stove in the living room, basking in the heat. He was a lovely, gentle dog and a beloved part of the family.

Conor loved how their home was always warm and welcoming. It smelled of laundry detergent and baking, and there was always a hum of activity. It was a million miles away from the cold lonely house he'd grown up in. His poor mother had worked all hours to keep food on the table for him and his brother, but it meant she was never there. There was never enough money to heat the house properly. It was a rented place, and the landlord had no interest in making it more comfortable for a deserted wife and her two kids.

Lionel jumped up to greet him, delighted he was home.

'Hi, Dad,' chorused his blond twins, still in their hurling gear.

Jamsie had taken them to training and collected them. They were both sports mad.

'Hi, lads.' He bent and kissed their heads. None of the fathers Conor knew growing up were tactile with their sons – it wasn't the done thing back then – but he and the boys were very easy with each other. They came into his and Ana's bed every Saturday and Sunday morning for a cuddle and to watch cartoons. He knew they would soon grow out of it, but he would keep it going as long as they wanted it to.

'I told Tim that we probably wouldn't be able to play in the match at the weekend,' Joe announced, ''cause Mammy had the baby and we're all very busy with Lily. And he said that's a problem 'cause he has a bet on with the trainer of Ballydangan that we can beat them and he needs me and Artie so he can win a tenner.'

'He needs you more than me,' Artie said without a hint of self-pity. Artie was a good hurler, better than most kids his age, but Joe was brilliant. He was agile and fast and had great intelligence when it came to the game. Artie was the one who did better in school. Joe got a bit of extra help from the resource teacher, but he was managing fine. Neither Ana nor Conor ever made a big deal of either of their boys' abilities or lack thereof; they just got on with things.

'I'll have to move you two to Dublin. I can't have you facing the Dubs as inter-county players in Clare colours when you are grown up,' Jamsie joked.

This set the twins off on the usual banter with their granda as to how the Dubs, his team, would never beat Clare once the O'Shea twins made the county team, which they had every intention of doing.

'I'm sure between us someone can drop you.' Conor smiled at his sons and took Lily from her *babusya* for a cuddle.

'She smiled at Joe,' Artie said, rubbing his sister's head gently.

'Did you now?' Conor gazed in adoration at his daughter. 'Did you smile at your brother?' He kissed her head. 'How's the most wonderful girl in the world today? I missed you, Lily O'Shea.'

'Will I dish this up?' Jamsie asked, stirring the delicious meaty stroganoff.

'Great. Where's Ana?' Conor looked around. Danika was putting her coat on; Artur was waiting outside for her. 'Thanks, Danika. *Dyakuyu tobi.*' He waved Lily's little hand. '*Do pobachennya, Babusya.*'

Danika grinned. She loved to hear Conor speak Ukrainian. After years in Ireland she still spoke only rudimentary English, but she was a wonderful woman and Conor loved her.

'*Do pobchennya, Divchynka.*' She kissed her granddaughter's head, and Conor could tell she was inhaling the lovely baby smell of her. '*Do pobachennya khloptsi.*' She waved goodbye as she ruffled the boys' hair affectionately.

'Bye, *Babusya*! See you tomorrow,' the boys chorused.

'Mammy is in the bath,' Artie said, rubbing out something from his copybook with an eraser. Joe would never do that; if it was done at all, it was good enough for him. But Artie was known to wake in the middle of the night to go down to fix something in his homework. Though they were identical, in so many ways they were like chalk and cheese.

'Righto. I'll go up to her.' Conor handed his daughter to Jamsie, who smiled down as the baby nestled in his arms. 'And then we'll have dinner, OK? Are you nearly finished with your lessons?'

'Dad, nobody calls it lessons any more – it's homework!' Artie rolled his eyes at his brother.

'It's not the olden days, you know,' Joe quipped, and Conor threw a cushion at him, hitting him in the back. Joe picked it up and threw it back, and within a minute, both boys were wrestling with him on the couch.

'Who are you calling an auld fella, eh?' Conor joked, pinning both boys down at once and tickling them.

They screamed with laughter till he released them.

'Right. I'm going up to Mammy. Finish that *homework* and set the table, and we'll be down in five minutes.' He ruffled their heads as he pulled them up.

'I'll look after Lily,' Jamsie said, then gave him an enquiring look. It was clear he wanted to know how the meeting with John Gerrity went. Conor surreptitiously shook his head and Jamsie nodded. They would talk later once the boys were asleep.

Conor went upstairs and into their bedroom. The door to their en-suite bathroom was slightly ajar, and he tapped on it, pushing it open slightly. Ana was resting her head back on a bath pillow, bubbles up to her neck; her entire body was under the warm water. She was dozing and looked so peaceful that he didn't want to disturb her. Her eyes fluttered open and she smiled sleepily.

'You don't need to come out,' he whispered, leaning down to kiss her. He lit one of her scented candles and turned the lights down. He was so glad they'd installed a large corner bath in their bathroom – they could both fit in it.

'I wish you could come in with me.' She smiled. 'But I suppose the boys would be so horrored.'

He grinned. Sometimes, even after all these years, she got English words wrong. She was always asking him to correct her, but he never did, as he thought it was adorable.

They'd explained about the pregnancy to Joe and Artie, and inevitably the questions about where babies come from popped up. Though he had cringed a bit, they told the boys the truth, and now the look of terror on the boys' faces if they so much as held hands was a source of much amusement to him and Ana.

'Do you really, or are you saying it to be nice?' he asked.

'Really, I would love it, but I better get out. There is dinner on the stove.' She started to heave herself out of the water.

'Stay there,' he said with a smile, and took out his phone. He opened the text app and scrolled to Jamsie.

Need some time alone with Ana. Can you keep boys busy?

Jamsie answered instantly.

Of course. Lily gone for a snooze in her basket. Don't make another one just yet though

Conor laughed and relayed the messages to his wife.

'No, now he thinks we are up here...making love when I am just out of hospital...' She coloured with embarrassment at the thought.

'He doesn't really, and even if he does, so what? We're married.'

He crept over and turned the key on their bedroom door. He added more hot water to the tub and lit another candle. Then he stripped and got into the bath behind her. She rested her back against his chest as he kissed her neck.

They chatted, and he told her some of what John Gerrity had said. They had promised never to keep anything from the other after the problems they had a few years ago – one of the gardeners had taken a shine to Ana and it nearly killed Conor – but he didn't know what to do.

He played down the grim prospect of the repairs as much as he could, assuring her he'd get it sorted. He neglected to mention the need to find three million Euro somewhere.

They talked about their new baby, how lovely she was, and calm, though she didn't enjoy sleeping alone for longer than twenty minutes at a time. She slept on Ana's chest the first night and on Conor and Ana's the second, and it had continued like that. She slept soundly once she could feel a heartbeat. Other than that, she was a serene little girl.

'It's so funny having a girl, isn't it?' Ana mused as Conor gently massaged her shoulders.

'It is, all that pink stuff everywhere.' He chuckled. 'I think that's because all we know is boys. We had no idea what a girl baby is like, so we couldn't imagine it.'

'I think now that I have a little girl, I'll have someone to dress up and who would like to go shopping and watch romantic movies with me, not always with the sports and the films with explosions.' She chuckled. It was a constant battle to get the boys to watch anything but cartoons or films with lots of loud bangs.

'I watch romantic films with you,' Conor protested.

'You start watching, and then after ten minutes, I hear the snore.' She slapped him playfully. It was true; he fell asleep most of the time.

'Ah, but that's because no film could be as romantic as my own life...' He nuzzled her neck again and she hooted with laughter.

'Oh, yes, it is, the stretching marks and the haemorrhoids and the flabby tummy – it's *so* romantic.' She sighed.

'I love you, Anastasia O'Shea. I loved you before you ever gave me my beautiful boys, but now that you made me a father to Lily, well, there are no words to describe how much you mean to me. And nothing, no hotel or anything else, is more important to me than my family.'

'I know.' She smiled. 'But I know also you are worried, Conor. You don't need to pretend all is OK so I won't worry, you know. We're a team, remember?'

'We sure are.' He sighed and felt her relax against him.

Later that evening, as Ana fed Lily and the boys were in bed, Conor found his father in the sitting room watching the news. As he sat down, Jamsie flicked the TV off with the remote.

'Well?' he asked.

'It's bad.' Conor explained the situation, apologising that there would be no dividend of the profits from the hotel going to Jamsie.

His father listened as he told him his fears, especially the idea that there would be no money to pay the wages after the end of the month. Then they sat in silence for a few moments.

'Right. Listen carefully now,' Jamsie began. 'I didn't lend you that money or invest it in your hotel. I gave it to you. So that's not a debt to be repaid. It's a legacy if you want to call it that. I made that money and I wanted to give it to my son. Liz got her share too, so unfortunately it cleaned me out of the big money I had. So if I had three million, I'd give it to you with a heart and a half, but I don't. What I can do though is lend you the money to pay the staff until at least March, and hopefully we'll be up and running again. I'll need it back at some point, but there's no rush.'

'I can't take that from you. You've done enough –' Conor began, but Jamsie raised his hand to stop him.

'It's sitting in the bank ready for the day I need to go into a nursing home or whatever, but until then, I don't need it and you do. So please, Conor, just take it, and you can pay it back whenever you can.'

'Thank you.' Conor put his hand on his father's broad shoulder. 'You'll only go into a home if it's what you really want. You'll always have a home here with us.' Conor's voice cracked at the emotion of it all. 'We're your family.'

If someone had told him that he would not only welcome his father who abandoned him into his life once more but that he'd offer to take him and care for him when he was old, he would have said they were mad, but life was strange.

'Thanks, Conor. You've got a lot of your mam in you. I don't know what I did to deserve your forgiveness and the welcome you've given me – God knows I don't deserve it...' He swallowed. He rarely mentioned Conor's mother. 'But I'm very grateful.'

CHAPTER 6

*A*t three a.m., Conor sat at the kitchen table as Lily slept peacefully in the sling on his chest. She'd been restless and Ana needed her sleep, so he'd taken the baby downstairs.

Opening his laptop, he began researching all he could find about types of flood defences. Whichever way he went about it, the price was going to be way beyond what they could afford. Even repairing the wall was going to be too much, let alone the removable barriers. The bank was the only option. Maybe they would lend the money to him, but it was doubtful. Credit was hard to get and the hotel was run on a tight budget, so his repayment capacity would be a problem.

He scrolled on; the information made for grim reading. There was a company in the Netherlands that specialised in flood management. Maybe it was worth getting in touch with them as they might have some ideas, he mused as he tried to figure out all the different engineering terms and jargon.

Lily stirred and he gently rubbed her temple; it seemed to soothe her, and she went back to sleep. Ana had expressed some breast milk and he'd tried to feed Lily from a bottle, but she wasn't remotely interested. It meant Ana had to do every feeding, and Lily at three weeks old was going through a growth spurt so was hungry all the time. If he could keep her happy for even a few hours, Ana could rest. He was tired too. Sleeping was in fits and starts since Lily arrived, and when she was asleep, he was awake worrying about the hotel. Where was he going to come up with three million?

Maybe he should have stayed on as a tour driver. Life was simple then, and he'd had no real responsibilities. He had a little place in Spain and an apartment in Ennis, and he spent most of the year on the road, living in hotels and guiding groups of Americans around Ireland. But that was no life for a man with a family. Meeting Ana, getting married and having children had transformed his life in ways he could never have foreseen. He was so grateful for his family, but the burden of owning such a huge concern as Castle Dysert, a place that so many people relied on, was exhausting.

He fought the urge to make a cup of coffee; he really had to cut down. With a sigh, he opened his email inbox. The insurance people had got back, and John Gerrity was right almost to the letter. They'd cover the damage but not the remedial work, and a new policy would be subject to an inspection so that they could be assured that such events could be managed in the future. That meant flood barriers.

Every day there were meetings to attend regarding the refurbishment, and he really needed to sit down with Carlos, Olga, Artur and Katherine to work out a plan of action, but he had been putting them all off, hoping he'd have something more optimistic to say. Maybe Eddie was right – maybe he should just tell everyone the truth and see if all their heads together could come up with a solution. Because he sure as anything couldn't.

He started reading the next email, a series of questions from Daniel Coffey, the architect, on the plans for the refurbishment. Conor chose him, though he was a bit of a pain, because he did the original job and Conor wanted everything exactly as it was. It exasperated him that Daniel kept asking questions, suggesting they change things, and Conor replied with a firm email telling him to please find the original specifications and stick to those.

The money Jamsie was going to lend him to pay the staff was a relief. If he could keep everyone on salary until they reopened, then that was something. It didn't solve the biggest problem, but at least he would defer the panic at everyone being out of work. Katherine knew things were bad, but he'd kept it from everyone else up to now. But enough was enough. He'd tell the staff the bare minimum: that their jobs were safe for now but that a big job would need to be done and they were looking into options. But he'd get his main team together and tell them the truth – that he was all out of ideas.

CHAPTER 7

*C*onor pulled into the car park of the Old Ground. Everyone at the neighbouring hotel had been so good since hearing of their flood, and the manager had insisted he use the conference room at no charge for the meeting. Conor liked that about Irish tourism – people had a lift-all-boats attitude rather than petty jealousy. There was room for everyone, and so people in the business helped each other out as much as they could.

It was good news for the most part; they were keeping their jobs and the hotel would reopen in March. That was all the main staff needed to know for now. How they could do it without insurance was a whole other story, but he'd arranged to meet with the management team after this in his office, and they'd work something out. What that was, he had no idea. It might seem less daunting if he wasn't exhausted, he conceded, as he located a space and suppressed a yawn.

Since Lily and Ana had come home from the hospital there had yet to be a night of sleep in the house. Lily was angelic during the day – a sweeter-tempered baby could not be found – but she seriously objected to sleeping at night. She wasn't fussy about which of her parents sat semi-upright as she snuggled on their chest, but the moment they moved to put her in her crib, she yelled the house down.

Conor knew Ana was right, that there was nothing wrong and she just liked the comfort, but while Conor secretly loved the feel of his little girl on his chest, he did need to sleep.

Lack of sleep meant he was barely functioning during the day. Time was pressing on with the refurbishment of the castle, and he knew his silence on what the future held was unnerving the staff. They were used to him having all the answers, or at least pretending to.

The birth of his daughter had, if anything, made him more determined to find a solution. His family and many others relied on him to make this work, and he would do whatever it took.

The meeting was short and he got right to the point. The relief on everyone's faces that their jobs were safe and the hotel would reopen tore at his heart. The Old Ground had even laid on tea and scones for free, so there was a buoyant atmosphere.

'What about rebuilding the wall, Conor? Surely we have to do that?' Mariusz, one of the head gardeners, asked.

'We will for sure, and probably more flood work as well as some work to the drains and sewage – I'm still looking into how and when that can be done. But you're right. There's a lot to be done, and we need to be aware of costs now more than ever.' He scanned the room. He knew he had the loyalty of every one of them; they loved the hotel as much as he did. 'We do a good job of providing luxury accommodation and food on a very narrow margin of profit. I'm going to ask you all now to help us in whatever way possible. There is going to be considerable upheaval, a lot of dirt and mess generated by the repairs, so we need to stay on top of that. I know Sheila is meeting with all the housekeeping staff after this to allocate jobs.' He smiled at Sheila Dillon, head of housekeeping. 'Artur is heading up the grounds teams, and same there – lots to be done and we need to be frugal, so making the best out of as little money as possible. And the bar and kitchen staff likewise. We need to diversify labour because we won't have guests, but I know each and every one of you will be willing to lend a hand in whatever we need.'

Sheila raised her hand, and Conor looked down at her again. 'Yes, Sheila?'

'Conor, I just wanted to say, on behalf of everyone, I'm sure, how much we appreciate you keeping our jobs and paying us while the castle is closed. It is a huge burden on you financially, and I want to assure you that we are all behind you a hundred percent. We'll all pull together and do whatever is necessary. You can rely on us.'

'Just so you know, I can't iron,' Harry, the head barman, joked and everyone laughed.

'Don't worry, Harry, ironing and laundry lessons begin on Monday,' Sheila retorted with a grin.

'Seriously though, Conor, thanks,' Harry said. He was a charming redhead and a huge hit with the ladies. 'We'll all pitch in wherever we're needed.'

Conor smiled and nodded. 'I know you will. We're a team, and we have been since the start. Nobody here is afraid to get their hands dirty, I know that, myself included. And I won't lie to you – it's going to be an uphill struggle. But we survived a fire and came back even stronger, so we can overcome this too.'

He left them to enjoy their tea and scones and made for the castle. He wanted to speak to the management team there, away from listening ears. The story he'd told the staff wasn't a lie exactly, but it was certainly a lot more optimistic than the reality they faced. He would be more honest with Katherine, Olga, Carlos and Artur.

He wished Ana were there with him, as she was such a calming influence on everyone. She could manage Katherine when she was being snarky, or Carlos when he was about to eat the head off one of the staff. She managed to defuse the situation without upsetting anyone. She worked on the reception desk, but the truth was that she was his sounding board for new ideas, as well as his eyes and ears. He knew every single thing that went on behind the scenes because Ana was universally loved and trusted by everyone.

She had said that morning that she might pop up with Lily to see the progress of the work, so he wanted to be there when she got there. The boys were at school; Jamsie dropped and collected them. They loved him, and he enjoyed taking them to training or swimming. He had a place in Dublin, but Conor and Ana had discussed asking him if he'd consider moving down to Clare to be closer to them. There was nothing keeping him in Dublin really.

As Conor pulled in to the car park that resembled a builder's yard now with machinery and materials everywhere, he saw Ana's car was already there. Artur had been on-site from the beginning of the work – no corner could be cut under his watchful eye – so she was probably with her dad someplace. Olga and Carlos lived on-site in the staff quarters, and Katherine was coming to the management meeting scheduled for two p.m.

He let himself in and went to his office, which now contained just a desk and a chair and his coffee machine, which was perched precariously on a makeshift ledge made with scaffolding boards. His regular furniture had been stored upstairs, and the timber floor needed to be sanded and varnished.

He looked out the window to see Ana and her father pushing Lily in her pram and examining the new polished stone garden furniture that was being delivered. It was Carlos's idea – stone was waterproof and fireproof, and they could put cushions on the furniture in the summertime.

Builders stopped to admire the baby and Conor smiled. Lily O'Shea charmed all who met her. Old ladies on the street stopped Ana to tell her what a beautiful child she was, and whenever Ana brought her anywhere, she was instantly surrounded with people oohing and aahing over her. She had a full head of dark silky hair, as dark as Conor's had been when he was a kid, and she hardly ever cried. Her eyes had changed since she was born to the exact sapphire blue of Conor's, and she lit up whenever she saw him. Ana was back to her old self, and while she loved being at home with her baby, she was anxious to get back to her life after a long pregnancy.

Artur took his granddaughter out of her pram and waved Ana away. Conor watched his wife pick her way across cement mixers and scaffolding before she disappeared as she presumably headed to the front door of the castle. He went out to meet her. The normally serene and luxurious reception area of Castle Dysert was a hive of activity, and the constant noise of sawing and drilling was relentless.

'Hello you.' He winked at her.

'I brought you a sandwich,' she said, then kissed him. 'How did the meeting go?'

'You're a star. Thanks, love. It went grand. They were all happy to hear their jobs were safe – for now anyway.' He put his arm around her shoulder and led her to his office. 'I'm actually starving, but I needed to get back here straight away because yesterday the foreman and Daniel were about to knock each other out over the cornicing. If I'm not here to stop it, one of them is going to hit the other a clatter and drive off. I don't care who hits who so long as they all stay working.' He chuckled gratefully, then took a bite out of the home-made tuna and cheese sandwich, his favourite. 'They can batter each other to kingdom come once we get this finished. In fact, I'll join in, as they're both driving me mental. Honestly, Joe and Artie are more mature.'

'I know,' Ana sympathised. 'Papa told me they are fighting every day. He had to stop the gardener quitting yesterday too because Daniel said one thing and the foreman said something else, and he is sick of it.'

'I know. But we're getting there, slowly. I saw your dad going off with the micro-queen.'

'Being showed off by her *didus* to everyone,' Ana said as she made them both a coffee from his machine.

Conor accepted the cup, took a sip and grimaced. 'What the hell is that?'

'It's decaf. You are drinking too much this strong coffee. It's better for you.' She shrugged.

'It's disgusting is what it is,' Conor grumbled.

'Katherine told me she took all the proper coffee away, and all is now this stuff. Not my decision, but I agree with her.' Ana grinned as he took another sip and made a face. 'It's not that bad. You'll get used to it.'

'I won't.'

'So today you tell everyone and it's OK, so now what?' Ana perched on his desk as he sat down behind it.

'Well, the staff are back tomorrow, trying to get things back to normal, cleaning, gardening, all that sort of thing. They all said they'd pitch in wherever, and there's plenty to be done if we want to open in March. We're putting ourselves under savage pressure, but we need to make up for lost revenue as fast as we can. It's going to take some heavy advertising to get us back where we were, but we can do it, I think.'

Ana turned to face him, and he knew something was on her mind.

'Conor,' she said firmly, 'I don't want to hear any arguments now. Lily will finally take a bottle, so my mother is going to look after her every morning for a few hours and I'm coming back to work.'

Conor knew that look in her eye, the one that said she was going to do this regardless of what he said, so he decided just to go with it. Lily was only a few weeks old, but they could be flexible. She slept a lot in the mornings anyway since she was awake half the night, and it would be great to have Ana back in the castle even for a few hours a day.

'That's brilliant.' He beamed. 'I really need you here, and so does Katherine, and we can't afford to take on any more staff. So if Danika is happy to look after the micro-queen, then that's great.'

He saw her relax; she'd obviously been prepared for a fight.

'Yes, she's happy to do it. And I'll express so she can give her a bottle and all of that, so she'll be fine.'

'Wonderful.' Conor gave her a hug. 'Now if you can, will you stay for the meeting this afternoon? We need all ideas and input.'

'Of course.' She cleared away his undrunk coffee. 'I'll get *Didus* to find that gas heater we had to use to heat up the third floor before the fire, and some more chairs. We can bring them in here, make it a bit cosier for the meeting.'

'Already you're running the show. Welcome back, Mrs O'Shea.' He put his arms around her waist, pulling her towards him gently, and kissed her.

At two on the dot, the team arrived. Ana had his office looking much nicer. She got clean cups from the kitchen and sent one of the junior gardeners for biscuits and milk.

Conor addressed them all. 'So as you know, I told the staff today that they would be paid until we reopened, which between ourselves is down to a loan from my father. Look, lads, I had to sugarcoat it a bit with them. I don't want wild panic, but the truth is we are in a bad way.'

Katherine stared at him intently, her face a mask that he knew was hiding her anxiety, while Carlos and Olga just looked worried. Artur knew how bad it was; Conor had explained it to him a few days ago. Ana had just finished feeding Lily, and she put her in her pram, where mercifully she decided to sleep.

'So the situation is this. The insurance are going to pay to fix everything up in here and in the grounds. They won't pay for the repair of the sea wall, nor will they pay for the removable flood barriers we'll need to buy. The other thing is that they won't insure us until we have the wall back in place and the flood barriers installed and available for inspection. And we can't operate without insurance obviously.'

The silence hung heavily in the room.

'What sort of money are we talking about?' Carlos asked.

Conor inhaled, then sighed. Staying positive and being awake half the night was taking its toll. 'Somewhere between three and four million.'

'But that's preposterous!' Katherine snapped. 'To fix a wall and put in some barriers? It can't be that much surely. Have you shopped around?'

'It's not like buying a barbeque, Katherine. We need a procurement expert, a quantity surveyor. John Gerrity has done lots of research for me on what we need and how to cost it, so yes, we have, and that's the best we can do. The stone for the wall is the biggest issue because we need to comply with the preservation order and only use original stone. Now we can reinforce it with steel so it won't collapse again, but it must be faced in original seventeenth-century stone, and we need several thousand tonnes of it. Even in Ireland, that's going to be a tall order.'

'All right, so how do we get that kind of money?' she asked.

'I've no idea. That's what this meeting is for, to see if there's a way, because if there isn't, we'll have to close. I don't even know if we could sell it – whoever bought it would face the same issues we do – so we need to explore all of our options, which from where we are now aren't that many.'

'All right, let's brainstorm.' Olga took out her notebook and pen. 'My first idea is could we try for an international investor, some venture capital company or even a chain of luxury hotels that sees the potential and would back us to do the work for a share in the business?'

'Possibly,' Conor replied. 'I won't rule anything out, but it would mean that we no longer own the hotel. And we've all seen what can happen when a family business is bought out by a chain. And that's even if a chain would be interested. The sums involved in future proofing the place are not inconsiderable. That said, it's worth a shot, I suppose, as a last resort.'

Carlos nodded. He and Katherine had both previously worked at a lovely old hotel called the Dunshane. A French chain had bought it, and soon it was all self-check-in and everything that had been standard became an extra charge. It was all about profit and nothing to do with customer service. Both of them ran out the door of the place.

'That would be a last resort. We saw what happened to the Dunshane,' Carlos said.

The small, neat South African and Conor had crossed swords many times over those years, going back to when Conor stayed at the Dunshane as a tour driver and Carlos was the manager. If it had been up to Conor, Carlos would never have been hired as duty manager, but Conor had to admit that the man was excellent at his job. His attention to detail was second to none, and the two men had eventually developed, if not a warm relationship, then at least a cordial, professional one.

'Is digging drainage ditches not a good idea?' Artur asked. 'Maybe a pump, to pump out the water before it comes close to the castle?'

Conor was glad Artur was participating. Ana had told him her dad had been researching online day and night in Russian and English since he heard about the problem.

'We looked at that. If the source of flooding was a river, then yes, that might work, but in our case it's the ocean and rising tides. So according to the engineers, pumping wouldn't work, so it's not an option for us, unfortunately. But keep the ideas coming, lads. As I said, nothing is ruled out. We'll consider all possibilities.'

'What about Corlene?' Katherine asked.

Corlene was Conor's former business partner, and was now living the life of Riley in the south of Spain with a former Irish government minister.

'I thought of her, and I'm trying to track her down to see if Colm might use his influence with the department of the environment to get even a partial grant to cover some of the cost of the work. But taxpayer money for flood relief is in short supply, and there are schools, hospitals, not to mention thousands of private homes in constant threat of another flood, so a luxury hotel won't elicit much sympathy with anyone. Nor should it, I suppose.'

'Worth asking though.' Carlos was thinking. 'What about Liam Seoige? We could use our influence with him. I mean, we could put a bit of pressure on him, given what we know about his situation?'

Last year a young American woman had come to Ireland looking for her father, a man she'd never met. Her mother had a summer romance in Boston with a young Irish student who was working on a building site. The lad had outstayed his welcome and was in the USA illegally, but he'd been caught and immediately deported, never having a clue that his American girlfriend was pregnant.

That girl was called Billie Romano, and through a serendipitous series of events that seemed to have blessed Conor's career, Conor had managed to make the connection between Billie and her father. The only fly in the ointment was that the man was a government minister. Seoige was tipped to become the next Taoiseach, Ireland's prime minister, and so the whole thing had to be handled discreetly.

Conor had facilitated the first father-daughter meeting in the hotel and kept it all out of the public eye, and now Liam and Billie were very close. Liam and his wife and children had even met Billie and her fiancée, Noah, at the castle for dinner on a number of occasions when Billie and Noah visited from the States.

'It's not the worst idea,' Katherine said quietly, raising an eyebrow at Conor.

'Absolutely not.' Conor was firm. 'I'll ask Liam to help – in fact, he rang me two days ago when he heard what happened, so he might be able to do something – but we are not using our position of knowing about his personal life to put pressure on him. I'd rather lose the hotel than do something as horrible as that, so that one's a flat no, I'm afraid.'

'Well, even without pressure,' Olga interjected, 'Minister Seoige is nothing if not a canny politician. He must be acutely aware of how the saving of so many jobs for the region would be a help in the upcoming election. How about you make it clear that if he helps us, we'll make sure everyone knows about it? That's not underhanded. That's just business.'

'Indeed. But even with a grant, it's only going to be a drop in the bucket. We need to come up with the money ourselves for the most part.' Conor sipped his coffee, forgetting it was decaf, and made a face.

'Don't mind your whining,' Katherine said. 'We've enough on our plate without you keeling over with a heart attack from all the caffeine, so it's decaf or nothing.'

'You'd never think I was the boss,' Conor muttered.

Everyone laughed, easing the tension in the room.

'OK, any other ideas?'

Ana spoke then. 'What about that TV company – remember – that wanted to make some show here but we had to turn them down because we were full? Maybe we could approach them again?'

'That was ages ago though,' Conor replied. 'I'm sure they've found someplace else by now. It might have worked though. Pity, especially since we've no guests. Maybe they could have filmed in the bits we've fixed up.'

Katherine coloured and everyone turned to her. 'Well, actually the programme was called *Grandma Says We're Irish* and it was put on hold, but now they have a new celebrity lined up and they're still looking for a location.'

'How do you know all this?' Conor gave her a quizzical look.

'Look, I saw it in one of those celebrity magazines, all right, if you must know, and the celebrity they have lined up is none other than our own Fintan Rafferty.'

Conor caught Ana's eye and suppressed a grin. Katherine must really want to save the hotel if she was willing to admit she liked something as frivolous as celebrity gossip. Ana had told him that Katherine got *OK!* and *Hello!* magazine every week but would rather die than have anyone find out.

'Go on,' Conor encouraged her, as the two pink spots on her cheeks reddened further.

'Well, just that the producer is Xavier Gonzales, and he and Fintan Rafferty are friends for years and years. Gonzales is the king of reality TV and wanted to do this project, but it fell through because they couldn't find a location.'

'But surely Fintan Rafferty is too big a star for reality TV?' Conor asked. 'Didn't he win Oscars and all sorts? He surely wouldn't do something like that?'

'Well, he used to be, but...' Katherine swallowed. 'This is common knowledge anyway, but his wife left him for a friend of his – not Xavier Gonzales, some other man – and they basically have been saying terrible things about him. He's hitting the bottle fairly hard and has lost some major roles recently because of his drinking. He was arrested last month for fighting in a nightclub in Miami.'

'And you're sure they don't have a location?' Olga asked, getting excited now.

'Well, as of last week's interview with *CelebSpy*, they didn't anyway.'

'But his brother lives outside Ennistymon, doesn't he? We can contact him, ask him to speak to Fintan, and invite them here to do the show.' Olga grinned.

'Ah, I don't know. The poor man sounds like he's been through enough. We shouldn't be badgering him –' Conor began.

'No.' Ana put her hand up to stop him. 'I agree we should not say we will tell everything about Liam Seoige's life, that is wrong, but Conor, this man, this Rafferty, is a world-famous actor and he's from here. He might want to help his old place. And they asked before, so it won't be any harm to contact him. He has sad life now, it is true, but this is what reality TV likes, you know, and we can't afford to be all…I don't know…what is the word?'

'Overly sentimental and polite.' Carlos helped her out.

'No, look,' Conor said, 'I'm not comfortable calling the guy up, but we will get back to whoever contacted us first and say the hotel is now available, OK?'

'I know you're not one to press your advantage, Conor, but we really need to use all we can now –' Katherine began.

'No, Katherine, it's not fair. Fintan Rafferty's life is in ribbons, he's got a drink problem, and us going with the begging bowl and asking for special favours because he's from here doesn't sit well with me. We will ask, but through the proper channels. Agreed?'

Katherine looked mutinous, but Carlos just shrugged.

'OK, so, Olga, will you reach out to them? I'll speak to Liam Seoige about a grant, and I'll keep on trying to track Corlene down as well.' Conor smiled. 'Herself and Colm might have a couple of million Euro in a biscuit tin under the bed. In the meantime, how are the renovations coming along? I'm aware that it's Christmas week, and with the new baby and everything going on and fielding phone calls and emails all day, I'm leaving the overseeing of that to you all.'

'We get more done when you're not here anyway,' Katherine replied tartly, a hint of a smile playing on her thin lips.

He knew her of old and took no offence. He'd invited her and Jimmy over the night Ana and Lily came home, and he knew how much his family meant to Katherine. She had no family of her own; Jimmy and the O'Sheas were her whole world.

She and Jimmy had bought Lily the most lovely antique rocking horse they'd found at an auction, and the boys were mesmerised by it. When Conor asked her if she'd like to hold Lily, she almost refused, but once he settled his daughter in her arms, Katherine's face softened in a way rarely seen by anyone. She was besotted with the little girl, and that night Ana suggested that they ask Katherine to be her godmother. They planned to ask her on her own – she'd hate a fuss – after the meeting.

They each gave him a progress report for the different aspects of the castle, and he was pleasantly surprised how much had been done. It looked like the reopening could be sooner than he'd expected, and that cheered him up to no end.

'How are you getting on with Daniel?' Conor asked with a grin, knowing the architect from a very trendy Dublin suburb tended to look down his nose at anything not urban and chic.

'He is insufferable,' Katherine answered bluntly. 'Worse than when he was here for the original refurbishment, if such a thing is possible. You would think we had flooded the castle deliberately to annoy him the way he goes on. Apparently he asked Paddy Mac why he couldn't get a decaf skim flat white in the coffee machine at the petrol station. Poor Paddy asked him what language he was speaking. Daniel was so put out that he brought a stupid big coffee machine down from Dublin and installed it upstairs.'

Conor suppressed a smile. He could just picture the scene: Daniel in his designer suit and handmade Italian shoes conversing with Paddy Mac, owner of the shop and garage near the castle. Paddy had two brown hairy suits – a good one for funerals and hurling matches and an old one for work, shiny with age. He cut his own hair and regularly had bits of toilet tissue stuck to his face where he'd cut himself shaving.

Olga and Carlos exchanged a look. Carlos Manner didn't like anyone, yet those two were thick as thieves.

Conor had heard from Katherine what had happened. Apparently Daniel decided to try his luck with Olga – she was a lovely girl, so Conor didn't blame him – but she turned him down flat. He'd been very disgruntled and had said during the work tea break that he thought she was probably a lesbian. Unfortunately for Daniel, Carlos overheard. He gave Daniel short shrift, explaining that a person's sexual orientation had no relevance in the workplace, but that Olga most certainly was not gay, for the record, and that only a pathetic loser of a man would say such a thing. He quoted the equality act as well, and all of this in front of the builders who had been giving the architect a teasing about being knocked back. It was all high drama, and Daniel walked off the site in a huff. But Conor wasn't supposed to know any of this.

'Fine,' Carlos said curtly. 'He is getting the job done, though the builders are always complaining about him. His people skills are very poor.'

Conor coughed to hide the chuckle. Carlos Manner pointing out anyone's poor people skills was hilarious. The man rubbed everyone the wrong way.

Artur jumped in to save him. Conor felt a wave of affection for his father-in-law, who was self-conscious about his heavily accented English, especially in groups.

'The gardens is fine, resodding is finish and beds are all resetted as well. We have to buy some seasonal colour because it all look empty and bad. But now is fine, and in few weeks when spring flowers come, it will be much better.'

Conor shot his father-in-law a glance of gratitude. 'Well, I want to say thanks to all of you. These last weeks have been crazy, for me personally and of course for us all professionally, but I couldn't have left to attend to my family if I wasn't so confident in you all. I know I'm always saying it, but you are amazing, and we will figure this out, however we do it. We thought after the fire that we were finished, but we came back stronger than ever. We'll do the same this time.'

'First a fire, then a flood. What's next, a plague of locusts?' Katherine said with a wry smile, and they all laughed. They'd get through this.

As they filed out, Conor looked up. 'Can you hold on a sec, Katherine?'

She turned and shut the door, resuming her seat. Ana took Lily, who had just woken up, out of her pram.

'Ana and I wanted to ask you something,' Conor said. He stood in front of her, his hands in his pockets. He shot Ana a glance.

'Well? Get on with it,' she replied. 'If it's to do with the new bar stools, I told you the upholsterer is in Lanzarote and his son is doing them but he –'

'It's not about the hotel. It's personal.'

'What?' She swallowed.

Ana had told him that Katherine was afraid he was going to ask her to retire. She was coming up to the age but didn't want to go.

'Two things actually. The first is to do with retirement.'

Her face was inscrutable, but he knew she was nervous and wanted to reassure his old friend.

'I want you by my side in this place until you want to go. I'll hate to lose you whenever that time comes, but only one person will decide when you retire and that will be you. Is that OK? So birthdays and all of that are none of my business, but there's a job here for you for as long as you want one.'

'Thank you, Conor,' she replied, her dignity not allowing anything else. 'And the other thing?'

He sat beside her and took her hand in his. Ana stood in front of her, the baby in her arms. They didn't have a very tactile relationship – to say Katherine was prickly was to understate the case – but he gave her the odd hug anyway.

'What? You're both worrying me now.'

'We would love it if you'd be Lily's godmother,' Ana said.

'I...' Katherine opened her mouth but closed it again. 'But...but I have no experience with babies or children or anything, and I'm not that religious,' she spluttered. 'I mean... I...'

They were afraid that she would refuse.

'We want you,' Ana said sincerely. 'Lily loves you already, and you know we all love you. We may not be blood, but you're family to us, and we think you'd be a wonderful influence in her life. So please, will you do it?'

Conor never let go of Katherine's hand, and his gaze held hers as she turned from Ana to him, her eyes bright with tears. She'd had a tough life, rejected by her family as a child, then abandoned at the altar by her first fiancée, and she'd cut herself off emotionally for many years. Conor O'Shea, the tour driver as he was then, was the only one brave enough to risk trying to get under her granite exterior, and it had paid off with a lasting, loyal friendship that had sustained him through some very difficult times in his life.

She swallowed. 'It would be the greatest honour of my life.' Her voice was choked with emotion. 'Thank you.'

'It's I should thank you, Katherine, for everything. None of this' – Conor waved his hand around – 'works without you.'

She smiled, a rare and beautiful thing, and her face transformed.

'Right. Back to work,' Conor growled jokingly.

Katherine stood up and walked to the door, placing her hand on the knob. She never turned but said, 'I want you both to know...'

'Yes?' he asked.

'I love you all too.'

Then she walked out and quietly closed the door behind her.

CHAPTER 8

'So that went well,' Conor said as Katherine closed the door behind her. 'If this TV show is an option… We never got as far as talking money, but they'd surely be willing to pay, you'd think. Right?'

'I've no idea, but we can try to find out.' Ana bit her thumbnail as she always did when she was deep in thought. 'Remember a few years ago, we went to the cinema – we were invited by the hotel to see this comedy film about a haunted house in Ireland. Like, it wasn't haunted but they were pretending it was or something?'

'I do. It was set in Ballybracken House?'

'Yes, this one. Could you call them and ask how much they got to film there?'

'Well, my little communist, I could ring and gently bring the conversation around to it and try to enquire subtly.' He chuckled. Ana had a directness to her that was at odds with the Irish way of doing things. Sometimes people saw her as too abrupt, but it was just her way. Her parents were the same. It was something to do with the Soviets.

She rolled her eyes. He knew it drove her crazy how Irish people didn't say what they thought or what they meant. She complained constantly that it was impossible to get anything done with everyone speaking in code. It wasn't really as bad as she made out, but the straight-talking way of those from the Ukraine was at odds in West Clare.

'Well, the end result is same, just my way is quicker.' She grinned.

'And as subtle as a bag of hatchets.' He kissed her head.

'I should probably know, but tell me about this Fintan Rafferty.'

Conor knew Ana wasn't a big fan of films, and the only TV she watched was a dreadful soap opera in Ukrainian that she and her mother were addicted to – in which everyone was either screaming or crying as far as Conor could see.

'He's an Irish actor, kind of a heart-throb fella, I think, at least he was. He was the one in that thing we watched... What's it called? The one set in the South of France and he was an architect and your one – you know, the one with the long red hair – was in it?'

Ana rolled her eyes. 'And this, my dear Conor, is why I don't watch films with you.'

'You'd know him if you saw him.' Conor did a quick Google search and showed her a picture. One of the photos, clearly a press shot, was of a ruggedly handsome man with dark wavy hair, designer stubble, smouldering eyes and a powerful physique. But the next photo was totally different. In that one, his face was puffy, he was wearing a winter jacket and a woollen beanie hat and he looked very much the worse for wear. The photographer was clearly intruding.

Conor read the copy aloud. 'Hollywood A-lister Fintan Rafferty left court today clearly shaken after the divorce hearings between him and his ex-wife, actress Nikita Amos. The star of the hit show *The Unbelievers* claims Rafferty was emotionally abusive and is demanding a huge settlement amount, a source close to the couple revealed.'

Ana looked at the picture again. 'The poor man looks terrible. What an awful thing. But maybe he was bad like she said – who knows?'

'I remember reading something about that last year, when his missus went off with some other fella, but I don't keep as up to date with celebrities as Katherine.' Conor chuckled as he tried to remember. 'I don't know the details exactly, but it sure has shaken him up by the looks of things, hasn't it?' Conor closed the article.

'And does he come back here? Have you seen him?' Ana asked.

'Not for years, but maybe he does and nobody notices. You know how many famous people we get here and nobody notices them. I think it's why they enjoy Ireland – they know they'll be left alone.'

'I know,' Ana mused. 'Irish are weird in so many ways, but they respect people wanting to be private, I think. Remember last year when that comedian – you know, the one on the TV – came here and she was a bit cross that nobody recognised her?'

Conor laughed. 'Do I remember? She had me tormented for weeks before she came, asking about security and all the rest of it. In the end, nobody batted an eyelid. You're right, Irish people don't generally bother celebrities, not because they are so respectful though. It's because they wouldn't give an actor or a singer or whatever the satisfaction of them knowing that we knew who they were.'

He drained his cup, grimacing in disgust. 'Honestly, pet, can you smuggle some proper coffee in for me? I can't stick this muck.'

'No, I will not. For one reason, Katherine would kill me, and for the other reason, it is bad for you. You are old enough and you have a small baby now, so I need you to stay alive forever.' She reached up on her tiptoes and kissed his cheek.

'Speaking of small babies, give me my little one for a cuddle before I intervene in the tenth fight today, this time between Daniel and the digger driver.' He pointed out the window to where a large man with two sleeves of tattoos, a bald head and an enormous red beard was gesticulating threateningly at the architect.

'OK. And so I'm coming back tomorrow. Mama said she will be fine, and if there is any problems, I can pop back.' Ana sounded amazed he'd given in so easily.

'Brilliant, I can't wait. Katherine can't stand Daniel, and makes no effort to hide the fact, and you've a much better way with people. Carlos and herself are like the odd couple, one crankier than the other, and poor Olga is firefighting constantly. To be fair to her, she only brings it to me if it's looking like a blood injury, but they are all too frequent. You manage everyone with a smile, and they all love you. And as you say, if Lily is upset or whatever, one of us can go for her.'

They walked out into the building site, and it seemed impossible to imagine it would ever be the idyllic resort it once was.

CHAPTER 9

*T*he next afternoon, having checked the time in LA, Conor punched the number into his desk phone, having given strict instructions that he wasn't to be disturbed.

He was returning Fintan Rafferty's call, which was strange considering Olga hadn't even emailed the production company yet.

Ana was back on the front desk, and Katherine was in the back talking to the advertisers, planning the promotions that would be needed to get the hotel full again. Carlos was checking on the rooms with Sheila. Chef was back in his kitchen, trying to reassemble everything. New equipment had been ordered, and installation was proving a problem. The new ovens were tripping the electric, and Artur was trying to figure out where the problem was. Meanwhile, the bar staff were together varnishing the floors, and the whole place was a hive of activity.

The number rang, the long dial tone of the United States, and after two rings, a deep but tentative voice answered. 'Hello?'

'Hello, Mr Rafferty, my name is Conor O'Sh –'

'I'm not speaking to anyone, and if you call again, I'll have my lawyer all over you!'

Conor heard static and then beeping. Rafferty had hung up.

Conor sat, holding the receiver. Whatever was going on with the man, he didn't want to talk anyway. Conor wondered if the number was a landline or a mobile.

He opened his messenger app and typed a text message.

Hi Mr Rafferty. My name is Conor O'Shea, and I own Castle Dysert in County Clare, Ireland. I was just returning your call. Anyway, this is my number, so if you want to give me a call, I'd love to hear from you, or you can email if you'd prefer. conoroshea@castledysert.ie.

All the best.

Connor was deep in thought when he saw his phone flash. He opened the message and saw that it was from Rafferty.

Hi Conor. Sorry I missed your call. Yes, I do have something I'd like to talk to you about. If you want to try me again, I'll pick up. FR

Conor dialled the number again, and it was answered on the second ring. A man with a cultured Irish accent answered.

'Hi, Conor. Apologies. I've been getting a lot of press calls recently, and frankly the only way to deal with them is to hang up. You're what the Americans call over here "collateral damage", I'm afraid.'

'No problem, I understand,' Conor replied, unsure whether to mention that he knew the story.

Rafferty saved him the awkwardness. 'You've probably seen something about the circus I'm stuck in over here?'

'Yes, I read an article. I'm so sorry to hear it...' Conor wished his words didn't sound so hollow. Apparently Rafferty's wife had posed nude in *Playboy* last week to 'celebrate her freedom'.

'Yeah, well, hell hath no fury and all that. Hard enough. Anyway, that's not why I wanted to talk to you.'

'I'm all ears.' Conor was relieved to be off the topic of the man's sordid personal life.

'So my brother Eugene got a call from Father Eddie – I think you and he are friends? Anyway, Eddie has known me for years – he was very good to my mam when she was dying – and so he asked Eugene to contact me when he heard about your predicament. He told me you're in a bit of bother and that you're a decent person and you've provided a lot of employment around the place. He also said you are good at dealing with Americans and that you know a bit about genealogy.'

'Well,' Conor said, 'we do have a lot of local people working here, and we are facing a bit of a disaster. The place flooded. We're getting it sorted this time, but it's happening more and more frequently and the insurance won't keep paying out. And anyway, we can't keep going with this level of disruption. So yeah, we're in trouble all right.'

'OK. Well, I have a proposal.'

Conor heard some noise on the line and realised Rafferty was lighting a cigarette.

'A production company is looking to make a reality TV show. That's where the money is these days, morons looking at other morons doing stupid things, but who am I to judge? They sent out some tentative feelers about a location a few months back, yours and a whole heap of other places, and they even went over there and had a look around. But between one thing and another, they couldn't find the right place and so they shelved it.'

Conor heard the exhale of the smoke.

Rafferty went on. 'So the producer is a friend of mine, and now that my life is officially a train wreck and I need cash badly to pay off that witch before she does any more damage, I'm reality TV gold. Rock bottom, I think they call it.' He laughed. 'Anyway, my agent wants me to do it. I'm kind of allergic to the idea, but beggars can't be choosers. Havie – that's my buddy – pitched it as a kind of *Who Do You Think You Are*–themed show. Basically, they'd gather a bunch of celebrities – and I use that term very loosely – all who have Irish heritage, and have them find out about their families and all of that, as well as doing challenges or some other such nonsense. As I said, I hate the idea, but I need the money for my legal bills and I thought if we did it in Ireland, then at least I'd get away from this media hell for a while. The company would potentially book out the hotel, give you a ball of money for the use of the castle, and everyone's a winner. What do you think?'

Conor thought quickly. 'I'm certainly interested, and thanks for thinking of us. I really appreciate it. But the thing is, the castle is in a bit of a state right now. We probably could get enough of it looking OK to film in, and the accommodation is fine, but would that be a problem, do you think?'

'I've no idea. I'd imagine it would be a good thing not to have guests, but look, you and Havie can talk that out.'

'Great. I'd love to sit down with someone, look at the numbers and see if it would work, but I'm definitely open to the idea.'

'Grand so. I'll tell you what. I'll talk to Havie – Xavier Gonzales is his proper name – and get him to put a proposal together on their end and send it over. If it's something you can work with, then we can take it from there.'

'That would be fantastic. Thanks again, Fintan.' Conor's brain was going a million miles a minute.

'And, Conor' – Fintan exhaled again – 'Havie may be a buddy of mine, but he's a shark. So as they say here, play hardball, OK? He's a multibillionaire, so he can afford it, and he's excited about this. He's Argentinian but his mother is Irish, so he's big into all that family tree stuff. He's convinced one of his Irish ancestors was some kind of republican hero, but you must get that all the time, eh? If everyone here who claimed to have a high-ranking IRA man in their past actually did, we'd have been occupied by the British for ten minutes, not 800 years.' He laughed. 'Anyway, humour him, I'd say. His is one of the only production companies that has no shareholders. He owns the whole thing, so he decides, nobody else. I'm going to be in the bloody thing because I need the money, and he listens to me to a point. He's got a girlfriend, a human rottweiler called Kayla, gorgeous but terrifying kind of woman, and she seems to be pulling the strings too. So if he brings her on board, she'd better like you. All of Havie's reality TV things up to this one have been very racy, and Kayla's behind them all. Their last huge success was with a horrific-sounding thing called *Kiss, Marry, Kill*, where a bunch of people are divided between a beach house in Malibu and a deserted factory on some dock, and they have to make alliances of every kind to get to the beach house and out of the factory. It sounded like my worst nightmare. Then there was another one called *Midnight Whispers* – people have to sleep with strangers in the dark or something... I don't know, I never watch them. But just so you know what you're dealing with.'

'Thanks for the tip. I appreciate it.' Conor thought Rafferty sounded genuine and Kayla's programmes sounded like utter muck, but he had no choice.

'And one last thing.' Fintan paused. 'This is Hollywood, not Ireland. The same rules don't apply. Get yourself a good lawyer, one that's not afraid of blood sports.'

'I will, though you're making me nervous, Fintan.' Conor chuckled.

'Forewarned is forearmed, my friend. Good luck. I hope we can make it work.'

CHAPTER 10

*C*onor changed his tie. Then he wondered if a suit and tie was the right look – perhaps something more casual would be better.

'Pull yourself together,' he muttered as he knotted a green silk tie in his private bathroom, located off his office.

Havie and Kayla were being collected from Shannon. He was going to do it himself, but Carlos insisted it looked better if he did it, that it made Conor look more important. Carlos, Olga and Katherine were full of advice as to how to deal with the TV producers, but for the most part, he ignored them. He'd spent his entire career with American visitors to Ireland, and he knew what he was doing.

They were mithering him day and night because there was so much at stake. Everyone was working hard to try to recoup some of the losses caused by the flood closures, but they were still closed. Even if they had a good season when they eventually did open, they would be in the red this year for sure, unless they could pull off the TV deal. And that was not even considering the insurance issue.

So far, things had gone smoothly. He got a contact at RTÉ, the Irish broadcasting network, to brief him on what he should charge, and the sum involved would cover the costs. Havie agreed, although not without a squabble, and Conor had engaged a solicitor known to be virtually unbeatable. He didn't like the woman – she seemed to lack scruples of any kind, her client being one hundred percent her priority regardless of guilt or innocence – and Conor had been reluctant to employ her at first. Her reputation for defending all sorts of dubious characters and winning preceded her, but she was the best, and he was assured by everyone that she was what was needed. She specialised in contract law, and the prospect of a high-profile negotiation like this one seemed to excite her. She was often seen in the society pages apparently, so she probably thought there would be a few photo opportunities with celebrities in it for her.

So the negotiations went ahead and the sum was agreed upon. The company would begin filming shortly, and they would take all of the self-catering accommodation for the crew and rooms in the hotel for the stars. Filming would happen around the hotel and on the grounds. Conor assumed they would hire a genealogist to research the people's families, and it actually all sounded very interesting. He resisted the urge to seek assurance that the show wouldn't be of the shock-TV type the producer seemed to specialise in, but from the sounds of it, it was all fairly straightforward: a group of Irish Americans looking to find their ancestors. How racy could that be? He didn't know who they had lined up yet apart from Fintan, but he had a great feeling about it. As an added bonus, it would showcase the hotel in the American market. He just needed today's meeting to be a success; once they were happy, then it was all systems go.

His phone beeped with a text from Carlos.

Ten minutes.

Conor exhaled, forcing himself to calm down. He knew the hotel looked splendid. The work was ongoing but what was left was either in maintenance, far away from the public eye, or some decorating that could be done unobtrusively. Thanks to Artur's diligence and research into water-loving plants, the grounds were blooming. The flowerbeds were a riot of early colour. Danika had put an 'Infant Jesus of Prague' statue in the garden, an old Catholic superstition for fine weather, and it had worked. Last week it had bucketed down every single day, but today the sky was blue with white puffy clouds scudding across the bay. Though it was still chilly, it was as idyllic a day as you could imagine.

Ana and Katherine were on the desk, and he joined them, placing an arm on each of their shoulders. 'Showtime.' He grinned.

'You will be wonderful,' Ana said, giving him a quick kiss on the cheek.

'Don't say anything controversial or tell them any jokes,' Katherine warned. 'And for God's sake, act like you knew who they were before they contacted you.'

Conor rolled his eyes at Ana behind his old friend's back, making her giggle. Katherine was as anxious as everyone to make this work. Only the management team knew what was going on, as the excitement of a big TV show would drive the place wild with hearsay and rumours. He would wait to make an announcement until it was all in the bag, and he was hoping nothing cropped up last minute.

'I won't,' he said. 'Chef has a fabulous lunch menu ready for when it's all signed and sealed, though he's like a cut cat at the moment, whatever's wrong with him. We're going to have coffee and scones first in the library, followed by a tour of the hotel and grounds. How can they not love the place?'

'They will love it, and they will love you.' Ana straightened his tie. Only she knew how nervous he really was.

He went to the library, just to make sure everything was in order. Olga was going to be one step ahead all day, smoothing any wrinkles, and Carlos had every staff member on high alert. They'd told everyone the health and safety people were in doing an inspection and that everything needed to be perfect.

He heard the car pull up on the gravel outside and went to meet his guests.

Carlos got out and immediately went to the passenger side to open the door.

Conor saw her legs first, slim, toned and tanned. Then a woman emerged, who looked, to Conor's mind, simply bizarre.

She had huge fire-engine red lips, her dark eyes seemed to be weighed down with metallic eyeshadow, her eyebrows were thick and dark and a completely unnatural shape, and her face didn't move. She had a permanently startled expression, and though Conor knew nothing about women's cosmetic surgery, he'd bet his house that this woman had been altered somewhat. Her dark glossy curls cascaded down her back, reaching almost to her waist, and she had an extremely thin figure. She was wearing a silver outfit that seemed to be made up of tiny shorts and a frilly oversized shirt, and on her feet she wore large red shoes with thick black soles that were like tyre tubes – they looked like the beetle-crushers from back when he was a kid.

'Conor!' she screamed, flinging her arms around him as if he were some long-lost relative, and he winced as an enormous shoe landed on his toe. Her perfume reminded him of a combination of cats, mothballs and lemon juice.

'Oh, you are so like I imagined – a sexy, hunky old Irish guy. I told Havie, if he's not hot, I'm getting back in that car, but I knew you would be. I watched some promo stuff you did for this place.' She theatrically wiped non-existent sweat from her brow. 'Hot! Even hotter in person.'

She ran her hand down his chest, and Conor was totally taken aback. Whatever he'd expected, it wasn't this.

'Y'know' – she winked at him, the heavily made-up eyes making the gesture look ridiculous – 'I record our calls – your accent gets me so turned on – so I can listen to your voice. Sometimes I play it when Havie and I are –'

'Kayla, baby…enough.' Havie walked around and offered his hand to Conor, who'd been mercifully released from Kayla's clutches.

'Hi, Conor, thanks for inviting us. Your place is really something.' Havie looked up at the ramparts and the ivy-covered turret in admiration.

'Hi, Havie, welcome to Castle Dysert.' Conor smiled and hoped the man wasn't upset by the enthusiastic greeting his girlfriend had given him.

Standing behind Havie, suppressing a grin, was Fintan, who

looked considerably better than he did in the photo Conor and Ana had seen. He was rangy and thin and his brown leather jacket hung on his frame, but Conor could see why women thought he was attractive.

'Hi, Conor,' Fintan said, offering his hand.

Conor took it. 'Welcome, Fintan. Some changes since you were last here, I'd imagine?' Conor gestured at the grounds.

'For sure. It used to be all overgrown, bramble and briars everywhere. People said it was haunted, but that just made it more attractive to us as kids.' Fintan gazed up at a huge horse chestnut tree that stood to the right of the castle. 'We used to knock conkers out of that tree, me and my brothers.'

'The local kids still come up here in September and climb that tree, driving the gardeners mad. My own lads love them too, and the competition to have the best one is just as fierce.' Conor chuckled.

'You guys are too cute!' Kayla squealed. 'Say something else.'

Conor exchanged a look with Fintan.

'Oh my gosh, your accents are *adorable*!' Kayla wrapped herself around Conor like a cat.

'Put him down, Kayla,' Havie said good-naturedly, obviously used to her. 'Let's take a look around.'

CHAPTER 11

*H*avie was medium height and slight. He had dark eyes, wavy black hair and caramel-coloured skin. He too was dressed in a manner that caught people's attention, in cream skinny jeans with more rips than fabric and a petrol-blue oversized silk shirt. On his feet were green and gold crocodile-skin slip-on shoes without socks. Around his neck was a delicate silver chain with a diamond angel hanging from it.

'Havie, Fintan and Kayla, you are all very, very welcome to Castle Dysert,' Conor said. He could handle them.

'Havie, look, there's a suit of armour!' Kayla squealed as she ran up the worn stone steps into reception.

Conor caught Ana's eye as she lifted the vizor of the suit to gaze inside.

'Do you think these walk around at night?' Kayla addressed Conor, and because of all the Botox, she lacked facial expression, so it was impossible to tell if she was joking or not.

'I wouldn't know, Kayla. Sure we're all tucked up in bed at night here.' He smiled.

'Alone?' she asked, unabashed, her smouldering dark eyes gazing at him.

'No. Not alone. With my *wife*.' He emphasised the word in the hope it would get her to back off, and felt himself blush slightly.

'So you're married?' She pouted. 'Pity.'

'I am, to Ana. Let me introduce –'

'No, it's OK. I don't want to,' she said offhandedly as she stepped closer to him and placed her hand on his cheek. That horrible smell again made him cough.

'You're not meant to like it – it's pheromones,' she purred. 'We're attracted to each other based on pheromones, so you can get it in a perfume now.' She slid her hand down his face.

Havie was walking around the circular reception. There was a door off to the bar, another to the orangery tea room, and the lifts and stairs to the floors above were tucked behind the huge circular dark-mahogany reception desk. The ballroom, dining rooms, gymnasium and pool and the eighty bedrooms were all upstairs and hidden from view.

'This place is phenomenal!' Havie exclaimed, approaching Conor, Fintan and Kayla, who was standing much too close to Conor, her hand on the small of his back.

'Kayla,' Havie growled quietly, and she grinned and moved away, taking her hands off Conor, but then she pretended to pout.

'Thanks. We love it,' Conor said, glad to get away from her. She was terrifying; Fintan was right.

The staff served freshly baked scones, warm from the oven, with home-made jam and whipped cream. There was coffee and tea and sparkling water, and as Havie and Kayla tucked in, Conor noticed Fintan didn't eat anything. He excused himself to go outside onto the stone patio; Conor guessed it was for a cigarette.

Though he looked better than he did in the shot taken outside the courthouse, he was still gaunt and a million miles from his movie-star image of ten years ago.

Havie began to explain the format of the show. 'So here's the idea. We take six celebrities – Fintan being one – with Irish heritage, and we bring them over here. Basically they uncover their family histories and hopefully meet their Irish relatives if we can find any, and we see what unfolds. The thing about reality TV is the uncertainty – you don't really know where it's going to go. And some of the people we have lined up, well, let's just say they could be volatile.' He grinned and Conor found himself warming to him.

Now was his chance. It was going to be awkward, but he had to say it. 'I'm not much of a man for TV, to be honest with you, most of my viewing is with my kids, but I just wanted to say – and I hope this doesn't cause offence – that we have a reputation here for discretion and as a luxury destination, a place to go to get away from it all. So I hope we can keep the show in that theme and not stray too far into the scandalous end of things, if you know what I mean?' Conor felt so self-conscious and feared he was coming across as a prudish spinster aunt, but at the same time, there was no way he was going to allow the salacious cavorting that was a feature of Havie's other shows to be associated with Castle Dysert. They'd worked too hard on their branding to have it destroyed.

Conor and Ana had watched some of the previous shows, and to say they were car-crash television was to understate the case. They were a torturous mix of screaming, sex and swearing, and Conor was afraid that potential guests seeing the show would be put off coming if they thought that type of behaviour was what went on. The women seemed to be dressed constantly in bikinis that left nothing to the imagination, and the men were not much better. Ana did point out it would have to be a hardy man or woman who would consider baring all in Ireland when filming started in January.

'Oh, don't worry, Conor.' Havie winked. 'It's all going to be squeaky clean, I assure you.'

'Everyone will be fully dressed, and no F-bombs, we promise,' Kayla simpered, her red-taloned fingers resting on his jacket sleeve.

Conor knew neither of them meant a word of it. He was being used and knew he would probably have to intervene at some point, but they needed the money so badly.

He changed the subject. 'Fintan told me your mother was of Irish extraction?'

Kayla was now on her phone, scrolling intently, allowing the men to talk.

'Yeah, Mom was an O'Bride from Tipperary.'

Conor heard the note of pride in Havie's voice.

'Her folks came over to the US in the early twentieth century and settled first in New York but followed the gold out West. My ancestor was an Irish freedom fighter – he left with the British on his heels. My father's family came from Argentina – he's third-generation US born though, so it's far back. It all fascinates me, so this is kind of a pet project of mine.'

Conor wondered if he should clarify the fundamental error and decided he would. If Havie stayed around, someone would eventually tell him his mistake. 'Well, I think your mother's family were probably McBride rather than O'Bride.' He watched for signs of Havie taking offence, and when there was none, carried on. 'All Gaelic – or Irish as we say – names are either O or Mac names, so my name, for example, O'Shea, or O'Mahony, or O'Leary, O'Brien, they just mean "of". So I am Conor of the O'Shea clan. And then the Mac or Mc names mean "son of", so MacBride, McGann, McSweeney, McCarthy, would always be Mac and never O.' He decided to leave the Irish freedom fighter to another day. It might be true, but he was inclined to agree with Fintan – people liked to invent romantic pasts for themselves. Who was he to question it?

'Really?' Havie was intrigued. 'I wonder how it went wrong. She was sure they were O'Brides, and I've looked at old claim stakes for gold and things like that and it says O'Bride too, so the mistake goes far back.'

Conor sipped his coffee – thankfully full strength as it was laid on for guests – and made a note to get his coffee from the kitchen himself from now on rather than drinking the disgusting stuff Katherine had put in his office. 'Well, that's anyone's guess. Many of the names were changed for pronunciation purposes or by accident when the clerk couldn't understand the immigrants. Mostly they were illiterate, so they just said their names, and so with accents and what have you, it often got confused. For example, Ellis Island. The new emigration station there opened in 1893 and was active until 1943, and their records often have incorrect spelling, or totally different names altogether – it makes finding roots really tricky. It's not just an Irish problem. It was the same for all immigrant groups.'

'You know a lot about this,' Havie said approvingly. 'Are you a professional genealogist?'

'Ah, not at all, just an amateur, but I spent most of my career with Americans who were looking for their Irish heritage, so I have an idea how to go about it. In Ireland, families don't move much, so you could take a guess at where on the island different people came from. Round here, for example, it's all O'Briens, McNamaras and O'Connors. Down in Cork where I come from it's all O'Sullivans, O'Donovans, names like that in the west of the county, and McCarthys, Barrys in the city. Dublin is where all the Kellys are, and so on.'

Havie sat back and thought, absorbing what Conor said.

As Fintan returned, a waft of cigarette smoke hit Conor's nostrils. He'd never smoked himself as he loved swimming and hated the idea of having poor lung function. Since smoking was banned in public buildings, it made going out so much more pleasant. It was rare now to meet a smoker, he realised, and perhaps that's why the smell seemed so pungent.

'Tell me more,' Havie said smoothly.

'Well, we can accommodate all the crew in the self-catering section of the hotel, and we can allocate some space for equipment if needs be. There are several large lock-up garages that could be –'

But Havie interrupted him. 'Yeah, that's all fine. I want to do it here, so we have a deal. But tell me about genealogy.'

Conor was nonplussed. He suppressed the urge to jump up and punch the air. The deal was done. It was happening. The hotel would be saved. He longed to tell the others – they would be on tenterhooks outside waiting – but he thought he'd better not.

'Well, it's interesting on several levels. I mean, we had mass emigration during the famine, obviously. In the middle 1800s, the population went from eight million to five million. A million and a half died, but the other million and a half, the lucky ones, emigrated, largely to the US and Canada, Australia too, and of course to England. But people think Irish emigration is a famine story, and that's only partly true. We have always left – it's in our blood, wanderlust, I think. In each century, regardless of prosperity or the lack thereof, people have emigrated from Ireland, and they always will.' Conor could feel all three pairs of eyes on him as he carried on. 'It's why the best pub in any city, be it Beijing or Boston, is an Irish pub.' He chuckled, and Kayla and Havie caught each other's eye.

'It's gotta be,' Kayla said, and went back to her screen.

Conor had no idea what was going on, but something was being decided.

'Conor,' Havie began, 'I've employed a genealogist – a guy from Pennsylvania, very good at this stuff – to be the glue that holds this whole show together. There's nothing this guy doesn't know about finding roots, so it's all done behind the scenes as it were. I'm going to base my show here. The money it will generate is going to save your hotel and build whatever you need to build out there and then some.' He waved his hand in the direction of the Atlantic Ocean. 'But there's one condition, and its non-negotiable.' He smiled.

Conor was reminded of Fintan's warning. 'What is it?' he asked, wary, though it was hard to imagine any demand he would not meet to save the hotel.

'You've got to be the host, the frontman, the glue. It's got to be you.'

Conor's heart sank. He didn't really enjoy seeing himself on screen, and any promos he did for the hotel he kept very short. This was different, and what if it turned into the kind of show Havie and Kayla specialised in? There was no way he could be stuck in the middle of that rubbish. 'Look, it's very flattering that you think I could, but –'

Havie raised his hand. 'I want you. You want this deal. You can make it happen, but I won't budge on this.'

'But I'm not even qualified –'

'We'll have a team of researchers. Hell, I'll bring that genealogist guy over and he can do the work, but you've got to be the face.' Havie was adamant.

'But why me? I could find you someone –'

'Because, Mr Sexy Irish Guy, you are funny and charming and American women will drool over you,' Kayla said, never looking up from the phone. 'Say yes now. Save yourself the trauma. He won't back down.'

'I'll have to think about it,' Conor said, hating the feeling that he was being railroaded.

'No time,' Havie said quietly. 'It's yes or no. If it's no, I walk out the door and find someplace else. If it's yes, we shake on it now, and soon Conor O'Shea will be a household name all across America.'

Conor looked out the library window. Artur was explaining to Aidan O'Connor where he wanted the new topsoil put. Aidan was one of the best gardeners they had, and his wife, Gill, was a waitress in the restaurant. They were expecting their first baby in the summer. Clearing the coffee things was young Saoirse Mullane; her sister Aoife was the riding instructor, and their father, Tony, supplied the kitchen with vegetables. Out in reception, Ana, Artur, Katherine, Carlos and Olga were waiting to hear if he'd pulled off a miracle. It was so close. So many people relied on him, so many families, not just his own.

He could do it. He'd hate it, but he could do it. He'd been a showman on the tours for so many years, telling stories, singing songs; it probably wasn't that much different. And he was in no doubt that Havie wasn't bluffing.

'All right,' Conor said. 'I'll do it.'

'Awesome.' Havie grinned.

CHAPTER 12

*I*t's extraordinary,' Katherine remarked as she and Conor were walking through the hotel on their morning rounds, 'that a television show needs so many people and so much equipment.'

The hotel was almost back to normal. It was early January now, and they'd had a lovely family Christmas. Normally Conor would have to be at the hotel for most of the holiday because there would be so many guests, but since it was closed, he decided to make the most of it. Santa Claus came, even bringing something for Lily, and they'd had a big family dinner.

As a surprise for Conor and Jamsie, Ana had arranged for Liz and Damien to come back for a few days, so they joined in and the noise and fun was tremendous. Jamsie, Artur and Danika, as well as Jimmy and Katherine, joined the O'Sheas for Christmas dinner, and it was wonderful.

'I suppose you heard Olga and Carlos went away for a few days.' Katherine paused. '*Together.*'

'I did,' Conor confirmed. Ana had filled him in on their plans to go skiing in Switzerland for Christmas. 'Do you think there's something going on there?'

'Well, I don't know.' Katherine sounded dismissive. 'I mean, she's a lovely girl and he's as odd as two left feet, but there's no accounting for taste, I suppose.'

'Ana reckons they're just friends. He'd probably like it to be more than that, but she is a bit out of his league all right.'

'She'd want her head read to get tangled up with him – he's daft. You know he told Martin Lowry that he was putting too much baking powder in the scones?'

Conor chuckled. 'And how did the charming Martin take that bit of constructive criticism?'

'Exactly as you'd imagine he would. Carlos was lucky Martin had his hands full with a load of vegetables or he'd have brained him.'

Conor made a point of calling to each department every day, just to say hello and see that everyone was all right. It was more important than ever to do it now. He used to do it alone, but in recent months he asked one of the management team to accompany him. So many issues were being raised by the arrival of Acorn Productions that he needed someone to keep track of it all and chase up any problems.

Together he and Katherine opened the doors of the newly refurbished kitchen, and immediately Martin started in.

'Conor, the list of allergies and intolerances are getting entirely out of hand. I can't be expected to cater to every single nonsensical whim of people with nothing better to do than dream up conditions for themselves.'

Katherine soothed him. He was a wonderful chef but dramatic and inclined to be grumpy at the best of times; however, in recent weeks he had been worse.

'He's got gout,' Katherine murmured as she and Conor left the kitchen after listening to a fifteen-minute rant. 'Apparently he's been put on a strict diet and told he's to give up drink, so he's like a briar. Best just humour him for now.'

'Are they being difficult though?' Conor asked as they walked around the grounds on the way to the landscaping meeting that Artur held every morning at eight thirty to allocate the day's jobs.

'Not especially,' Katherine answered. 'Mostly they are very nice actually. And so young. I can't believe these kids that look like they should still be at school are production assistants and head of this or that. And there are so many of them. Though they all say when the celebrities show up tomorrow, that's when the real fun and games will start.'

Conor heard the tinkle of excitement in her voice. The normal acerbic Katherine was getting giggly at the idea of celebrities arriving.

'Hmm,' Conor replied, then sighed deeply.

'Ah, for God's sake, Conor, would you cop on!' Katherine stopped and rounded on him, startling him with her vehemence. 'Going around like you're being sent to the gallows and everyone dancing on eggshells around you. If anyone is being a diva, 'tis yourself. It's only a television programme, Conor, and you said it yourself – we need to do everything we can to raise the money. So this is your bit. Everyone else is flat out making sure this is a success, and it's not easy trying to run a luxury hotel when you've people wanting to tape electrical cables to 300-year-old oak floors. But we are managing, and the castle is holding up, so just get on with it and be your usual self. They tell me you're charming apparently. I can't see it myself but...'

Conor grinned. Trust Katherine to give him a good talking to. The more he thought about it, the more he dreaded the coming weeks. Kayla kept dropping hints that it was going to be explosive and how people would be glued to their TVs to see what happened next, which didn't fill him with anything but terror. He had no idea what she planned, but it was definitely not a gentle, semi-academic show about genealogy, that was for sure.

There were to be six episodes, each focusing on a different celebrity, and they would all be filmed simultaneously. Carlos and Olga assured him that they would run the hotel so that he could just focus on doing the show.

'I've booked Laoise and Dylan for the wrap party, by the way. They are so busy these days, you need to book them months in advance. They're playing at Radio City Music Hall in New York next week, can you believe it?' Katherine beamed with pride. 'Jimmy and I might go back to New York for a long weekend once everything dies down. Even though he was born and raised there and loves to go back, he's happy to leave after four days. He says the west of Ireland is in his blood now and he can't keep up with the frantic pace in the Big Apple. But if we timed it for when Laoise and Dylan were there, it might be lovely.'

Dylan and Laoise, a young couple, were loved by everyone at Castle Dysert. Dylan had come on a tour of Conor's with his mother Corlene, when he was a teenager and had fallen in love with the Irish uilleann pipes, a sort of Irish bagpipe, while simultaneously falling for a wild young Irish virtuoso, a harpist and fiddle player with tattoos, piercings and multicoloured hair, called Laoise. They were both incredibly talented musicians and had carved out a huge career for themselves playing a kind of Celtic rock combined with haunting pipes and harp music, and they were in great demand internationally.

'I know. Laoise rang and squealed down the phone with excitement when she heard I was going to be in it,' Conor said. 'She loves Havie's shows, wouldn't you know, so she was winding me up saying I'd be stuck in love triangles and other total rubbish. But she thought it was hysterically funny that I was going to be getting involved with any of it. Anyway, I told her this was nothing like that, that it was a show about people tracing their Irish roots and nothing more. She wasn't convinced.'

'Well, with all due respect, Conor, I think you're a bit long in the tooth for any of that silliness, and I doubt people would be sitting on their sofas waiting for you to get yourself into anything untoward. So you're safe enough, I'd say.' She smiled, a rare occurrence. 'Look, I know you're nervous and I wouldn't do what you're doing for all the tea in China, but this is no different than standing up in front of a crowd and talking about what you know. You've been doing it for years, so just be yourself and they'll be mad about you.'

'I don't care if they're mad about me or not, that's not the issue, but I…I don't want to be a celebrity. I know it sounds so…like I've notions of myself, but I honestly don't. I like my life as it is and I hate going on television, you know I do, and I avoid it when I can. And I've had to do some stuff for the hotel that I don't enjoy, but this… That mad lunatic Kayla has something up her sleeve – I know she does. This is not me being self-indulgent, but have you seen the way she's always pawing me and how rude she is to Ana? I can't stick her. And Havie seems oblivious. I mean, if my partner was going on like she does with another man, I'd get out of that situation right away. But he doesn't seem to mind that she flirts and makes suggestive remarks all the time.'

Katherine didn't say anything but listened intently to every word.

Conor went on. 'It's like she's trying to push my buttons, to get me to react to her, and I won't do it. You know better than most, Katherine, I've had all sorts of people on the tours and in the hotel over the years, and I can manage most of them, but she's in a league of her own. She stinks of that horrible perfume stuff she wears, and it feels like I'm a mouse and she's a cat just toying with me. If we didn't need them so much, I'd have put her in her place long ago, but I hate that I have to put up with it.'

Katherine gave a wry smile. 'Now you get a glimpse of what women all over the world have had to deal with since God was a child. Not all men are like that of course, but some definitely are, and there are enough of them to make it a real feature of working life for women. It is predatory sexual harassment, but most women are unable to do or say anything for fear of losing their jobs. And you know, one of the hardest things is that good men often don't see it, so they don't know it's a real problem. Any woman who complains is made to feel they are imagining it, or worse, inflating their own attractiveness. Or often it's passed of as a joke and a woman presented as being an angry feminist man-hater if she refuses to accept it. It's horrible but it's the reality.'

'I know it is. I saw plenty of it myself over the years. I don't know how ye stand it, it's ridiculous in this day and age. I can't bear her, Katherine, seriously. She just gets under my skin and I want to tell her to back off...' Conor realised his fists were clenched in frustration.

'I know you do. And you'll get your chance when the cheque is in the bank. But for now, we need to be prudent and just endure, all right?' She linked her arm through his, a rare gesture of affection. 'I know she's a pain, and you're not imagining it – she has a thing for you. She does deliberately try to rile you, but so what? You have no interest, and Ana knows you wouldn't look sideways at her. You have great people skills. Kayla is testing them, but just ignore her.'

'I'm trying,' Conor said with a sigh. 'I'm worried too that she's not going to go from near pornography and emotional meltdowns to something as sedate as they are telling me this is going to be, and I'm nervous I'm walking into something I'll regret.'

He shoved his hands in his trouser pockets, gazing out over the bay. It was an overcast day, but even then it was unspeakably beautiful and atmospheric. The early morning mist was still on the furze-covered hills to the right, and the ocean was calm, gently lapping over the pebbled beach that bordered the castle.

'But we have to do it.' He sighed, his eyes on the sea, so calm now but capable of such destruction. 'You're right. It'll pay for the repairs and the flood barriers, so I'll just have to get over myself and get on with it, I suppose.'

'You will.' She patted his arm. 'Now let's see how our gardeners are getting on, shall we? And hopefully they're not as cantankerous as the kitchen staff.'

* * *

THE WEEK since Acorn Productions arrived had flown by. They were filming every day and scouting locations and so on in anticipation of the celebrities' arrival. They had to be curtailed on occasion when they tried to place cameras on antique furniture and one memorable occasion when Carlos nearly had a heart attack as they asked Jason, one of the grooms in the stables, to take his shirt off as he worked so they could film him. Jason was a body builder in his spare time so was happy to oblige until Carlos passed the stable yard and found a member of staff covered in oil and wearing the tightest riding britches imaginable. Carlos had come down like a ton of bricks on Jason, threatening instant dismissal for bringing the hotel into disrepute and all sorts. But generally it was all fine.

Havie, Fintan and Kayla had gone back after two days – they'd return with the celebrities. The entire crew would be back tomorrow to begin filming.

Conor had had meetings with wardrobe, who thankfully agreed that a suit was the best option for him, so at least he'd look like himself. He had a few suits that had been made by Louis Copeland in Dublin and he liked them, and the wardrobe department seemed happy they looked good on him. They had some shirts sent over, tighter than he normally wore, but they insisted. They explained how he would need to wear make-up, but they assured him they'd keep it subtle. He'd had his hair cut by the stylist and had his nails manicured for the first time in his life. He'd grumbled to Ana that he felt like a prize pig at the County Clare Show, but she, like everyone else, thought it was funny and had no sympathy for him.

'They actually said it was lucky I was tanned or else they'd have to put me on sunbeds,' he complained as they had dinner one evening. 'Can you imagine? And they told me not to shave tomorrow in case they want to go with a stubble look. They can forget that anyway. I've never had a beard in my life, and I'm not starting now.'

Even the boys thought it hilarious that he was being primped and prodded.

CHAPTER 13

*T*aylor Davis gazed down at the expanse of Atlantic Ocean as the plane made its way to Europe. The man beside her had introduced himself as Professor Douglas Wilson, but the conversation seemed to kind of dry up then. That woman, Kayla, who seemed to be in charge, told her that he was the genealogist for the show. He seemed nice, and at least he, like her, wasn't a celebrity. She felt such a fraud. Who on earth cared about her ancestors? She was a nobody, only interesting because of her father's nefarious goings-on, nothing to be proud of. Professor Wilson seemed nice at least, not too scary. If anything, he looked a little awkward too. He was younger than most of the professors she knew at college, but he looked every inch the real thing. He wore a Harris tweed jacket and had light-brown hair that fell in front of his eyes, which seemed to need to be pushed back often. His wire-rimmed glasses framed kind brown eyes.

He caught her glancing at him and smiled. He had a nice smile.

'Is it your first time to Ireland?' he asked.

'Yes.' She swallowed. 'And you?'

'I was there once for a conference at Trinity College, but I didn't see much because the work took up all of the allocated time. But what I saw was very nice.' He coloured.

She hoped he would bring the conversation around to the family tree stuff. She would need to rely heavily on him, having absolutely no idea about any of it.

The idea that she would be on TV made her feel sick, actually physically sick, and she wished more than anything she could get out of it. But it seemed there was no other way. People had been kind so far, and nobody mentioned the scandal to her, but she knew everyone knew about it. How could they not? It had been in every single newspaper and on every TV show for weeks.

She tried to focus on her dad's face, him pleading with her to do this thing for him. She could refuse him nothing, much to her mother's disgust.

Marcia Davis was a cold woman. She was not a good mother. Taylor deserved better. It had taken a lot of therapy to get to the point where she could say that.

She didn't have a good relationship with her mother – actually, strike that. She had no relationship with her whatsoever. Her dad was the one she could talk to. And everything was on the line with this show. He was convinced she could restore his position with the Irish vote by doing this. The democratic senator from South Boston who had so badly damaged his relationship with the people he was meant to represent that he needed to use his only child to charm them was in serious trouble. He'd even hinted that not only was his political career over but his business interests would go south too if this situation weren't turned around. She wasn't political in any sense – she hated the constant wheeling and dealing that went on, you do this for me and I'll do that for you – but this was family and her dad needed her. She longed to be back at school, immersed in her studies. She was involved with Amnesty International and was considering a postgraduate course in international relations.

Her father's faith in her was completely misplaced. She knew it was. But she was his last and only hope, so she had to try.

If the Irish connection was on her father's side, it might have been better, but it wasn't. It was on her mother's. Marcia's family had come over to the US from Ireland sometime in the past. That was it, all she knew. But her father had jumped on the Irish thing and played it for all it was worth. Taylor remembered their house on East 4th Street in South Boston – every year on St Patrick's Day it was all done up in green, inflatable leprechauns on the lawn, the whole lot. Everyone in Boston had some Irish in them, but the Davis family were next level. Her dad often joked about changing their name to O'Davis. At least she thought it was a joke; she prayed it was.

She felt such a fraud. She wasn't really Irish, she wasn't a celebrity, and this was a farce. Right up to the moment she set foot on the plane, she fought the urge to bolt. The only thing stronger than her abhorrence of the TV show was the vision of her dad, defeated, holed up in the house, his life in tatters, drinking again. Marcia was staying at their apartment downtown, according to her personal assistant at the advertising company she owned, not answering his or Taylor's calls.

The last few months had been hell. She was shocked when her father finally opened the door to let her in a few days after the story broke. He was always so well-turned-out – hair nicely cut, the best tailoring for his suits – but the man before her that day wasn't her dad. He was puffy-eyed and unshaven, and the house was in darkness. The whiskey bottle on the table made her heart sink.

Ted Davis had been sober for nine years, but she was old enough to remember him as a drunk. Never in public, and never so anyone but his family knew, but she remembered the rages, the broken things, the crying, the begging for forgiveness from his only daughter, and Marcia's cold silence. He'd fought it, went to AA, the whole thing, and had become clean and sober. She was so proud of him. But this new disaster… She just didn't know how to deal with that.

'You're in college, aren't you?' the genealogist asked as he accepted a cup of coffee from the steward and passed her one.

'Yes. I'm a literature and politics major at Boston College. Senior.'

'Ah. My old alma mater.' He offered her a cookie from the selection they had been given. 'Do you enjoy your courses?'

'I do.' She felt relieved. This she could talk about, though she glanced nervously as Kayla, who had been prowling the aisle like a satisfied panther, perched beside them, talking to some of the others on the other side of the aisle. Her butt was level with Professor Wilson's face. There was a rip across the fabric that exposed her bottom, and a scarlet thong was clearly on show. She had an enormous cell phone sticking out of the pocket of her jeans. Taylor wondered what it was like to be that confident.

The professor seemed oblivious to her charms and a little uncomfortable at having her rear end in such proximity to his face. 'What classes are you taking?' he asked, sipping his coffee and shoving his hair out of his eyes.

'This year I'm taking lots of classes in Old English – *Beowulf*, Anglo-Saxon texts, what's left of them – and I love it.'

'Ah, yes, "The Dream of the Rood" and "The Wife's Lament" are particular favourites of mine. There was a marvellous show a few years ago, a one-man show would you believe, where this man, I think he might have been Australian actually, performed the entirety of *Beowulf*.'

'The original or Seamus Heaney's translation?'

If he thought it unusual that a twenty-two-year-old woman knew the difference, he gave no indication of it. Taylor had spent a lifetime trying to hide her academic passion, or nerdiness as the girls at school called it. She'd always felt like an outsider. Her parents were not bookish, and while they left her to her own devices and seemed pleasantly surprised that she was more interested in Molière than mascara, they found her a bit of a mystery and she knew it. Her mother was a beauty, but to Taylor she was like a piece of marble, perfectly carved but cold to the touch. She never looked anything but poised and perfect, never a hair out of place, and Taylor couldn't remember even one cuddle. Her dad had never loved Marcia – he ranted about it often enough when he was drunk – and she certainly despised him, so it was a lonely childhood. Their life was perfect on the outside, of course – they were both wonderful actors – but Taylor found the connection she craved in books.

'The Heaney translation. Excellent work, remarkable. And that he dedicated it to Ted Hughes was a nice touch.'

'I agree. Especially since Hughes was the subject of so much pain and suffering in Sylvia Plath's work, it was nice to see him represented kindly in literature for a change.'

He nodded. 'Indeed. Plath was no doubt a genius, but I always got the impression that she sought to blame Hughes for the collapse of their marriage. Undoubtedly he wasn't faultless, but she was a woman with serious mental illness, and that can't have been easy either.' He took a bite of a chocolate chip cookie. 'I think nobody knows what goes on in anyone's relationships, families and so on, and yet we are so quick to judge. It makes life very difficult for those normal flawed humans who find themselves in the public eye.'

Taylor wondered if his remarks were general or referred to her family. She had no idea how to respond, but he saved her by going on.

'We all make mistakes, but to have them played out in public is particularly hard.' His brown eyes settled on hers and held them for a moment.

'I agree,' she said quietly. So he *was* talking about her. But something in his tone was kind. It didn't feel like an attack. She trusted him. She focused on his long fingers around the coffee cup. His arm touched hers where they shared the armrest, and while she was quite comfortable, he probably wasn't as he was so tall – his knees almost reached the seat in front. Apparently some mix-up meant they all had to travel in economy. Something about the way Kayla delivered the news made Taylor think it wasn't an accident but a way to rattle them, get them to react.

She swallowed nervously. 'Professor Wilson,' she began, keeping her voice low and relieved that everyone seemed to be busy doing something else. She needed someone in charge to know the truth or else this was going to turn into an even more mortifying fiasco, and she might not get the chance to speak with him alone again. He was giving her the opportunity to come clean, and she was going to take it.

'First, call me Douglas.'

'All right, Douglas.' She felt herself blush but forced the words out. 'Look, I wanted to say, before we start the research, that the truth is my mother is the Irish connection, not my father. Though you'd think he had green blood in his veins from the way he goes on, he's actually

Slovenian. And my mother and I, and my parents, don't really get along, so my mother only gave me very minimal information and that was all she was willing to say about her family. So I honestly don't know how that could look good on the show, for me to be so hopeless.'

She was desperate and felt way out of her depth. She might as well tell him the whole story – he probably knew it anyway – as him wasting his time digging around for non-existent Davis relatives would add another layer of embarrassment to an already excruciating situation. Best to be honest now.

'It's quite all right. Please, don't worry,' he said, but she needed to tell him everything.

'I'm sure you know the story, but for the record, my father is the sitting democrat for South Boston, and being Irish and having Irish roots is very important. He married my mother – Marcia O'Hara – for her Irishness, I think. Anyway, they've never been close, but they stick together because it suits them. Or at least it did until recent events.'

'Taylor...' He paused. 'May I call you Taylor?'

'Of course.' She nodded.

'I know this is difficult for you, but you don't have to go into it if you don't want to...' Douglas glanced around, but everyone else was talking or sleeping.

'I don't really. In fact, if there was a parachute available, I might just take my chances down there.' She sighed ruefully and nodded at the ocean below. 'But if you're doing the research, you need to know. I'm doing this to try to regain some position politically for my dad. I think it's a stupid idea, but he really wants me to try. There were taped conversations and video of him with a woman, and in the tape he's talking about how dumb his Irish constituents are, how ugly Irish women are, how Ireland and the Irish are just a bunch of morons, all sorts of horrible stuff. He didn't mean it. He's an alcoholic. He'd been sober for nine years, but he had an affair with this woman and started drinking again. A journalist got a tip, suffice to say, and the whole thing exploded. It's been horrific. My mother has effectively left him, and so she's not keen on helping him to regain anything. But she's not stupid and likes her life and the money, so a divorce will be more profitable if he can get back in the good books. So she told me that there was some Irish relative but that she had no idea who or when.'

'Right,' Douglas said.

Taylor realised she was crying. She'd not shed one tear since the whole mess happened, but now, with this kind man, she couldn't help it.

He handed her a clean but old-fashioned handkerchief from his tweed jacket pocket and patted her hand. 'It sounds like it was a horrible time,' he said gently. 'Please don't worry. Nobody can force you to do anything you don't want to do.'

The conversation might have carried on, but Kayla whipped around and saw that Taylor was crying.

'Tears already?' She grinned. 'Don't waste them! We try to keep all crying for when the camera is rolling.'

The pilot then interjected, making some announcement about the need to fasten seatbelts because of turbulence, and Taylor thought about how metaphorical that was.

Douglas seemed to read her thoughts. 'Buckle up. It's going to be a bumpy ride.' Douglas spoke quietly, out of Kayla's earshot. 'But remember, in the end, what happens is up to you. Don't be bullied. She's a formidable person and very sure of herself. You'll need to be strong.'

'Thanks,' Taylor said as she fastened her seatbelt. It felt good to have one ally at least.

CHAPTER 14

*C*onor had driven to Shannon with a bus to pick up the group. The paparazzi were gathered, and he cursed himself for not thinking of it. Of course the red-top newspapers would be all over the arrival of celebrities to Ireland in the depths of winter.

He thought quickly and said, 'Siri, call Shannon security.'

The phone was answered on the second ring. 'Security.'

'Hi, my name is Conor O'Shea. I wonder if I could speak to Derry Bradley, please?'

'One second.'

A click on the line and he was connected.

'Conor, how's things?' The head of security at Shannon Airport was a golfer and he and Conor and Eddie often made up a three-ball.

'Grand, Derry, but I'm in a bit of a corner and I was hoping you could help me out.'

'If I can, I will.'

Conor briefly explained how he needed to get the people off the plane, into the coach and away, all without the press, and Derry understood immediately. This was a common feature of life in Shannon.

'Right. They'll smell a rat if I try to corral them, so here's what you'll do. I'll get the lads to divert traffic out of the coach park, and if you can get one of your former colleagues on board to coordinate, I reckon there are enough tour buses there to block them in long enough for you to escape. Meanwhile I'll get your people out through the diplomatic gate, so if you go round the back, you can load them up there and be gone before they know it.'

'Derry, I owe you a pint.' Conor grinned.

'I'll hold you to that.' Derry chuckled and hung up.

Conor scanned the coach park and recognised several coaches. The press were gathered around the exit gates, hoping to catch him on the way out. No doubt several more of them were inside the arrivals hall.

'Siri, call Carolina,' Conor instructed as he pulled in.

The phone rang and rang and he was afraid she wasn't going to pick up, but then he heard, 'Well, stranger, how are you?'

He and Carolina Capelli had worked together many times on tours and had kept in contact.

'I'm grand, Carolina, and you?'

The press had spotted the bus with the discreet Castle Dysert logo on the side.

'I need you to do me a favour.'

Carolina sprang into action as he knew she would, and asked all of the guides inside to contact the drivers waiting in the buses for their groups that week. They'd enjoy creating a bit of havoc; it broke up the monotony of waiting endlessly. Within ten minutes the coach park was a complicated gridlock of buses. The news vans were entirely blocked in. Carolina texted Conor a thumbs up.

He drove around the back of the airport, to what looked like the freight offices, and parked. Nobody could have followed him, as all of the press vehicles were stuck.

Inside the airport, he ducked in to the security office.

'Hi, Aidan, how's your mam? I met your granda and he said she was getting the hip done?'

'Hi, Conor. She's grand, up and around already, in fairness to her.

Come here. Derry rang. Your group are going through gate L, so I'll bring you in because you'll need a fob to get through.'

'Good man, Aidan.' Conor followed the young security officer through the bowels of the airport, emerging at the private arrivals hall used for diplomatic or sensitive arrivals.

'They've landed and they'll be directed to come this way, so if you just wait here, they won't be long.' He hesitated and looked like he was deliberating about saying something.

'Spit it out, Aidan.' Conor smiled.

'It's just my girlfriend is looking for a job. We're both in college in Galway but we come home at the weekends, and she applied to the castle but didn't get an interview. She has loads of bar experience 'cause her parents have the pub in Inchintaggart, you know?'

Conor thought for a moment. 'Well, I don't know what we have going, but tell her to send her CV in again, this time to Katherine O'Brien, and tell her to put a cover note on it saying you were talking to me and I said to apply. I'm not promising anything. We get so many applications every time we advertise, we can't interview everyone. If she has the right experience and all the rest of it, I'll ask Katherine to make sure she gets an interview anyway. Is that fair enough? What's her name so I'll be on the lookout for it?'

'Jenny Mulligan. Thanks so much, Conor. We'd really appreciate it. I wouldn't normally ask, and she gets a grant for college, but her dad died a few years back and her mam has Parkinson's, so she could use the money.' The lad looked uncomfortable asking, but Conor knew his family well and wanted to put him at ease.

'This country, rightly or wrongly, works on favours. I'm getting my people out here because your boss is doing me a turn, so that's how the world works. So you were right to ask. A dumb priest never got a parish, as they say, so leave it with me and I'll see what I can do, OK?'

Conor made a mental note to tell Katherine to hire her unless she was terrible altogether. He doubted that she was though; Aidan was a solid lad.

He thought about the old days as he stood in the empty arrivals hall. Normally he'd have been in the main terminal, chatting with former colleagues, men and women he'd worked alongside during his years as a tour driver. He contemplated how his life had changed. All those years, he was single and living mostly in hotels. He was happy, or so he thought, but now, married with three children, owning his own castle, well, it was like a dream come true…except he could never have even dreamt of a life so full. Even the worries of the hotel, the staff, the flooding, all seemed to pale into insignificance in the light of his happiness. He was not looking forward to the TV thing, and he could just imagine the roasting he'd get from those fellas outside once the first show aired, but it was going to be worth it, and he'd just have to get it done.

Havie and Kayla shepherded the group through. There seemed to be enough luggage for fifty people, but he greeted them with a smile.

'Havie, Kayla, welcome back.' He was careful to only shake hands; he didn't want a repeat of the stinky long hug he'd endured from Kayla last time. The dynamic he observed between the couple bore out Fintan's warning. Kayla was an enigma. She came across as aggressively sexual, and looked, in the words of his wife, like she wanted to eat Conor with a spoon, but she seemed distant as well. When she wasn't touching him or making comments that would surely have had any man up in court for harassment, she was scrolling on her phone or laptop, seemingly oblivious to her surroundings. Ana couldn't stand her, and Kayla behaved as if Ana simply wasn't there. Ana was perfectly secure in their relationship, but nonetheless he reassured her that he found Kayla nothing short of terrifying and smelly, and they'd laughed about the pheromone perfume. He knew that if the situation were reversed, he wouldn't like it either. But like everyone else, they had to just endure it for the greater good.

Fintan was right though; Havie did everything Kayla suggested, and Conor found their relationship intriguing.

She seemed to reserve her appetites just for Conor, and though Havie reprimanded her when she got too outrageous, he did so gently. She would just pout for a moment and then return to her old ways. When she wasn't flirting with Conor, she was needling him, and several of their video conferences left Conor gritting his teeth due to her ridiculous demands.

In terms of business, Havie was forceful but charming, the iron fist in the velvet glove. Conor liked him but was wary. The solicitor had been all over the contract and assured him it was watertight, and the first tranche of the money had already been lodged, so the company doing the wall and the flood defences had been engaged to start work as soon as possible.

They had toyed with the idea of waiting until after the filming, but the company assured him that the work would not impact the hotel in any way. They would set up a worksite on the grounds, but they would landscape so that it was unseen by the public. A temporary access had been granted by the council for the machinery, so he was assured it would all be very unobtrusive.

John Gerrity had retired from the Civil Service, so Conor had offered him the job of overseer of the project and liaison between him and the engineering company. Thankfully, Gerrity took it, so Conor relaxed knowing that Gerrity would not let anything go. It felt like everything was falling into place.

'Conor.' Kayla ignored his outstretched hand, instead walking right up to him and putting her arms around him, her hands running up and down his back. She nuzzled her face into his neck, and he decided he would need to nip this in the bud. She was playing with him, and he wasn't having it.

Havie was busy helping the group to manoeuvre their over-stacked trolleys, so Conor took his chance. He took her hands from around his waist and gently but firmly removed them. 'I think it would be best if we were professional, Kayla, so let's just keep it to shaking hands, all right? I don't hug any of my other colleagues, so I'd better not start with you. I'd get nothing done if I had to go around hugging everyone.' He smiled to take the edge off his words, hoping he had been clear enough.

She looked up at him, her dark eyes deep and unfathomable. She wasn't hurt or even admonished. Her lips curled slowly. 'We'll see,' she drawled.

They were interrupted by Fintan, who looked dreadful. Conor got a fright to see him so haggard – how had he deteriorated so much in just a few weeks?

'Hi, Conor,' Fintan said

'Fintan, great to see you. How've you been?'

Ana had shown him an article last week where Fintan's ex had gone on TV to do a tell-all documentary accusing him of being a drunk. She didn't explicitly say he'd been violent, but she hinted heavily at it and kept going on about how no matter how hard she begged, he refused to go to rehab. She even managed to squeeze out a few tears. Several high-profile people condemned her, one going so far as to call her a gold-digging tramp, and another claiming the accusations were entirely fabricated. Conor was inclined to believe Fintan was largely innocent, though no doubt he was drinking very heavily now. He'd watched a bit of the show and was surprised to notice Fintan's ex looked so fake. Nothing about the woman seemed real, and something about her didn't feel right to him. Whatever the truth of it, it was a horrible story and Conor's heart went out to the poor man. To have a relationship fall apart was hard on anyone, but to have it all played out in the newspapers and online was just too much.

Fintan shrugged. 'You know yourself, not too bad.' He smiled, and Conor suppressed a wince at his stale breath. What the wardrobe and make-up people were going to make of this cadaver-like celebrity, Conor couldn't begin to imagine.

'Well, folks, let's go make *Grandma Says We're Irish*!' Havie called from the front of the group as Kayla walked behind.

Havie seemed excited. He'd explained on their last night in Ireland, when he'd gone to dinner with Conor and Ana, that he was not an executive who was afraid to get his hands dirty. He had a reputation for working very hard, and he could be found in make-up and wardrobe just as easily as behind the camera or in the marketing room. He did everything, and everyone answered only to him. It was the secret of his success.

Once outside, Conor started loading the bags. Like Havie, he was a hands-on kind of man too and never felt like any job was beneath him. He was reminded of the days when he did back-to-back tours, and found he was actually enjoying himself. Once the bags were loaded, he stood at the top of the sumptuous tour bus he'd indulged in for the hotel. The black coach with darkened windows was emblazoned with the small gold Castle Dysert logo on the sides, and he loved it. Ana jokingly called it his midlife crisis. But he told her it was better than a silly sports car in which he'd look like the oldest swinger in town.

'Good morning, everyone.' He smiled warmly at the exhausted group, though why they would be, having flown first class all the way, he had no idea. 'Welcome to Ireland. My name is Conor O'Shea, and I own Castle Dysert where you will be staying and where we'll be making this TV show. I'm really looking forward to it and hope you all have a wonderful time. And of course if there's anything I or the staff can do to make your time with us more comfortable, please don't hesitate to ask.'

Some of them smiled; more ignored him.

'Thanks for that, Conor.' Havie stood up. 'I know we're all excited to be here and get this project going. Let me introduce everyone. We met briefly in the airport, but it was all a bit chaotic and then everyone was sitting in different parts of the plane, so it will be good to do formal introductions. Conor is going to be the host of the show, so you'll all know him well by the end of this. Now I'm sure that Conor will know who all of you guys are – your reputations precede you all, of course – but let me give a little bio of everyone for the benefit of the whole group. Conor has helpfully done his own.'

Havie pointed at a woman sitting in the front seat. 'This is Shannon O'Cleary, otherwise known as the Celtic Colleen. She's wowed audiences all over the world with her shows, so for her this is just a trip home, I guess. I think her show has been touring for five years straight now?'

The woman smiled. 'Eight actually. I'm just back from an eleven-week tour of Asia.'

Conor had never heard of her, but that meant nothing. Ana was always telling him about famous people he'd never heard of. Havie had refused to tell anyone who the final line-up was, so he couldn't google them in advance.

She certainly looked the part. She was in her forties, he guessed, with long curly dark-red hair – though even to his untrained eye, the colour looked a little unnatural – and wore what looked to Conor like some kind of a Celtic robe. Her dark-blue eyes and pale skin made her look like images he'd seen of Grainne Uaile, the famous Irish pirate queen of the Middle Ages. His eyes moved to a little carrying case she'd placed on the seat; there was something moving in it.

'And this is Princess Bellachic,' the woman said, extracting a tiny little dog, no bigger than a kitten, from the case. The animal was tan and white, a tiny ball of fluff, and had pink bows on its head and around its neck. Conor couldn't believe his eyes, but it also looked like the dog had had its claws polished with sparkly glitter polish.

'She comes everywhere with me.'

Despite that, she didn't seem to show any affection to the animal who looked miserable as it was put back into the case.

Havie didn't remark on the dog but moved on with the introductions. 'And here is Fintan Rafferty. You all know Fintan – three times Oscar nominated, won it twice, for his portrayal of John F Kennedy in the biopic of the same name, and also for his role in *African Symbols*, which won five Academy Awards that year. Am I correct, Fintan?'

Fintan was sitting in the other front seat, gazing out the window, making no effort to engage with anyone. His clothes were crumpled, and frankly, he smelled awful. He looked up, clearly not having heard the question. 'Sorry, what?' he asked.

Havie brushed over it. 'Not to worry. I'm just telling everyone how successful you are. I don't expect you to listen.'

There was a dutiful chuckle from the crowd.

'Sorry, Havie,' Fintan apologised. 'I'm just…'

Conor saw the concern in Havie's eyes. Havie and Fintan were good friends, he could sense it.

'It's cool, man, it's been a long flight.'

Havie moved on to the young woman sitting behind Fintan. 'And behind Fintan we have Taylor Davis, daughter of Ted and Marcia

Davis, who has graciously taken a semester off college to participate in our show.'

Conor saw several people exchange a look. Again, he had no idea who these people were, but that name clearly struck a chord.

'And Taylor asked that she introduce herself to the group, so I'll let her do just that.'

Conor watched as a young woman in her early twenties stood up. She seemed bookish if anything and was dressed very conservatively for someone her age, in a pink cardigan and cream top and a grey and pink tartan skirt. Her sandy hair was pulled up in a ponytail.

'Hi, everyone.' She smiled nervously. 'I know I'm not famous like you guys, but I guess you've all heard of my dad. I just want to say that I'm honoured to be here and I'm looking forward to meeting you all properly, but that I can't answer any questions about my family or the political situation right now, as it's subject to an ongoing investigation. I hope you understand.' Her cheeks flushed deep crimson and she swallowed, betraying her nervousness.

A man in a tweed jacket sitting in the back seat seemed to give her an encouraging nod.

She sat down, and Conor felt like the speech had been learned off. He felt sorry for the girl; whatever her father was famous for, it wasn't a good thing.

'Yes, well, we'll all respect that, and this is to research your Irish roots, which come from your mother's side, so we'll be focusing on that,' Havie said kindly, and the girl nodded gratefully. 'OK, moving on, we have American national treasure Bob McCullough.'

Conor realised who the man was as soon as he took off his battered cowboy hat, raised it in a gesture of greeting and gave a broad grin. Bob McCullough was a household name in the US but also all over the world for his music. He sang and played bluegrass banjo and had had a long and varied career. He'd also been a political agitator and was still very vocal on the need to avoid wars. The man had shared stages with Willie Nelson, Johnny Cash, Flatt and Scruggs – all the greats – and was much loved.

He was dressed in blue jeans and boots and a frayed old t-shirt emblazoned with the words 'Life's Too Short'. His thinning grey hair was long, and his tanned and wrinkled old face was covered in stubble. He really looked the part.

'Howdy, y'all!' He waved and grinned.

Everyone murmured a greeting.

'And behind them we have Ryan Farrell and his parents, Joel and Julie, and you'll all remember Ryan from his breathtaking performance at the Grammys with rapper SilliB, after they swept the boards this year for the musical *Virtuosilli*.'

This kid Conor had heard of. Joe and Artie loved the film in which a child piano prodigy made friends with a female rapper from the wrong end of town and they joined forces to produce an album without either sets of parents knowing about it. They were signed by a big record label and became overnight stars. Ryan played the piano prodigy.

The boy, who looked about ten, gazed unhappily out the window and jerked away from his mother's hand as she tried to straighten his hair. His father was on his phone. Wherever young Ryan wanted to be, Conor was fairly sure it wasn't here.

He was reminded of the first time he met Corlene and Dylan. Corlene had heard that tours were a great place to meet men and so was looking for husband number five; she'd dragged her son along for the trip. He was mortified, but if she hadn't brought him, he would never have met Laoise or discovered his talent for Irish music. Conor's heart went out to Ryan. The boy looked miserable.

Julie Farrell looked like she was going to say something, but Havie moved on to the last person, cutting her off.

'Last – but of course by no means least – we have Shelby Maguire, the face of America's most popular architectural show, *Roomy*. Would you like to tell us a bit about yourself, Shelby?' Havie asked.

SHELBY WAS DRESSED CASUALLY in a white button-down shirt and pale-blue Ralph Lauren jeans that clung to her perfect figure, but her precision-cut short blond hair, polished nails and perfect make-up told everyone there was nothing casual about her. She had that sheen that extreme wealth brought. Her skin was honey coloured and she was Barbie Doll perfect. She was probably thirty and spoke with a cultured East Coast accent; Conor guessed she was from the Hamptons.

'Hi, I'm Shelby Maguire, and as Havie said, I'm the presenter and main architect on *Roomy*. The show has recently been syndicated internationally, so it's a very exciting time. But that said, I'm super excited to be here and to find my Irish family.'

The last person, who sat at the back of the bus, was a thin man dressed in a tweed suit. He had brown hair on the long side and a scholarly disposition. Though Conor knew he was only in his early forties, he looked older.

'And down there at the back is Professor Douglas Wilson, resident at NYU but also visiting professor at Cambridge and the Sorbonne. One of the many strings to his bow is that he's an expert genealogist who'll be helping you all research your families. You should go to him with any questions about your roots and all of that.'

Douglas smiled and nodded, but he seemed shy.

'OK, so you all know me and Kayla, so we're done. Let's go make our show!' Havie patted Conor on the back as Conor pulled out of the airport car park, taking the back entrance and avoiding the gathered press completely.

CHAPTER 15

'Ah, Conor, are you serious? I'm trying to run a kitchen here.' Martin Lowry was fuming as he stood in Conor's office, looking out of place in his chef's whites, his normally florid complexion positively puce now and his oiled hair, normally combed back, hanging down unattractively over his forehead. Nothing about the man looked healthy. According to staff gossip, though he created amazing dishes, all he ate himself were sausage sandwiches, washed down with litres of fizzy drinks. His body and skin had all the signs of it. He was overweight, his belly testing the seams of his tunic to the limit, and his skin had a grey pallor.

Conor's patience was wearing thin with the chef's bad mood. Gout or not, chef or not, he had a policy from the top down that everyone at Castle Dysert was cordial and helpful, not just to guests, but to each other as well.

He hated to pull rank and avoided it when possible, but the new commis chef had left in tears yesterday and the wait staff were terrified of him.

Martin Lowry had the highest references. He'd worked in Paris, Nice and New York, and he had trained alongside Laurent Le Claire, one of the most famous chefs on the planet. But Conor had had enough. He'd called Martin to his office.

'I am serious, Martin. The participants in the show have to perform challenges. It's just a bit of a laugh really, but they have to do tests of their Irishness alongside the finding of their roots, and the first challenge is to bake a loaf of soda bread.' Conor kept his voice even.

Martin puffed up in indignation and glowered at Conor. 'And they can't do it somewhere else? My kitchen is for professional chefs and their staff, not spoiled brats with nothing better to do with their time, famous for being famous or some such rubbish.'

Conor sat back and considered his next sentence. Martin was exceptional, there was no doubt about it, and he was the reason they'd been awarded a Michelin star, the much-coveted badge of approval for any eating establishment. But he needed reining in. Conor needed to gamble, and the first rule of gambling was not to bet anything you couldn't afford to lose. Could he afford to lose Martin? He decided he could. The hotel was in a healthy financial state due to the cash injection from Acorn Productions, so he could headhunt someone excellent and provide them with an enticing package. It wouldn't be ideal, of course, but if it came to it, it could be done.

'Firstly, Martin, almost all the participants in *Grandma Says We're Irish* are all accomplished people who have had international recognition for their talents, and secondly, they are guests here at Castle Dysert, so I'd prefer if you spoke about them in a more respectful manner.'

Martin just rolled his eyes and sighed. He was so immature for a grown man, Conor thought, so filled with the idea of his own brilliance, he thought it gave him a licence to be horrible.

'And while we're talking, I'm not happy with how things are being run in the kitchen.'

He waited for a reaction and saw the incredulous outrage on the chef's face; the man was used to much more respect.

'What do you mean?' Martin was immediately on the defensive, which indicated he knew exactly what Conor meant.

'The wait staff are frightened of you, the commis chef I hired only last week left in tears after you roared at her for her entire first shift, we've failed to keep a pastry chef more than three months since you started... The list goes on and on, and frankly, I won't put up with it. It's not how we do things here.'

Martin snorted. 'I wouldn't expect you to understand, but that is how kitchens work – the good ones anyway. If they can't deal with it, they are in the wrong business. When I was at *The Fitzley* in Mayfair –'

Conor stopped him. 'I'm well aware of your credentials and where you've worked, but that's irrelevant to me in this matter. I don't care what a person's title is, here at Castle Dysert, we speak respectfully to each other. This notion that chefs get a pass on that, and that it's part of the job to be rude and aggressive, holds no sway with me whatsoever. So consider this a verbal warning. There won't be a second warning. Are we clear?'

'You can't speak to me like that,' Martin spluttered. 'If I leave here, I can guarantee you that Michelin star I got won't be long behind me.'

'It is Castle Dysert's Michelin star, not yours. I actually have another chef in mind if you decide we aren't the right fit.' That was a lie, but this guy really wound Conor up and part of him wished he would leave. He was sick of him.

'Oh really?' Martin sneered. 'Who?'

'That's not your concern.' Conor knew he shouldn't enjoy rattling him like this, but the man was such a pain, it was good to give him a taste of his own medicine.

'Now are you staying, and changing how you interact with people here, or are you going?' Conor asked bluntly, his tone indicating he was not pushed either way.

'I won't be spoken to like this –'

'Look, I hate having these conversations. I just want everyone to pull together, and for the most part, that's how things go here. But I own this place, and you're upsetting my staff, you're rude to guests, and to be entirely honest with you, if you walk out the door today, there won't be any tears shed. But make your decision carefully, Martin. I'm a long time in this business and there are very few people I don't know, so making an enemy of me is not a smart move.'

Silence hung between the men. Martin would never apologise, or even say he would stay, so Conor assumed his silence was agreement and went on.

'So this morning after breakfast they will gather in the kitchen. We need six work stations, and one of them is only a little lad, so he'll need help. I've asked Evie, the *new* pastry chef, to give the demonstration and all of that. She'll make sure each person has the correct ingredients and whatever else they need. You can carry on as normal, but if the camera is on you, or even if it's not, no roaring or being sour, right?'

Conor knew the inclusion of Evie would drive Martin wild. He loved the limelight – the man took a tour of the restaurant each night accepting congratulations from each table for every dish – so having a junior of his on TV would drive him daft. Conor suppressed a smile.

'And am I meant to prepare lunch with all this going on?' he asked sullenly, and Conor knew that, at least for now, he'd won.

He decided to soften a bit now that he had the upper hand. 'Just the usual menu for the crew and participants. They were all raving about the fish pie last night.' He smiled. 'Look, Martin, it's really important that this works out. You know the situation with the flooding, so it's in everyone's interest that *Grandma Says We're Irish* is a huge success. Each department of the hotel will be asked to do their bit. The landscaping team are designing a native flora challenge around the grounds, they have to learn a bit of Irish, learn a tune on the tin whistle, all sorts of things like that as well as the genealogy. On the face of it, it's just a bit of craic, but the reality is all of our futures are on the line here.'

Martin said nothing, which Conor again took for reluctant acquiescence.

Martin was single, unsurprisingly, and lived in the apartment building purpose-built for staff. Apart from his job, Conor doubted he had much else going on. He was a workaholic, arriving early and staying late, but he didn't seem like a happy man. The only person he wasn't rude to was Ana; he seemed to have a soft spot for her, but then everyone did.

'Right, so we're all good?' Conor asked, ending the meeting and opening the door.

Martin walked out past him with as much dignity as he could muster, and Conor knew he'd better start lining up a replacement, just in case. He could just imagine Martin this evening over a bottle. A line from 'Tam o' Shanter', one of his favourite Robert Burns poems, came to mind as he imagined the chef going over and over the conversation, getting more outraged with each passing hour, nursing his 'wrath to keep it warm'.

He checked his watch. The first of the genealogy searches was to begin today. They'd chosen Bob McCullough for the first episode because he was by far the most well known and best loved of the group. Conor was to have a meeting with Douglas Wilson about Bob's family and the research already undertaken.

Kayla was in charge of the challenges, and Conor was giving her a wide berth. His gentle admonishment at the airport had had absolutely no effect whatsoever, and she still tried to paw him every time they met. She seemed to never touch Havie. Unless one knew they were together, there was no way to guess. They were an odd pair if ever he saw one.

He had time for a quick swim. He had a locker in the hotel pool and spa and tried to swim every day. It was a habit he'd had for decades now, and if he didn't get to the pool, he missed it. Swimming was such a solitary sport, and he could just lap up and down, thinking his thoughts. With his goggles on, nobody even recognised him.

He walked to the spa, hoping he didn't run into anyone. He needed to be in the right headspace for the day ahead of him. Ana had advised him to forget the cameras were there, but that was easier said than done, with the lights and cameras, make-up and hair people all doing their best to make it all look natural and easy.

Thankfully the spa was empty apart from a couple chatting at the shallow end. He realised they were Taylor and Douglas. He wondered if they'd come to the spa together or had just bumped into each other.

He slipped in and changed. He was just about to step out into the pool area when he spotted Kayla on the sun deck. They'd installed a solarium, which had large glass panels overlooking the bay so guests could sunbathe effectively while enjoying the stunning view and without dealing with the reality of the cold outside. In fact in winter, when the ocean was rough and angry, the solarium was gorgeous.

Each heated lounger had a little table attached where drinks and magazines could be placed, and on each table were noise-reducing headphones in case the guest wanted to listen to music or a meditation. There were beautiful mohair blankets, made in a cottage industry up the coast, on each lounger for additional comfort. On a marble table to the side were teas and coffees, fresh fruit and sparkling and still mineral water. Guests often mentioned this space in their online reviews, and Conor knew it was worth the investment.

Conor never used the sun deck – he just slipped into the pool, swam and left again – but Kayla was stretched out on a lounger wearing a tiny red bikini. He thought for a moment. Unfortunately he had to pass her to get in the water, but once he was in, she would never know it was him. No, he decided, it was too much of a risk. The thought of an encounter with her, both of them almost naked, was one that didn't appeal at all. Disappointed, he turned to go back and get dressed. It wasn't worth it.

'I can see you,' she called, and for a moment, he wondered who she was talking to.

He felt so foolish. A grown man, hiding from this woman in his own hotel. 'Hi, Kayla,' he said, walking past her to the pool.

'What happened to your back?' she asked, staring at the scars.

'The hotel caught on fire a few years ago. My children were inside, so I had to go in to get them.' He didn't like talking about that night with anyone, and especially not her, so he kept it short.

'Wow, heroic as well as sexy.' She panted dramatically. 'I'd have liked to see that. Maybe you could tell that story on the show – that would raise the temperature of the ladies in the US. We could maybe even do a re-enactment. It's amazing what can be done with CGI now. I'll talk to Havie, but yeah, I like that idea, you emerging from a burning building, naked to the waist, carrying some kid. Hmm.' She licked her lips.

'It was horrible and we were very lucky nobody was killed,' he said shortly. 'Those "some kids" were my sons and we were all badly affected by that night, so we definitely won't be revisiting it for someone's entertainment. Now I'm going for a swim, so I'll leave you to it.'

'Sure. You don't mind if I watch, do you?'

They were alone now, as Taylor and Douglas had left. He minded very much, and under normal circumstances he would have told her so, but she seemed to have some kind of power over Havie, so he'd have to use diplomacy – although he really just wanted to tell her to leave him alone. He ignored the question.

'I'd better get on. See you, Kayla.' He dived into the deep end, hoping he splashed her as he did so.

When he got out after swimming a hundred lengths, he was relieved to see she was gone and he had the pool area to himself.

After changing, he headed to his office. He was meeting Douglas Wilson at midday for a briefing, and the filming of Bob's story would begin tomorrow. He knew everyone was excited that he was going to be such a big part of the show, and the staff were giving him a right old ribbing about it. He had to laugh it off, and only Ana and Katherine knew how uncomfortable he was with it.

The professor arrived exactly on time, and Conor invited him in. He carried an old leather satchel with the initials 'DW' stamped on it. He looked every inch the academic.

'Professor Wilson, welcome.' Conor smiled. 'Can I get you a coffee, or some lunch?'

'No, thank you, Conor, and please, call me Douglas.' He sat on one of the sofas Conor had installed. His office, located at the base of the side turret, was circular in shape, and the entire room was cut stone with a large ornate fireplace. It lent itself to the mismatched furniture Daniel and the interior designer had selected. He was really happy with it. He had a desk but disliked sitting behind it when he spoke to people; he preferred to sit on one of the two gold damask sofas he'd chosen himself. With its moss-green carpet and dark wood fittings, the room looked cosy and most un-office-like. Diamond-shaped leaded windows looked onto the rose garden and side lawns.

'This is such a beautiful castle, and you've done wonders keeping it in character and authentic. I love it.' Douglas Wilson spoke quietly and deliberately, and he exuded sincerity and dignity. Conor liked him immediately.

'Thank you. Yes, well, we try our best, but also every inch of it is under a preservation order, so even if I wanted to, I couldn't do anything to alter the appearance.' Conor chuckled. 'So the authenticity is intentional but also compulsory.'

'Well, whatever the motivation, I'm very pleased with the result. Now, to business. And let me say how relieved I am that it will be you presenting this and not me. Havie approached me because I'd done some genealogical work for him previously, but then I met Kayla. Understandably, she wasn't so sure I was the look they were going for.' He smiled ruefully. 'And to be honest, I'm thrilled it's you and not me.'

'Well, I'm not exactly over the moon about it, but they insisted.'

'And what Kayla wants, Kayla gets,' Douglas said with a wry smile.

'Exactly. And to be honest, I'm not that comfortable on screen, and as for all the make-up and nails and the rest of it…'

'Nonsense. You look much more the part than I do, and I guarantee you the US market will love you and your accent. I understand that you are something of a genealogy buff yourself, so it will be a joint effort, I'm sure.' Douglas opened his bag and extracted a buff-coloured file, with 'Bob McCullough' written in exquisite copperplate on the cover.

They spent a pleasant hour examining what Douglas had unearthed, with Conor adding what he knew, and the end result was certainly enough to fill a show, they thought.

'I hope they're all this easy,' Conor said as they packed away the sheets of paper.

'They're not, trust me,' Douglas said ominously. 'We are going to run into some problems with some of them, but that's all part of the show apparently.'

'Well, don't tell me. I'm nervous enough about today as it is, so we'll start with an easy one and see how we go.'

The conversation moved to other things. Conor found himself relaxed in the other man's company. He'd never been to university, and it was something he often wished he'd had the opportunity to do, so talking to such a learned man was a treat.

'So what do you do when you're not finding people's relatives?' Conor asked.

'Not much.' Douglas shrugged. 'My elderly mother lives with me. She's gone into a rest home for the few weeks I'm here, but generally I care for her.'

'That's quite a commitment.'

'Yes. She's in her eighties now but still sprightly. She lost her family in the Second World War – they were Jews, you see – but she and her sister got out. They were children at the time, and I promised her when I was a young boy that I would grow up to find her family, as some of them must have survived somewhere. So that's how I got started in genealogy.'

'And did you find anyone?' Conor was almost afraid to ask.

Douglas shook his head sadly. 'No, not one. They were from Warsaw in Poland. The Nazis killed them all.'

'That must have been hard news to deliver,' Conor said quietly.

'It was. She loves me, and my brother too, and I think she was fond of our father. He was a Protestant from Wisconsin, and they met at a dance for returned servicemen. She married him in 1948, but I think it was more out of gratitude than love, I don't know. It was as if the biggest part of her was left in Poland, and she gave us what she could, but it wasn't much.'

'I suppose we can't ever imagine what it was like for those people, how it felt to survive,' Conor mused.

'Yes, indeed. My father died of cancer thirty years ago, and my brother married a woman from the Yukon and spends all his time up there, so it's just been me and my mother for a long time.' He shrugged.

'And you never married, had children?' Conor wondered if he shouldn't pry, but Douglas was being so open, it felt all right to ask.

'No, I never married. And I've no children. How about you?'

Conor knew from his tone that he was unwilling to elaborate further on his personal life so he answered,

'I'm married to Ana – she works on the front desk. You would have met her.'

'Ah, yes. She is from Ukraine?'

'That's her. And we have three children, twin boys aged ten and a new baby girl called Lily.'

'You're a lucky man then, Conor,' Douglas said, and Conor could hear the note of regret.

'I certainly am,' he agreed.

CHAPTER 16

*C*onor and Bob walked into the old graveyard. To Conor's astonishment, Havie had sent the film crew all the way to the actual graveyard, in County Tyrone in the North of Ireland, to get shots of Bob's ancestors' graves, but now they were filming him and Bob wandering around an entirely different cemetery. It was an old one just a few miles from the hotel, and there were very few burials there now. The new cemetery in town was where all the local funerals were, except in the case of a few old local families that had family plots. The place was atmospheric on the cold, bright morning. Lichen- and moss-covered tombstones, many leaning precariously, dotted the ground, seemingly at random. Some wealthier families had tombs, so large stone structures were scattered here and there, and every so often there were holes where the grave had collapsed and you could see down. Conor explained that the graveyards of Ireland were often very old and used for so many generations that to find human bones wasn't that remarkable. They walked through the ruins of the chapel, its once wooden or straw roof long gone and the stones open to the skies and the vagaries of the Irish weather. Statues stood in alcoves, their faces, once carved with such love and care, now unrecognisable through erosion.

He and Bob had had a chat the night before in the bar, and Conor instantly warmed to the man. He was a natural agitator, had a lot of opinions on the state of the world and was deeply critical of politicians. It was refreshing to listen to him because, unlike younger people in the public eye, he couldn't care less what people thought of him. He spoke his mind. He was so loved and respected over his fifty-year career, he could do no wrong.

The two men picked their way through the cemetery, chatting amicably, and Conor found it wasn't as bad as he thought it might be. The cameras were rolling, but he took Ana's advice and pretended they weren't there and just spoke normally.

'Wow, some of these go way back, don't they?' Bob tried to make out the worn carving on a lopsided stone. The ground underfoot was very uneven, and they stood beside one of the larger tombs, which had cracked, exposing a dark cavernous hole inside. Ivy, star jasmine and holly, still bearing its berries, crept all over the graveyard unchecked, and there seemed to be a mixture of large plots, ones with just a single stone and some with no marking at all.

'They do. The burial of the dead is an important ritual here. It's always been an important part of our culture, even going back into pre-Christian times. Some of the tombs in the east of the country are over 6,000 years old, and there is evidence to suggest the people believed that burying their dead with certain objects of value was a way to ease their passage to the next world.' Conor hoped he didn't sound too much like a schoolteacher.

'Like the Greeks and the River Styx, huh?' Bob smiled.

'Exactly. There are lots of similarities between all ancient cultures, I suppose.' Conor tried to ignore the cameraman, who was moving a bit too close for comfort. Havie had instructed them just to chat normally; the crew would edit it all afterwards.

'Take the engineering, for example. The pyramids remain – it's a mystery how they did it. And we have constructions here that also baffle archaeologists. All sorts of theories abound. I met a guy once who was convinced aliens had set it all up.' Conor chuckled. 'And of course there are all kinds of superstitions here even now. Irish people believe in the presence of the dead in our everyday lives, and it's not something you'd be ridiculed for here. It's a very ancient belief and kind of transcends religion in lots of ways. Púcaí – that's the word for ghosts, fairies and the souls of the dead – are kept at a respectful distance.'

Bob stopped. 'When I was a kid, in the Smoky Mountains, it was the same. I remember my mama used to make my daddy touch up the haint blue every year.' He laughed. 'I ain't thought about that for years.'

'What was that?' Conor asked.

'Haint is the Black word for a ghost, and those folks sure believed in the need to keep evil spirits away. They reckoned the dead couldn't cross water, but they couldn't build a moat like you guys have here in your castles, no money for that. But they would paint the outside of the house this kinda greeny-blue colour, haint blue, to make it look like water and keep the place safe.'

'That's fascinating.' Conor smiled. 'I never heard that.'

'My grandma lived with us – she's the Irish connection – and she had so many old things. There had to be a mirror in the hallway, and boy, would she be holding her breath in here, scared the recently dead would try to get into her body. She sure had some crazy ideas.' He chuckled at the memory. 'But us kids loved her. She smoked a pipe and let us puff on it when our folks wasn't looking, and she carried a little bottle of Tennessee whiskey up her sleeve. She could sing...man, could she sing, and she played the fiddle, Irish tunes, y'know? "Devil music", the preacher called it. He didn't like her one bit. I guess he never got over her missin' his ass with buck-shot by an inch that time he tried to get her to give up her sinful ways. My mama was a righteous woman, and she was so embarrassed. She and Grandma Mac were like oil and water, but we loved the old lady.'

'She sounds like a character.' Conor smiled. 'And did she know much about her Irish roots?'

'Well, she said our people came over from the old country 'cause we were the music makers and the kings or whatever didn't like that, so the story goes. Supposedly her grandpa got run out of town, but she was a bit vague on the details.' Bob shrugged. 'Reckoned that's where I got it though.'

Conor felt this was a good time to get into his story. 'Well, she's not exactly wrong. As far as I can tell from researching your family, your branch of the McCulloughs were originally Ulster Scots. They were granted land during the Plantation of Ulster around 1610, and they were predominantly Presbyterians.'

'What does that mean, the Plantation of Ulster?' Bob asked, skirting around a huge tomb.

'Well, in an effort to quell the constant Irish rebellions and get some kind of control, as well as to reward loyal servants to the Crown, Scots men were given parcels of land in Ulster by the king – that was James the sixth and first.' Noting Bob's look of confusion, Conor explained. 'First of England, Sixth of Scotland. Apparently his Scottish accent was so thick, nobody in London had a clue what he was on about. Anyway, he wanted to "civilise" the Irish. The Gaelic lords were to be driven off their land, and everyone was forced to speak English and basically treat the place as if it were part of England rather than Ireland.'

'OK, so you reckon my people were those guys?' Bob looked troubled.

'Well, yes, but we are talking about the very early 1600s here, 400 years ago. Initially, they were forbidden from interacting with the Gaelic people, forbidden from employing them, trading with them and so on, but of course over time they integrated, and eventually, those Scots became the Ulstermen.'

'Well, my family was Baptist, but I guess they could have convert-ed.' Bob stopped. 'But if the king or whoever sent them over from Scotland to Ireland, how come the family story is that they were run out of there?'

'Well, that's where the whole thing gets a bit interesting. You see, in the 1641 rebellion, the Gaelic lords rebelled against the Crown, and instead of fighting back on behalf of the king, as the Crown would have expected the Scots settlers to do, many of them joined forces with the native Irish.'

Bob grinned. 'So we're the good guys again?'

'Well, yes, for a little while.' Conor grinned as well. 'Until the arrival of Oliver Cromwell to Ireland in 1649. He was anti-royal, so much so that he had King Charles beheaded, and even though the Ulstermen hadn't been exactly loyal to the Crown, he felt that they weren't supportive of his Rump Parliament after the English Civil War either. So once again they found themselves on the wrong side.'

'OK, go on.' Bob seemed fascinated.

'So then Cromwell conquered the entire island and installed his loyal Englishmen onto the land of Ireland, having first slaughtered all before him. This was land that was originally Irish, then Scots, now owned by English. The reality was, life was as bad for Scotsmen in Ireland as it was for the native Irish, and so after several more wars, uprisings and rebellions, and finally a Test Act in 1703 that further discriminated against anyone who refused to conform to the Church of England, the Scots decided to move in great numbers – estimates put it at around 200,000 people – to the United States. And your ancestors were most likely among those people.'

'And the music?' Bob asked.

'Well, the Scots who came over to Ireland from Scotland were Lowland Scots, and they had a very distinct kind of music. They were industrious people and excelled at everything they put their hand to – that's why they were chosen for the Plantation in the first place, I suppose – and they took their music, language, sport and culture very seriously. It's widely accepted that it's that Lowland Scots style of music, fiddle playing in particular, that formed the basis of the American country-and-western scene.'

'And is that music different from Irish traditional music?' Bob asked. 'I heard a guy on TV last night playing Irish music, and it sure sounded a lot like bluegrass.'

'A little bit, but over the years it's all been homogenised. The Scots would have different tunes, and a different way of using the bow – more staccato or something. It's hard to describe.'

'That's so interesting. So now all I got to do is find my guy.' Bob grinned. 'I mean it was only 300 years ago and there was 200,000 of them. How hard can it be?'

Conor smiled. Douglas had already found Bob's ancestor and he had quite a tale to tell, but that would be for later in the programme. That segment would be filmed in the library in the castle.

'And...cut!' Havie called, and the cameramen stopped filming.

'That was great, guys!' Havie came over and shook Conor's hand and then Bob's. 'Really great. You're so used to the camera, Bob, but Conor, you're a natural.'

Conor exhaled a sigh of deep relief. It wasn't as bad as he thought it might be.

'I love this graveyard.' Havie ran his hand over an old granite tombstone. 'I think we'll use it for some of the others, as well as the library and the castle grounds. We can recreate a different library, and I've got scouts all over the place looking for other locations, but this is great so far. Good job, you guys. Just talking naturally is the best thing. We'll do some library shots back at the castle, and then in a pub with you two talking it all out over a pint of Guinness. How does that sound?'

'I like the pub idea.' Bob chuckled.

CHAPTER 17

When Conor returned to the hotel, he found the door to his office shut, which was unusual. 'What's up?' he asked Katherine, but she gestured that he should follow her to the back office.

'What?' he asked as she closed the door.

'Ana is in there. There's been a bit of a rumpus here today. Ryan, the lad who plays piano, refused point-blank to do the baking challenge, and his mother got very angry at him. The father tried to intervene but got nowhere. She's a bit of a dragon, if you ask me. But anyway, the child got really upset and ran off. We've been searching for him all afternoon. Artur found him eventually in the stables, but he refused to come out.'

Katherine spoke in hushed tones, seemingly afraid that any upset would stop the filming.

'Ana went down,' she went on, 'and between her and Artur, they managed to coax him out. I let the mother and father know he's all right, but he's still very upset. Ana eventually convinced him to come back, and she and her father are in your office with the boy now. But he made Ana and Artur promise that they wouldn't let his mother in.'

'Oh, for God's sake. What are we meant to do now?' Conor ran his hand through his hair. He wasn't sure about having a child in the show in the first place. It felt wrong. Ryan should be in school, or playing with his friends, not hanging around with his parents, a tutor and a whole bunch of adults. He was such a good-looking child, which is why he was a Hollywood sensation no doubt, but to Conor he was a sad-looking lad, and his heart went out to the boy.

'That's not all. Your woman, the Celtic Colleen, has explained in no uncertain terms that there needs to be a dog groomer on standby every day to do whatever she does to that tiny snappy dog. She carries the ratty little thing everywhere, and apparently she was assured that a groomer would be on standby. She's coming back at three and expects a mobile groomer complete with all manner of implements to be here by then.'

'And does such a person exist on the west coast of County Clare?' Conor asked, guessing the answer.

'What do you think?'

'What about the man that we take Lionel to, out the Galway road? He's a grand fella, and Lionel doesn't mind going to him for a clipping.'

'I tried him, but when I explained the situation, he wasn't available. Anyway, she needs someone full time apparently. Did you ever hear such rubbish?'

Katherine wasn't a dog person and just barely tolerated the unbridled, licky affection of Lionel Messi O'Shea when she came to visit. People being silly over small snappy dogs would test her short patience.

'Well, why don't we bat this one to Kayla?' Conor suggested. 'If they promised something we can't deliver, then that's hardly our fault.'

'Well, I was going to do that. But she came up to the desk this morning and Ana went to see what she wanted, and she waved her hand and said, "Not you. The other one." And pointed at me. She's a complete nightmare. All sweetness and light when you or that Havie is around, but on her own she's dreadful.'

Conor inhaled and exhaled slowly. Kayla harassing him was one thing, but being rude to Ana wasn't going to happen.

'OK, I'll speak to Havie now. Leave it with me.'

'And the child in your office?' Katherine asked, her hand on the doorknob.

'Um, we'll let Ana deal with him for now. She's much better at that stuff than me.'

'This is harder than we thought it was going to be, Conor,' Katherine said quietly. 'Martin is like a demon below in the kitchen. He's not talking to anyone, and he completely refused to have anything to do with the baking thing. I thought you were going to have a word with him?'

'I did,' Conor said grimly. 'I gave him a verbal warning and he threatened to leave. I kind of let on we had someone on the sub's bench.' He sighed.

'What? And what do we do if he walks out the door, would you mind telling me that?'

'Jump off that bridge when we come to it?' Conor tried to get her to smile, but she looked worried.

'It feels like the wheels are coming off. There was a big party last night between the crew and our staff down in the staff block. There's a lot of sick heads this morning. Sheila found one of the chambermaids asleep in the linen cupboard, and that Madden young one we hired for the glass collecting made a total show of herself and it's all over Instasnap or whatever they call it, so she can't face coming in. That Fintan Rafferty turned up as well, drunk as a skunk, and the porter had to pour him into bed at six a.m. He had to be dragged out of it again by Kayla this morning to do the baking challenge. These television people are really disruptive, Conor.'

'I know, but we've no choice here, Katherine. Your one Kayla is wrecking my head – it's like she's determined to wind me up – but we have to put a brave face on it. If the troops see the general despondent, it kills morale altogether.' He winked at her. 'So nail on that smile. And how do we eat an elephant?'

He was quoting Joe, who'd got a joke book for Christmas and was plaguing anyone who'd listen with his terrible jokes. Katherine had been a victim for twenty full minutes last Sunday.

She tried to look stern but failed. A tiny smile played around her thin lips. 'One bite at a time.' She sighed.

'Exactly.' He gave her shoulder a quick squeeze. 'We'll be grand, Katherine. I know it's a bit of a palaver, but we never died a winter yet. We'll survive.'

'If you say so,' she said sceptically as she returned to her post.

Conor decided to leave Ana and Artur with young Ryan and thought about which issue he should deal with first, prioritising the worst of the problems. He called Havie.

'Conor, what's up?' Havie answered immediately.

'Hi, Havie. I wonder if we could have a chat?'

'Sure, Conor. Kayla and I are in the bar, having lunch.'

Conor thought quickly. He needed to speak to Havie alone. 'Ah, don't worry, I won't disturb you. Finish your lunch, and when you have a minute, you might let me know.'

Havie paused. 'No, I'm finished. Library?'

Conor would have to hope he came alone. 'Sure. I'll be there in five minutes.'

The library had been commandeered for the duration of the film-ing. The once serene and tranquil room, lined with books and with a large Kilkenny marble fireplace that had an aperture large enough to take half a tree and long French windows that overlooked the cobbled courtyard and stables, now looked like a spaghetti junction of wires and lights. Conor picked his way through to one end of the large oval rosewood table and was just about to sit when Havie arrived, alone.

'What's up, my friend?' he asked.

'OK, we have some problems that we need to deal with.' Conor decided to get right into it.

'Shoot.' Havie plunged his hands into his tight-legged cream chino pants pockets. Today he was wearing a scarlet silk shirt, open halfway down his chest. On anyone else it would have looked ridiculous, but Havie managed to pull those outfits off.

'Firstly, young Ryan is in my office.' Conor briefly outlined the state the child was in, and Havie nodded.

'I guessed there might be problems there. That kid is a classic Hollywood brat, unlucky enough to be born pretty. He's being exploited by greedy and fame-hungry parents.'

Conor nodded. 'My lads love that film he's in with the rapper kid.'

'Yeah, well, that's not fake – he's really good. But the mother's a nightmare. The father can't handle her, and she's forcing the kid to do this stuff.'

'And you knew this? Before you started?' Conor was incredulous.

Havie shrugged and smiled. 'Sure. An over-pushy mom, a sensitive kid, and she's got her husband by the you-know-what 'cause the kid is their meal ticket. It's reality TV gold.'

'But he's just a child. This isn't right. If he doesn't want to do it –'

'Not our circus, not our monkeys, Conor. Yeah, it's crap for the kid, I get it, but we're not forcing her. She's up for it, she wants the cash, the fame, the whole lot. If I only made shows full of people who were morally above reproach, then those would be boring shows and ratings would plummet and you wouldn't be getting your flood wall or whatever it is.'

'But we can't just carry on –' Conor tried again.

'Conor, look, you're a nice guy, and you would never make your kids do this, of course you wouldn't, but people do stuff with their kids all the time that other people disagree with. Should they sit as judge and jury? Of course not.' Havie laid his hand on Conor's shoulder, giving it a pat.

Conor was confused. On one level he liked Havie, but on the other he disliked the sensation that he was being manipulated and patronised.

'Next problem?'

Clearly the Ryan situation was what it was and Havie was happy with it.

Conor explained about Shannon O'Cleary and the dog groomer, to which Havie simply replied, 'Hire one from Dublin or London or wherever. Just get them here and keep her happy. I don't care what it costs. Bill it to me.'

'All right.' Conor shrugged. After years of budgeting everything, this reckless spending didn't sit well with him, but it wasn't his money.

'OK, what else?' Havie asked.

'Fintan.' Conor knew Fintan and Havie were old friends, but Havie needed to be made aware that the guy was going off the rails completely.

On this subject Havie didn't appear to have a glib answer. He paused and then said wearily, 'Yeah, he's hitting it pretty bad these days. I thought bringing him here, away from all the media circus back in LA, would help, but it's made him worse if anything.'

Conor could hear the genuine concern in Havie's voice.

'He adored Niki, I mean, like absolute worship. She never appreciated him, a gold-digger, nothing more, but he could never see it. And she had the cheek to think she was slumming it. But y'know, without him she's nothing, and she's starting to realise that now. Schlepping around flogging her book full of lies to crappy third-rate TV shows might make a few bucks in the short term, but anyone who knows Fintan knows he's not the man she's describing.'

Conor nodded. 'It seems hard to imagine he's as bad as she's making out, all right.'

'The guy she left him for was a friend of ours. Him, me and Fintan were friends since Fintan arrived in LA. Fintan and I were roommates and met Bradley on the set of our first movie together. Fintan was his best man when he got married the first time, and Bradley was always at his and Niki's place. Bradley got divorced, and they were the ones to pick up the pieces. I knew from the get-go Niki had it in her, and Kayla can't bear her, never could, but I can't believe Bradley would betray Fintan like that. It's so hard to take in, you know?'

'No wonder the poor man is hitting the bottle,' Conor said.

'Yeah, but we both know that's not the answer. No, it's time to step in. Trouble is, we've had it out so many times since this happened. He won't listen to me. When he's in self-destruct mode, he just goes for it. That Irish melancholy, I guess.' Havie chuckled. 'He needs rehab but refuses to go.'

Conor wondered if a drunken volatile Irishman with a sordid personal life was also good for ratings. Would Havie use his friend's tragedy and addiction like that?

It was as if Havie could read his mind. 'If Fintan isn't ready for this show, I'll find someone else. We'll keep him till last, see how we go.' He locked eyes with Conor. 'Look, I know how you feel about what I do, and I don't blame you. It's not great Shakespeare, but people like it and I'm very good at giving the public what they want.' He paused. 'But I wouldn't sacrifice my closest friend for ratings. Contrary to what you might think, I do have some scruples.'

'I didn't think you would.'

'You thought I might though.' Havie smiled, and Conor knew why he was so successful at this stuff.

Corlene, Conor's former business partner, had remarked one time that Conor's strength was not in his charm or good looks – she was always going on with that stuff too – it was because he was emotionally intelligent. He understood people and could see beneath the surface, and Havie was the same.

'OK, is that it or is there more?' Havie asked.

Conor thought about Kayla being rude to Ana, and not caring in the moment what impact it had, he heard himself say, 'One more thing.'

'I'm listening.' Havie leaned against a bookshelf.

'It's Kayla. She's being very rude to the staff here, and in particular Ana, my wife.' He could have gone on about her constant harassment of him, but he could manage. He was totally impervious to her – she held no attraction whatsoever – but he would not have anyone being rude to Ana.

Havie averted his gaze and appeared to examine the floor. Long moments passed as neither man spoke. Eventually Havie pushed himself from a leaning position to upright. 'I'll speak to her,' he said, and hands in his pockets, he left the room.

Conor stood there, not sure what just happened. Was Havie upset? Furious? Did he think Conor was whining over nothing? It was impossible to know with him, as he was very guarded. If he pulled the project, they would be in trouble, and nobody would thank him for bringing the list of woes to Havie in that case.

CHAPTER 18

*T*aylor stirred her untouched coffee as she waited in the almost empty café off the main reception for the filming to begin.

'You look like someone going to the gallows, if you don't mind me saying so.'

She looked up to find Douglas standing in front of her. He wore a navy sweater and beige cord trousers today but still managed to look like a professor, albeit an off-duty one.

'I'd pick the gallows over that right now.' She nodded in the direction of the library, where her segment was to be filmed.

'It's going to be fine, honestly.' Douglas sat down next to her. 'Please, don't worry.'

'How can I not worry?' she asked. 'I've no idea what, if anything, they are going to say. My mother sent a one-line text, and my father isn't even Irish for God's sake.' She whispered the last bit, making sure nobody was in earshot.

'I can't say what or why, but please, Taylor, trust me, it's going to be fine. And Conor is a really nice man. He won't do or say anything to embarrass you.'

Taylor put down her cup and felt her cheeks flush. 'I wish it was you doing it with me,' she mumbled, and he looked at her awkwardly. 'I just mean...you know already and I wouldn't have to...you know, explain... Not for any other reason.'

She thought she might be sick. Did she really just say that to an NYU, Cambridge and Sorbonne professor? She was mortified. Clumsy flirting from an undergraduate was the last thing he needed.

Douglas swallowed, and she knew he'd rather be anywhere else.

'I'm not made for television, but trust me, it will be fine.'

He looked so sincere and honest, she longed to trust him, but her insides were churning.

They brought her in, and she tried to ignore the cameras, but the room was so hot. She regretted wearing her sweater.

'Let's take this off,' the wardrobe lady said kindly as someone else did her make-up and two others spoke inaudibly about her to each other, pointing at her hair and outfit. One of the women was Havie's partner, Kayla, who had not spoken to Taylor even once since they arrived.

Taylor allowed them to do as they pleased as she sat and wrung her hands under the table.

'So,' Conor began at Havie's order, 'let's start with what you know, and we'll work from there, shall we?'

She looked up into the Irish man's face. He seemed kind. He knew her whole sordid story too; of course he did. Her cheeks burned.

'Well, I just know my mother's family came from here, someone named Ned O'Hara, and he landed at Ellis Island in 1893. But...I don't know where in Ireland or when in that year...' Her voice trailed off. Marcia had begrudgingly given her that much. By text.

'OK, so let's begin.' Conor indicated she should sit closer to his screen so she could see what they'd found. None of the participants knew ahead of time what Douglas had unearthed; Havie was adamant their reactions must be genuine, whether good or bad.

'Edward O'Hara,' Conor read off the screen. 'Ned is a pet name for Edward. We have three Edward O'Haras arriving into the USA in 1893, so we'll need to narrow down the search. Luckily, in the case of one, "Ned" was written in brackets after the entry, so we can assume, for now at least, it was him.'

Taylor nodded. 'I guess so?' A camera mounted on what looked like a rail tracked around behind her.

'Now, do you have any idea what part of Ireland he came from? Or what his occupation might be?'

Taylor realised she'd have to tell him the truth too. When her father told her about this project, he assured her they would do all the research and that all she had to do was be her charming self on screen. But it was going to be much more than that.

'I'm sorry, can we stop?' she asked Havie, trying to keep her voice steady.

'Of course. What's up?' he asked.

'I need to tell Conor something. I thought I'd get a chance to speak to him before...' She waved at the cameras.

Conor held his hand up. 'Can you give us a second, please?'

The cameraman glanced at Havie, who gave him a nod, and he backed away.

Conor spoke very quietly to Taylor, sensing her rising panic. 'I know this is difficult and you may not want to do it. It's entirely your decision, and I wouldn't blame you if you didn't want to. But we did a bit of research on this Ned O'Hara before meeting you, and it turns out he was quite the character. He led an unusual life, and his is a good story, and dare I say it, it would show your family in a positive light were you to progress.'

Taylor blinked and wiped her eyes with the handkerchief. 'What did he do?'

Conor winked at her. 'Havie will murder me if I tell you – he wants authentic reactions – but I swear to you, it's not bad. It's really good in fact. I wouldn't do that to you, Taylor.'

'OK.' Taylor swallowed. She sensed that Conor was decent and trustworthy. 'Let's do it.'

Conor nodded at Havie, and the cameras started rolling once more.

'Well, your Ned O'Hara – and we are fairly confident it's your ancestor – set up a free school in the tenements of Hell's Kitchen.' He smiled kindly. 'He taught the children of immigrants English and basic skills, which allowed them to move up through society. At the time, access to education was difficult and cost a lot of money, so Ned O'Hara set up the Irish Free School. He held classes in the evenings and at the weekends as well as during normal school times, because many children worked during the day.'

Conor then opened a folder and extracted a grainy photograph of a man in a dark suit with thinning dark hair and an impressive moustache, standing beside several children. Written on the back was 'The Irish Free School. New York, 1900.'

Taylor gazed into the man's dark eyes. He was slight and looked quite stern, but the children gathered around him seemed very relaxed, many of them smiling.

'Now at that time,' Conor went on to explain, 'there were many Catholic schools that young Irish immigrants did attend, but this school was unusual in that it wasn't under the Catholic system and charged no fee. He ran afoul of the Catholics, however, because they didn't want anyone setting up in opposition to them as they saw it.' He handed her a document.

'What am I looking at?' Taylor asked.

'It's a newspaper account of the sermon given at Holy Cross Church on 42nd Street denouncing the school and Ned O'Hara as a Marxist.'

Taylor read the article. It was certainly forthcoming and held nothing back. The priest, a Father Gerald Dennehy, claimed that Ned was working on behalf of the devil and that anyone who sent their children to him was putting not just their moral character in this life but also their eternal soul in grave peril.

'And what happened next?' she asked, fascinated, all thoughts of her father's indiscretion forgotten.

'Nothing, it would seem.' Conor turned again to the file. 'Until two years later when Ned gets arrested. Here you see we have the name Edward – Ned – O'Hara tried on the 7th of May 1902 for disturbing the peace and sedition.' He pointed to another entry in a large book. 'This is a court document for the City of New York. Sedition was –'

'Openly defying the authorities,' she finished for him. 'But I don't understand. He was certainly annoying the church, but that's not an offence surely. I mean, they had no legal standing to have him arrested?'

'Well, technically that's true, but you're not factoring in Tammany Hall.'

'What was that?' Taylor asked.

'Tammany Hall, or the Society of St Tammany, was an organisation set up to help and advance the cause of Irish immigrants. They were a very powerful political force and were in operation from the 1780s right up to the 1960s. They effectively controlled New York City politics, and the organisation was made up almost exclusively of Catholics of Irish descent.'

'So the Church would have had influence with them, and so they joined forces to stop Ned and his school?' Taylor felt outraged on behalf of her ancestor, a feeling that surprised her.

'I can't say for definite, but it could be likely.' Conor went to the file once more. 'He served some time in prison, but then it looks like they managed to drive him out because the next we see of him is in Washington, DC, of all places, where it looks like he married and had two children. Here is a letter from a notable Tammany Hall politician, Charles P. Flynn. Unfortunately the letter is not in great condition, so we can't see the date or the person he was writing to, but you can see here what it says.' He handed it to Taylor to read.

The writing was smudged, so she read haltingly. 'It would be prudent to encourage O'Hara, using any and all means necessary, to depart NYC forthwith. His presence is disruptive and contrary to the vision we have for the city.' She put the letter down as Conor went on, pointing to an entry on the screen.

'We can see here on the register of births, deaths and marriages for the city.'

'Edward – Ned – O'Hara,' Taylor read. 'Oh look, he gives his address as 44th Street, New York, married to' – she peered at the old-fashioned writing – 'Cecilia Hamilton.'

'Yes, Cecilia Hamilton.' Conor paused and smiled. 'Who was an academic. She taught at Mount Vernon women's college in Washington, DC, and was a very active member of the National American Woman Suffrage Association.'

'Are you serious?' Taylor couldn't believe it.

'Yes. Ned and Cecilia are your great-grandparents. Your great-grandmother was a friend of Susan B Anthony, and she was very outspoken on the subject of women's suffrage. We know this because she was cautioned officially by the university for making her lectures too political. Also, she wrote several letters, not just to the university authorities but to the press, to politicians, anyone she could, really. They had two children – Alice born in 1906 and Jeffery born in 1908.'

Taylor was intrigued. Her mother had never mentioned her grandparents, not once, and the idea that they were such radical academics filled her with a feeling she couldn't identify, a sense of pride and something like belonging.

'So then we see' – Conor pored over a selection of documents that he'd spread out on the table – 'that she wrote a series of articles for the *Woman's Journal*, a periodical of the time. Here they are.' He passed a sheaf of photocopied pages to her.

Taylor leafed through them until she came to a charge sheet from the Washington, DC, police department. 'Ned and she both were arrested on two separate occasions. It seems he was as enthused by the suffrage movement as she was. I can't take it all in! I'm so interested in them, I can't explain, and it feels like they're the link, you know?'

Conor nodded. 'I do. So finally, Ned and Cecilia's son, Jeffrey, was your mother's father, and we can see that he had two daughters, Marcia and Estelle?'

'Yes, I have an aunt Estelle,' Taylor said. 'So this proves that Ned is our Ned?'

'It does.' Conor smiled and sat back.

Taylor looked at him. 'I had no idea what to expect, and I was kind of dreading this process if I'm honest, but this is amazing. Thank you so much. It's like detective work, isn't it?'

'It is. And sometimes you can be lucky and other times not. Your story was relatively easy.'

'Is it difficult if the person in the past turns out to be awful? You know, telling their descendants?' she asked, suddenly intrigued by the whole process.

'It can be. And sometimes it's sad. But often it's just interesting.'

'I've never fit in.' Taylor had forgotten about the camera and confided in Conor. 'I know this might sound silly, but I was always the geeky kid with the perfect homework, straight A's, reading constantly. People thought I was weird – even my parents did, if I'm honest. But hearing about Ned and Cecilia and their academic life and their political activism, it makes me feel like I'm not such a freak, you know?'

'I do know.' He nodded. 'I've found over the years that this journey of discovery for people is about more than finding out who went where and how many children they had. Often the process tells us about whose blood runs in our veins, and we can learn a lot about ourselves from it.' He stood and lifted the heavy file, passing it to her.

'Thank you so much, Conor. I can't wait to get into these.'

As she perused the file, Havie called, 'And...cut! Great work, you two. That was really something, wasn't it?' he asked Kayla, who was standing beside him, her eyes boring into Conor's.

'It was good,' she agreed.

'OK,' Havie addressed everyone. 'Maybe we'll leave it there for now and we'll shoot some scenes around the grounds tomorrow?'

Taylor was relieved he didn't seem annoyed the shoot was interrupted. 'I'm sorry for stopping... I just –'

'Don't worry, no problem,' Kayla responded. 'We have all we need.'

CHAPTER 19

Shannon O'Cleary entered the ballroom, the last of the group to arrive, Princess Bellachic under her arm as usual. The cameras were set up, and Havie was sitting in the director's chair.

Irish language lessons were about to begin as the cameras rolled. One end of the ballroom had been set up as an old-style classroom. They'd found a chalkboard, and much to everyone's amusement, the teacher was dressed in black robes and had small reading glasses perched on the end of his nose. The desks had been borrowed from a tourist attraction nearby, a village reconstructed as it would have been in the late 1800s, complete with inkwells and wicker baskets for their lunches.

The instructor was the Irish teacher from the local secondary school, officially called Mr O'Murchú but all the kids called him Mokie, the reason for which was about to become apparent.

Conor stood at the back of the makeshift classroom and watched in amusement. The task for the celebrities was to successfully conduct a short conversation in the Irish language using, among other things, the bane of every Irish teenager's life, the future conditional tense.

'I guess Fintan is going to win this one,' Kayla said as she sidled up to him and stood so she was touching him.

Without caring if he offended her, Conor took a step to the right. 'Well, maybe,' he agreed, subtly moving his head slightly to escape the pungent odour of her perfume. 'But to be honest with you, every person who ever did their leaving cert – it's the equivalent of your SATs, I think, where you need to get points in the final exam to gain access to university – has had at least one nightmare that they had to do their Irish oral exam again.'

'What was it?' she asked, her dark eyes focused intently on him. It was most disconcerting.

'It's a one-to-one conversation with an examiner. Learning the Irish language, what you call Gaelic, is compulsory here in this country, so there were three parts to the exam – a written part, an aural part, where they play a tape of different dialects within the country and ask you questions, and then the hardest part is the oral. That's what these guys are going to have to do. And several of the questions force you to use a very complicated future conditional tense called the *modh coinníollach*. It's kind of like an "if I had fifty Euro, I would go to town" idea, but in Irish the whole thing changes, the syntax, the words themselves. It's complicated.' He chuckled.

'Seems kinda dumb. Why do they force you guys to do that? That's a dead language, right? What's the point?' she asked dismissively.

Conor felt his hackles rise. She had no idea. 'The point,' he said, forcing his voice to remain neutral despite his frustration, 'is that it is our native language, and it would be the language of our country today were it not for the British occupation of our island for 800 years. We were forbidden to speak it, this beautiful language so much more expressive than English could ever be, and so now that we are finally free, it means something in our hearts, in our culture. It's part of who we are, and we are proud of it.'

Kayla shrugged. 'Seems dumb to me.'

Conor bit his tongue. How dare she dismiss the culture like that? She was truly insufferable. 'Well, it's not, but it's an Irish thing. I don't expect you to understand.' Conor turned to leave; so many things about her just annoyed him.

'So much of this place seems dumb. Like why can't you install underfloor heating in this place? Those stupid stone floors are cold, and you all try too hard to keep it looking like it did. But why? Why not just let it go? The past is over, gone, not worth our time.'

'As I said, you wouldn't understand.' Conor walked off, but she followed him, grabbing him by the arm. Deliberately, he removed her hand from his forearm.

'So why does everyone call him Mokie?' Kayla nodded at the teacher who was addressing the class now.

Conor would have loved to have been rude, but too much was at stake. He said shortly, 'Well, the tense is pronounced like *"mowkenee-loch"*, so it's shortened to Mokie.'

Conor looked around at the gathered pupils, sitting at old-fashioned desks, the kind he remembered from school. The teacher put the group in three pairs of two. Bob and Taylor, Shannon and Fintan, and Ryan and Shelby.

Poor Ryan was red-eyed from crying; clearly the situation wasn't improving. Conor had suggested to his parents that he could bring Joe and Artie over and they could kick a ball around or play a video game or something with Ryan, but his mother dismissed it, fearful that he might get injured or something would happen to ruin his perfect face. Conor had rarely seen such a miserable child, and he doubted Shelby was the maternal type. She'd apparently told the make-up people that she would do her own and refused to wear what wardrobe planned for her. Havie was very slow to intervene, but Conor noticed there always seemed to be a camera rolling somewhere.

The teacher handed out sheets with Irish sentences written phonetically and asked the pairs to say the lines to each other. Bob and Taylor were trying their best, but Bob's Southern accent made the complicated language sound even more incomprehensible, which reduced Taylor to giggles. Fintan was teaching Shannon without the use of the phonetics as he was fairly fluent, and Shelby had no idea what to say to the mutinous-looking Ryan.

'Ryan!' his mother hissed. 'Read the line.'

The child looked at her, his eyes filling up once more. Conor couldn't stand it. Havie had told him he could come on and off set during these tasks as he wished, so he got down on his hunkers between Ryan and Shelby and tried to jolly them along. His arrival turned a light on inside Shelby.

'Oh, don't say you're multilingual as well as all your other talents, Conor!' she trilled, though her blue eyes were fixed on the camera and not on him.

'Oh, we can all speak Irish here,' he answered, but then turned his attention to Ryan. 'Are you all right, Ryan? You look a bit sad.'

Immediately the camera was at his shoulder, practically in the child's face.

'Take that away,' Conor said to the cameraman, quietly but firmly. The man glanced at Havie, who gave a small nod, and backed away.

Conor whispered to Ryan, 'I've an idea. You say the lines after me, they'll record it, and then you and I will go for an ice cream in our coffee shop. How about that?'

The boy looked at him doubtfully, and though his mother was straining to hear what was going on, Havie had warned her not to appear in the shot. Conor knew it must have sounded strange, a grown man inviting a child for ice cream – his own lads were well versed on not accepting such invitations from anyone – but he wanted to reassure the boy, and seeing the kid so miserable was breaking his heart.

'My own boys, they're called Joe and Artie, are just a tiny bit younger than you. They chose all the flavours for the ice cream bar, so as well as the normal flavours, there are lots of weird ones. They're off school today actually, so how about I ask someone to pick them up, and after the ice cream, we could play football?'

Shelby looked directly at the camera as she pointedly read the lines, practising them aloud.

'I'm not allowed to play ball games in case anything happens,' Ryan said sadly.

Conor swallowed his fury. This was a child, for God's sake, not a meal ticket, and his parents were standing by and allowing his childhood to pass him by.

'How about tree climbing? Is there a rule about that?' he whispered.

Ryan shrugged. 'She never said anything about that.'

'Then let's assume that's OK.' Conor had no doubt in his mind whatsoever that Julie would have a stroke if she knew. 'So here's the plan. You say the lines – just copy me, I'll go slowly – and then it's ice cream and tree climbing. We've got some really cool trees behind the hotel, and Joe and Artie are good climbers.'

He stood up and beckoned one of the wait staff over. 'Maire, do me a favour. Can you ask Ana to send someone for Joe and Artie? Nothing wrong, just this lad needs someone to play with, but tell her to keep it quiet, all right?'

'No problem, Conor,' the girl murmured, then left.

They got through the Irish task easily enough, Shelby flirting with the camera and Ryan parroting what Conor said.

Once it was over, Conor approached Julie and Joel, who were standing off set. 'I'm taking Ryan to the ice cream bar, and then my sons are coming up to play with him for a bit.' It was a statement, not a request.

'Oh, no. Thank you, but he needs to prepare for a TV interview and we don't eat sugar –' Julie began.

But for once her husband interjected. 'Jules, the kid needs a break. Let him go.'

Conor shot Joel a look of gratitude.

'No, Joel. I'm sorry, Conor, but Ryan has a series of appearances lined up to promote the new movie, and he needs to prepare. Besides, and no disrespect to you or your children, but Ryan isn't really into that.'

Conor had no idea what she meant by 'that'. He gently led her away from the camera that was bearing down on them.

'Well, he'd be the first child in the history of the world not into ice cream, and my boys are nice, Julie. They'll play gently, and I'll be there to supervise. Surely you can see Ryan is not having a good time? He's surrounded by adults, and he never has any time just to be a ten-year-old boy.' His eyes met hers. 'It's not fair.'

Julie Farrell's face was a mask of disdain, and Conor thought he'd never seen such a hard-looking woman. She was short and not heavy exactly, but solid. Her dark hair was cut in an unflattering bob, stopping abruptly at her jawline, and she wore dark eyeliner and lots of mascara.

'My *son*, Conor' – she paused – 'is a gifted child and has to be nurtured. His talent is unprecedented, and while I appreciate that you think you are helping him, rest assured your intervention is unnecessary. Ryan is fine. He loves his life and has no need of the company of some random children.'

Conor rarely lost his temper, but seeing the abuse of this child as well as reeling from dealing with Kayla was really testing his patience. Ana had told him about how, after the incident when Ryan locked himself in the stables after the baking challenge, he'd sobbed in her arms and told her that he hated acting and wished he could just go to normal school and be a normal everyday kid. He'd told her he had no friends and played no sports, and how much he hated his mother.

'Ryan is talented,' Conor said quietly, looming over her now, 'but he is also a little boy, and you are ruining his life. He cried for hours the other day, did you know that? He told my wife how much he hated being here, hated being recognised, hated going on talk shows, all the rest of it. And I know you might think he's going to hurt himself or something if he's allowed to be a normal kid, but you have to stop treating him like a commodity to be exploited for money and start treating him like a child, your son.'

Her eyes left his and flicked upwards, where a large boom with a microphone was being lowered.

Conor knew the boom operator was standing behind him, but he didn't turn around. 'Take that away unless you want it inserted in you.'

He then walked over and put his hand on Ryan's shoulder. 'Come on, Ryan, we're going for ice cream.'

Julie Farrell nailed a smile on her face a moment too late as the camera panned over the scene. Conor wondered if he imagined it, but Joel Farrell seemed to give him the tiniest wink.

Over a big bowl of bubblegum, strawberry shortcake and cookie dough ice cream with extra sprinkles, chocolate sauce and whipped cream, Ryan opened up to Conor. He was a remarkably cheerful child once he was away from his mother.

'So, Ryan, if you could do anything, what would it be?' Conor asked, sipping a black coffee. He'd convinced Christoph, the barista, to make him proper coffee whenever he asked for a decaf. He'd had to agree to naming him employee of the month, which meant Christoph won a free weekend in the hotel for him and his girlfriend in return for his silence, but it was worth it.

'An electrician,' the child said without hesitation.

Conor smiled. 'Really? Why an electrician?'

The exceptionally handsome dark-eyed, dark-haired boy grinned, the first proper smile Conor had seen since he met him. His face was covered in ice cream, and Conor prayed his mother wouldn't turn up.

''Cause it's amazing. I mean, electricity, like, it gets generated by power, water, fuel or wind or even waves, and then we can harness it and manage it and get it into houses and hotels and factories to do so much cool stuff. I think it's amazing. What powers this place?' he asked. 'Are you off the grid or on it?'

'Well, Ryan,' Conor explained, glad the boy was opening up, 'this building is remarkable actually, because when it was built back in the 1600s, obviously there was no electricity. So we've had to retrofit all the power, but we had to do it very carefully. We can't spoil the look of the castle, so we can't have ugly old junction boxes or fuse boards visible. Artur, who is my boys' granddad, my wife's father, is the maintenance manager here, and there's nothing he can't do in terms of electricity or building or plumbing or anything like that – he's a genius.'

The boy hung on Conor's every word.

'But to answer your question, we're completely carbon neutral here. That means we generate all the energy we need ourselves through wind. We are in a fairly wild spot as you can see, so we have windmills, and we also use a waterfall on the property to generate electricity, so we feed into the grid as well.'

'That's so cool! And so what's your GEO disregarding in-house load?'

Conor chuckled. 'I've no idea, but I know a man who can help you with all of that stuff.' He pulled out his phone and dialled. 'Artur, hi. I have a young man here who is very interested in electricity and our…' He turned to Ryan again. 'What did you want to know?'

'The GEO, gross electric output,' Ryan said seriously.

'Our gross electrical output. So I said you might show him around our setup here.' He paused while Artur spoke. 'Perfect. You can go on a tour when you get here with the twins so.'

He turned back to Ryan. 'OK, so that was my father-in-law. He's collected Joe and Artie at my house, so they'll be here shortly too, and he's going to take you all to the maintenance department this afternoon, show you around and maybe even find a few jobs for you to do. How does that sound?'

'Really?' Ryan's eyes lit up, and Conor had never seen such enthusiasm in the child before. 'That would be so cool.'

'Well, I pay minors in ice cream, so when the jobs are done to Artur's satisfaction, then there's more where that came from.' He pointed at the now-empty bowl. 'He mentioned something about sorting cables?'

'I'd love that.' Ryan grinned.

Out of the corner of his eye, he noticed Julie searching the lobby, her face like thunder.

Through the window, he saw Artur pull up and his boys tumble out of the dirty maintenance jeep that they loved. Artur let them drive it in the fields; he and Ana weren't supposed to know, but the boys let it slip. It was harmless enough, he'd reassured his wife. Artur was very careful and wouldn't let anything happen to the twins.

'Now see those two boys getting out of the car with the football? They're my sons. Run out and introduce yourself.' He caught Artur's eye through the window, and Artur beckoned Ryan out.

With seemingly a combination of excitement and nerves, the boy walked outside as Joe and Artie kicked the ball to each other. Without any need for introductions, Joe kicked the ball to Ryan, who stood there nonplussed for a moment. In his immaculate cream chinos, tailored shirt and leather shoes, he was the opposite of the twins, who were dressed identically as always in soccer shirts, trainers and track-suit bottoms. They dressed up for Mass on Sundays but immediately changed the moment they got home.

Ryan kicked the ball awkwardly, but somehow Joe managed to get his head to it and nodded it to Artie, who kicked it back to Ryan. The boy was a little more confident now, and did a better job. Joe could easily have stopped the shot but let it get past him.

'Hey, take it easy on me!' he joked, and Ryan's face split into a huge grin.

He ran for the ball the next time Artie kicked it to him, and Conor felt a surge of pride for his boys.

He decided he'd better tackle the mother before she undid all his work by stressing the boy out again. He walked towards her as she scoured the area for her son, who was now safely outside. 'Julie, I was just –'

'Where's Ryan?' she asked exasperatedly. 'Look, I know you prob-ably mean well, but honestly, you don't know what's best, and he really needs to –'

'Would you come to my office?' Conor asked gently. 'Just for a minute? I want to show you something.'

'I don't have time. I need to find my son.' Her eyes scanned the coffee shop.

'You can see him. Please?' Conor asked.

'Julie.' Joel appeared. By the cold shoulder she gave him, the two had clearly had an argument.

'Is my son in your office?' she asked Conor, ignoring her husband completely.

'No, but if you follow me, I just want to show you something. Please. Both of you.' Conor stood back and gestured they should pass him. He ushered them across reception and into his office, which for once didn't have someone in it.

He led them to the window and pointed outside. Ryan's trousers became green on the knees as he slid to tackle Joe. He held the ball to his body rugby style as the boys descended on him, laughing and tumbling on the grass.

'Oh, for God's sake. He's filthy! Those trousers are Yves Saint Laurent.' Julie went to knock on the window to interrupt the game, but Joel gently held her arm.

'Forget the pants. Look at him, Julie, just look. When was the last time you saw him laughing? Really laughing? Or playing with other kids? Let him be. He's having fun.' He sighed, and Conor sensed the weariness. This wasn't the first time they'd had this conversation.

'He's not like other kids though! Why can't you get that through your thick skull?' Her eyes flashed with frustration.

'But he wants to be.' Joel shoved his hands into his pockets and turned to Conor. 'He's never been able to just be a child. He starred in his first movie at three, and since then it's been constant, bigger and bigger roles, more and more travelling, publicity.' His voice betrayed the emotion of it all, his sense of helplessness. 'We're doing wrong by him, Jules, we are.' Joel was gentle but firm. 'That's the kid he should be, playing and joking, getting dirty, kicking soccer balls. We've got him like a hothouse plant and he's suffocating.'

Julie Farrell turned to her husband. 'I'm not doing it for the money. Everyone thinks that's why, but it's not. I just want him...' She broke off.

'To be happy?' Joel suggested.

'To achieve greatness, to not just be some other guy, living a small life in a small town.'

'But what about what he wants? Isn't that something to consider?' Joel put his hand on his wife's shoulder. 'Look at him, Jules, he's so happy. He's just a little boy, playing. What's so wrong with that?'

They stood silently for a minute as Artie laughed and high-fived Ryan. Artie was doing some dramatic sidestepping with the ball as Ryan tried to tackle him.

'I guess, but he's so talented. Letting him waste it seems so wrong.' She watched the child she'd raised to never get a speck of dirt on him, who didn't go to school and instead had a tutor, for whom she'd prioritised fame over all else, who'd never had another child to play with, the kid that had an eight-figure bank account but was so sad. Her little boy kicked the ball so hard it bounced off a car, setting off its alarm.

'Oh no!' Julie's hand flew to her mouth, but Conor chuckled.

'That's my car. It's grand. It gets about fifty belts from footballs a day – it's used to it. Watch.' Conor pointed as Joe opened the car and disabled the alarm.

Ryan was talking animatedly to the twins, who were laughing at whatever he'd said. Ryan had a big smudge of dirt on his cheek.

'He doesn't look like the child that's been nominated for an Oscar and is going on The Movie Review Show next month, does he?' Julie said ruefully.

'Maybe not, but it's just a bit of dirt, nothing a scrub in the shower won't sort out,' Conor said. 'I've seen him act – he is incredible, no doubt about it.' But this wasn't his business. 'But I suppose all children need to play, no matter how gifted they are.'

As they stood there, Ryan kicked the ball through Artie's feet and into the makeshift goal of two hoodies on the grass and scored. Joe pulled Ryan's shirt out of his trousers and demonstrated how he should pull it over his head and do a victory lap. Ryan had to undo his buttons, the starched linen not being as stretchy as polyester sports shirts, but he did it, and Joe and Artie put their arms around him as they did a victory run. Artur then appeared with three bottles of water. The boys drank some and then squirted each other with the rest; within seconds they were soaked and chasing each other with the bottles. Julie and Joel stood, watching, and as Conor withdrew discreetly, he saw the tears rolling down Ryan's mother's face.

CHAPTER 20

The weather had turned bitterly cold. The roads were icy and the school's boiler broke, much to the children's delight, so classes were cancelled until it could be repaired. Thrilled with the impromptu holiday, the twins had taken to coming to the castle with Conor and Ana each day. Artur claimed he was happy to have the boys trailing after him doing 'jobs'.

The twins and Ryan had become inseparable, and it was lovely to see. Ryan was definitely more sheltered than the O'Shea boys, but they got along well. Ryan had never played a video game, and had never even heard of many of their games, but for Joe and Artie, he was a project, and they took to their task with enthusiasm.

Julie was still unhappy, as she was terrified he'd break his nose or get a cut that would lead to a scar, but then Havie intervened. He'd spoken to Conor and had seen how happy the child was with his new and first friends, and Havie told Julie that the friendship between Ryan and the much more boisterous and streetwise O'Shea twins was going to capture the audience's hearts. If she stood in the way, it would look very bad for her, so it was better to just go with it.

Ryan was reluctantly dragged away each day at three p.m. to talk to his agent or do some video interviews, and sometimes Joe and

Artie watched him through the window, amazed that this superstar was their friend. He didn't want to talk about famous people he'd met or stories from on set, but he asked Artur an endless stream of questions about the wiring of the hotel. He loved hearing about the boys' school, their teacher, their friends.

'Right, you two, you need to stay out of sight today,' Conor warned the twins on the drive in to work. 'They're doing lots of shots on the grounds today, and we want to do this in as few takes as possible.' Then he murmured, 'So we can get these people on a plane and out of our hotel as fast as possible.'

The boys giggled. Normally Conor spoke very kindly and respectfully about the guests, so it was unusual to hear him say a bad thing about them, but his patience was wearing thin.

Fintan was drinking heavily, though they had managed to clean him up considerably, but it was a worry. He never surfaced before lunchtime, staying up late into the night drinking, often alone.

Bob was really enjoying his stay. He'd found a bunch of trad musicians who played in a pub two miles away, so he joined the session there most nights. Nobody bothered him or tried to get selfies or anything, so he was having the time of his life.

Douglas had unearthed Shelby's family. She'd explained to Conor on one of her first days at the castle that she was sure there was at least some royalty connection, but he gently had to explain that Ireland was a republic for a start, so there was no Irish monarch.

She was often to be found explaining to the staff how she probably owned the castle they were working in, that her family were the high kings of Ireland, how they had all manner of antiquities in the family's possession, including suits of armour and swords, handcrafted in Birmingham, England. Nobody contradicted her though; the Irish were used to such extravagant ideas.

Conor wasn't looking forward to the filming of this one, which was going to start on the grounds and then move to his office. Havie had decided he loved Conor's stone-lined office and wanted to incorporate it into the show. When Conor objected, Havie upped the investment to include use of the entire castle, no areas off limits, and

Conor had to accept it, but with each day that passed, he was growing more and more frustrated. At least they were over halfway through. Bob was happy, and that entire episode, the pilot, was almost ready. Taylor's story had turned out to be a really super one, and he was glad it gave her some clarity on who she was. She'd told him all about her great-grandparents and was so excited to learn more about them, though what use that was going to be for her eejit of a father, he had no idea.

Ryan had endured his, with Joel and Julie sitting beside him, as Conor explained how their ancestor, a copper miner from West Cork, had moved to Butte, Montana, along with almost an entire community from the Beara Peninsula, and founded a huge Irish community there. It was the ancestor on Joel's side that the programme focused on, and he left Ireland in 1870, got married and had a bunch of children, all of whom stayed in the Rocky Mountains. Joel was vaguely interested, Julie not at all, and Ryan had no clue what they were talking about. He kept looking at Conor, seemingly wondering when he could go and play with the twins again. It was a huge mistake to have him on the show, but Havie insisted the interplay between him, Conor and his parents was good and that the genealogy was secondary.

The lad had been dreading the next challenge, which was to play hurling, because he'd never played sports, but Joe and Artie had decided to take him on as a project and now he was actually getting the hang of it. It was all unbeknownst to his mother, of course. If she saw the Irish national sport played, she'd definitely ban her son from joining in. The idea of children wielding three-foot-long sticks to try to hit a hard leather ball, no matter how skilfully the O'Shea twins managed it, would not be tolerated.

The cameras were rolling as Conor and Shelby strolled along.

'So where are the family crown jewels?' she asked, flirting with the camera.

'Cut!' shouted Havie. 'Are you wearing both your contacts, Shelby?'

The woman blinked self-consciously. 'Oh my, I'm not sure.' She turned to Conor. 'Are both my eyes the same colour?'

Conor was bewildered. What was she on about? He looked at her and yes, one eye was a pale blue, the other almost a vivid aquamarine. 'Er… One does seem a bit different, all right,' he said.

'Shoot, I forgot one contact.' She rushed off and returned several moments later, both eyes now that unnatural colour.

'Do you need them to see?' he asked innocently.

She pealed with laughter. 'No, Conor, I've got perfect vision. It's cosmetic.'

Conor shook his head but said nothing. Ana was grumbling only this morning about how she needed to do a bit of refurbishment, especially as the hotel was filled with such beauties, but he assured her that he loved her without make-up, just wearing jeans and a t-shirt, her hair short. Ana was naturally beautiful. She didn't need nor would she want to stick bits of coloured plastic into her eyes to change their colour. Shelby was good-looking, he supposed, but she was too polished for him. Almost everything about her, now that he looked, was fake: Her eyelashes were unnaturally long, her face was without one single crease or line, her eyes he knew were not the colour she presented, her nose was tiny and straight, and though he wasn't interested in examining them, he suspected those were not her own breasts either.

If anything, seeing that made him sad. He knew some women felt better about themselves after taking all kinds of measures, even surgery to enhance their looks, but he hated that the world made them feel that way. He thought of his tiny, perfect daughter and hoped she'd never feel like she needed to do things like that.

'OK, and rolling again!' Havie called, and they resumed their chat.

'So are my ancestors really the kings of Ireland, 'cause I could sure use a crown.' Shelby smiled.

Conor could see she was very used to cameras. He never got the impression from her that he had her attention; it was always someplace else, and she was usually looking for the camera or the microphone.

'Well, I'm afraid we haven't had kings here for a long time, Shelby, so if they were, it's a long time ago and I doubt any of their treasure, if they had it, would be available to anyone. All items of archaeological value are the property of the state and are stored in the National Museum in Dublin. If you want to visit there, you could, especially the Treasury, with its very impressive collection of precious things. But these days, we're a republic, and so our constitution cherishes all the children of the nation equally. We don't have anyone higher than anyone else here since 1916. But that said, your surname is associated with the Gaelic kings of old certainly.'

They strolled by the beach, the cameramen doing their best to keep the cameras steady in the wind.

Conor wanted to soften it up a bit for her to begin with, so he decided to tell her about the general history of her last name rather than specifically her family. He was used to doing it; it had been his stock in trade for so long while doing the tours. He knew the family history of most of the major clans and was able to tell people the stories of the O'Donovans and the McCarthys and so on with ease, which people liked to hear. But often they didn't realise that there were many branches and hundreds of thousands of descendants, so if the name was Murphy, for example, thousands of others held that name and it didn't give you a claim to the estate, even if there was one.

'So you're a Maguire, which is a derivative of the Irish Mac Uidhir, meaning son of the dark-haired one.' He watched her face change as he delivered the next piece of news. 'But according to legend, they are the direct descendants of Cormac mac Airt, king of all Ireland back in Celtic times, and of course the Maguires were the kings of County Fermanagh.'

She beamed. 'I knew they were. My father was so proud of his Irish heritage. He loved Ireland, and he had a huge aerial photograph of a castle on the wall of his office in the Battery that overlooked Ellis Island. He used to tell me how we came from that castle to the United States.'

'Did he visit Ireland?' Conor asked, assuming the answer.

'No, unfortunately he never got here. He planned to, but with work and everything...' Her voice trailed off. 'This is the first time anyone from my family has come here, I think.'

Though she was a bit of a show-off, never missing an opportunity to blow her own trumpet, something about her made him feel sorry for her. He got the impression she was raised with the need to impress in her DNA.

'Well, that's the Maguire line. Because that was many centuries ago, the family has several thousand lines of descent. But specifically your branch of it is this. Your great-grandfather and great-grandmother emigrated together, from County Fermanagh in the North.'

He knew it was far more likely they came from a tenant cottage rather than a castle, especially as they travelled as third-class passengers, but adding that wouldn't be helpful. Though what he had to say next would hardly be met with delight either. 'And they settled in New York.'

'Do we know where in the city?' Shelby asked enthusiastically. 'We lived off Union Square, and I think my grandparents lived in Midtown too. I don't remember them much – they died when I was young. I don't think they and my father were that close. We never knew anything about them.'

They sat on a bench overlooking the sunken garden, now lush and green, bordered by cyclamen and winter-flowering heather, and Conor took out the file Douglas had prepared.

They then moved inside, to Conor's office, and the cameras began rolling once more. He sat opposite her, with the small oak coffee table between them.

Conor hated ambushing people like this, but Havie insisted that reality TV only worked when the reactions were real.

'Well, we know they came into Ellis Island, actually relatively recently, in 1900. Your great-grandfather was a man called Aloysius Maguire, and with his wife, Elizabeth, and one child, also called Elizabeth, they disembarked and settled in New York.' He passed her a document listing their names.

'And how do you know these are my ancestors?' she asked, examining the document.

'Well, they had three more children, two more girls and one boy, William, while living in the Bronx –'

'The Bronx? Why did they live there?' She seemed incredulous.

Conor shrugged. 'I don't know why they chose it, but your great-grandparents had a laundry. Here's the deed of that property that they rented, with them listed as tenants. They lived there as well, as you can see, as the tenancy lists a laundry as well as three bedrooms and a shared kitchen and bathroom.'

'What? I... What kind of house was that?' She seemed very taken aback.

'It was a tenement,' Conor said kindly. 'The New York State Legislature in 1867 defined a tenement as any building rented out as a home for more than three families living independently. You see, Shelby, at the time, immigrants were flooding the city, all needing accommodation, so landlords were converting single-family units into apartments with lots of rooms to meet the demand. For around ten dollars a month, a family could rent around 300 square feet and up to seven people could live in that space.'

Shelby swallowed. 'Are you telling me my ancestors lived in a space half the size of a subway car?'

'Well, yes.'

Poor Shelby was appalled. 'I learned about these buildings when I was in college. They didn't have indoor plumbing, so no toilets or showers, or even running water. There was supposed to be an outhouse for every twenty residents, but nobody enforced it, so most people relied on chamber pots and just threw the contents out the window.' She shuddered.

'It wasn't an easy life, that's for sure, but people were tougher back then, I think.' Conor smiled, handing her a photograph of the building where the Maguire family were listed as tenants. 'It is a testament to those people that they were willing to endure anything to make a better life for themselves and their families. You come from strong stock, Shelby.'

'But I don't understand. I was always told that they were kings,' she said, gazing at the miserable-looking building. 'And yet they lived in this terrible place.'

'Well' – Conor glanced at Havie, who had three cameras on them – 'they didn't always live there. They moved.'

'OK, good, that makes sense.' She smiled.

Her relief was to be short-lived though, and Conor dropped the next bombshell as gently as he could. 'Aloysius and Elizabeth were arrested in 1908 and charged with larceny and assault.'

Shelby stared at him, speechless.

Havie gestured that he was to keep going. One of the legal terms of the show was that there could be no cherry-picking of the information; what was unearthed was going to be aired regardless of the wishes of the contestant. It was in the small print, and Havie made everyone aware of it again on the first day, after the contracts were signed and the first payments made of course.

'They pleaded guilty. They were both working in a house, a big mansion in the Battery actually. They came once a week to do the laundry it seems, and they robbed the owners. According to the court transcript' – he handed Shelby another document – 'the mistress of the house, a Mrs Ernest Gladstone, happened upon them in her bedchamber as they were rifling through her jewellery. She screamed and her husband came running, but apparently he was struck with something hard and was rendered unconscious. Some other staff called the police, and the pair were arrested. They were then charged with stealing from several houses where they offered their laundry service.'

Shelby gazed at the page from the records of the New York City police department.

'What happened to them? To their kids?' Shelby sounded shaken, and Conor placed his hand on her shoulder.

'Well, Aloysius and Elizabeth were each sentenced to seven years in prison, which they served. And their children were sent to an orphanage. Aloysius apparently got into an altercation with another prisoner towards the end of his sentence and had two years added on for brawling. He was killed in a fight in prison the following year. Elizabeth was released and did get some of her children back.'

He handed Shelby a newspaper clipping. It was from the society pages of *The New York Times* and contained a photograph of a bride, a beautiful woman.

Shelby read aloud. 'A radiant bride, Mrs William Maguire, nee Papadopoulos, who married Mr William Maguire of 132 7th Avenue, Manhattan, at St Francis de Sales Catholic Church on the 9th of June, 1928. The happy couple were married by Archbishop Corrigan at the beautiful church on the corner of Park and Lexington. Among the notable guests in attendance were the mayor of New York, Jimmy Walker, and his wife, Janet, Mr and Mrs Chamberlain of the Chamberlain Diamond Company and Mr Anthony Gauci and his wife, Violetta. Mr Gauci was recently released from prison, having served three years for money laundering and racketeering. Mr and Mrs Maguire have purchased a beautiful apartment on Fifth Avenue and plan to take up residence upon returning from their honeymoon at Cape Cod.'

She looked up at Conor, her face a mask of confusion. 'What's going on here?' she asked. 'Who is this guy? Surely not the son of a pair of criminals without a penny?'

Conor sighed. 'Well, it looks like William was the son of Elizabeth and Aloysius. He married well and had some...' – he paused, searching for the right words – 'notable connections.'

'And how did he go from being a kid in a tenement to living on Fifth Avenue and being married by an archbishop?'

Conor removed another article from the file. It was a cover letter from Sheehy, Canavan and Gold, Attorneys at Law, Queens, New York, addressed to William Maguire c/o Mr and Mrs A Gauci, and attached was a handwritten letter signed by Elizabeth Maguire.

Shelby read the letter and Conor waited.

'Oh my, am I reading this right?' she asked. 'My great-grandmother had her lawyer write to this William, who is my grandfather, at his adopted home?'

Conor nodded.

'Read it aloud, Shelby,' Havie instructed.

'My dear son William, I have not seen you for a long year and I hope this finds you well. I am now a free woman and your sisters are with me, but I want you to have a better life than the one I could provide, and so I will not seek to have you restored to me. I trust you are happy and well in the care of Mr Gauci.

'Your late father arranged for Mr Gauci to adopt you in the event that we could no longer care for you, and with him being a trusted business associate of your father's, we were secure in the knowledge that you would be cared for.

'As you are now eighteen years of age, please ask your adopted father to give you any heirlooms your father may have put by for you and entrusted to his care until you were of age.

'Take care, my dear son. I am not in good health and do not expect to live for much longer. Two of your sisters are married and settled, but the youngest, Jenny, is not, so should I die, please ensure she is cared for. Your loving mother, Elizabeth Maguire.'

Shelby sat quietly and absorbed what she'd just read. 'And this Gauci man, who was he? My grandfather's adopted father?'

Conor nodded.

'So my great-grandparents were criminals, thieves, and they arranged for this Gauci man to adopt their son, not their daughters, when they were in prison.'

Conor didn't respond, letting her work it out for herself. He then extracted a final document, another newspaper clipping dated 1935. He felt terrible and wished it could be different, but it wasn't his decision to make.

'Betsy Maguire Dead, but Where's the Money?' screamed the headline.

Shelby read aloud again. 'Convicted criminal Elizabeth – Betsy – Maguire died yesterday in her home on the Lower East Side of Manhattan. She and her late husband, Aloysius, were part of the notorious crime family led by mob boss Anthony Gauci, and served sentences for larceny and assault. At their trials in 1908, they both refused to give any evidence to implicate Gauci or any members of the crime family, nor did they reveal where the stolen money and jewellery, estimated to be valued at several hundred thousand dollars, the proceeds of crime amassed over several years, were hidden. The location of the proceeds of their life of crime remains a mystery to this day.'

SHE SAT BACK and gazed at the page, exhaling slowly. 'So my grandfather, this William Maguire was...'

'There's no evidence to suggest he was involved in anything nefarious at all,' Conor was quick to reassure her. 'He was adopted by the Gauci family, presumably because there was a connection between Anthony Gauci and your great-grandparents, but he made his own way in the world. There was never any scandal or anything about the Maguire family after that.'

'But he had a mob guy at his wedding,' Shelby said doubtfully.

'His adopted father, yes.'

'So I'm not descended from kings after all.'

She looked vulnerable, and he felt that pang again.

'I'm descended from criminals.'

'Well, those were difficult times. People did what they had to, I suppose.' Conor didn't know what else to say.

'Well, it's sure a story.' She smiled. 'And I think we can guess where my grandfather got the money to trade up from a tenement in the Bronx to a condo on Fifth Avenue.'

'Maybe he got lucky at the racetrack?' Conor smiled.

'Hmm. Maybe.' Shelby smiled back.

CHAPTER 21

Taylor threw the phone on the bed. She couldn't read another WhatsApp from her father demanding to be updated on the progress of the show. Then it rang. 'Dad' flashed on the screen. She'd replied to his last message only moments ago, so he knew she had her phone on her. He'd sounded anxious in the texts, so despite every instinct she had telling her to ignore the call, she slid her finger across the screen and answered.

'Hi, Daddy,' she said wearily.

'Taylor, baby, what's going on? I need to know what happened with the filming, and you're being so vague.'

Was he slurring? Possibly.

'I told you, I did the piece. It was all about this Ned O'Hara, Mom's ancestor, and how he was a teacher and set up schools. He fell afoul of Tammany Hall and the Church –'

'What!' he roared so loudly she had to pull the phone from her ear. 'Are you kidding me? Some guy that pissed off the Church and the government? Oh, that's just great, Taylor! That's exactly what I need when I'm trying to get back in the good books. For God's sake, Taylor, you had one job to do, how could you have let it go like that? You knew what I needed, someone good, someone loved, not some repro-

161

bate who is going to make me look worse than I already do. That's going to ruin me!'

She could hear the slurring clearly now. He was definitely drunk.

'But, Daddy, I don't control –' she tried to explain, but he was on a roll.

'Some bishop or a half decent congressman, something like that was what I needed. Surely you could have gotten them to talk about someone like that? Did you even manage to get in what a great father I am and how we love St Patty's Day and the Irish and everything? Did you highlight my achievements? Did you talk about the bridge I secured for the western suburbs? Tell me at least you managed to talk me up!'

Ted Davis cared nothing about the toll this was taking on her. She had a moment of clarity. She wasn't his beloved daughter; she was just someone to be used. That's what he was, a user of people. From somewhere deep within, she gathered her courage, and she heard her voice, stronger than ever before when speaking to him. 'Shut up and listen or I'm going to hang up and block your number.'

'Taylor? What are you...?' Ted Davis was shocked into silence.

'First, you have nobody to blame for this mess but yourself. It has nothing to do with me. *You* messed up, not me. Second, the producers research the histories, and I had no control over what the records show. And third, I did this for you, though God knows why when you didn't care about putting me in this awful position. So you texting and calling and blaming me is not fair.'

'But, Taylor, honey, you know what's at stake...' He was wheedling now.

'I know what's at stake for you. For me, nothing at all. Literally not one thing. I don't care if you get re-elected. I don't care if you and Mom divorce. I've had enough of both of you.'

'Ha!' he spat. 'You'll care when we stop paying for college, miss. You'll know all about it then –'

'I can apply for a scholarship to pay for my tuition, and based on my grades, I would stand an excellent chance of getting it. So I won't be taking anything from you in the future. And for the record, Ned

O'Hara and his wife were admirable people and I'm much prouder to have their blood in my veins than yours. I hope you sort out your drinking, Dad, but from now on, we're done.'

She ended the call, her hands trembling, instantly regretting her harsh words. He was trying so hard. She sat on the bed for twenty minutes, picking up and putting down the phone over and over. Eventually, she felt she had no choice, the guilt was too much, and she texted him back.

Daddy, I'm sorry. I shouldn't have spoken to you like that. I'll try to do better. I love you. Taylor xxx

There was no reply.

She moved to the window and saw Douglas walking around the grounds. It was cold but bright now after a torrential shower earlier in the morning, and the blue sky made everything look lovely, fresh and clean. A new day, a new start. She wished she could have one. She felt wretched.

Douglas looked up, saw her and waved. She waved back.

Without overthinking it – she'd back out if she weighed it up – she grabbed her coat and hat and left the room.

Douglas stood at the door of the coffee shop as she approached.

'Can I get you a hot drink?' he asked.

'Thanks, I'd love a hot chocolate.'

'Cream and marshmallows?' He smiled.

'Lovely. Are you busy or could we take a walk?' she asked as he handed her the paper cup.

'Not busy at all. I'd love a walk.'

They strolled behind the hotel, through the cobblestoned stables and into the woods that made up the eastern boundary of the castle.

'You can see where Yeats got his obsession with the occult and the esoteric, coming from such a place. One could almost imagine faeries and ghosts inhabiting these old woods,' Douglas said wistfully, and instantly looked embarrassed at expressing such a fanciful notion.

'I agree,' Taylor assured him. 'There is something other-worldly about this country, isn't there? And now in the depths of winter, it's so wild and untamed. It gives you such a sense of how we are merely passing through. This landscape has remained unchanged for centuries. We get ourselves tied up in knots about trivial things, but the trees and stones just watch and know they will be there long after we are all gone.'

As they walked slowly, she told him all about the conversation with her father.

To her astonishment, he said, 'If you need someone to support your application for funding, write a letter of reference or anything, I'd be happy to do it.'

'I couldn't ask you to do that! I mean, it would be amazing, but that's a huge ask and I –'

'I'd like to help.'

They came to a moss covered part of the path, where they had to climb over some rocks and he shyly offered her his hand to stop her from slipping. She took it and felt his fingers close over hers, she couldn't meet his eye.

Neither of them spoke for a few moments. She was recalling the feel of his hand on hers. As they rounded the bend in the path, she gasped. Before them was a torrent of a waterfall, surely at least sixty feet high, tumbling merrily over time-worn boulders, white at the centre where the water pounded relentlessly, but moss-covered on either side. At the base, just out of the spray, was a wooden deck, on which had been constructed a green and cream gazebo. The open parts had been glazed so it was enclosed, complete with a love seat inside. It was covered in variegated ivy and was the most romantic thing Taylor had ever seen.

'It's like something from a fairy tale, isn't it?' She wondered if she was dreaming.

'It really is,' Douglas agreed as they walked towards it.

They opened the door, and inside was a switch for a halogen heater. Taylor pressed it, and instantly warm heat filled the small space.

She sat and gazed at the waterfall, enjoying the warmth after the coolness outside, though several people that morning in the hotel had remarked to her how unseasonably warm it was. Irish people had a different opinion on warm she supposed. 'Thank you for listening,' she said shyly.

'I'm always happy to listen, Taylor. None of this is of your making, and you shouldn't feel responsible. It's not your fault that your parents behave as they do.'

She sighed. 'I know, but they're all I've got. I don't have any siblings, and while I know people in college, I don't make friends easily. I don't know, I just find it a bit awkward or something.'

He stared at the floor beneath his feet. 'I do too. It's just me and my mother, and I… Well, like you, I know people, colleagues and students mostly, but I never seem to know what to say.'

'I have never spoken to anyone as freely as I do you, actually. Maybe we're kindred spirits.' She'd said the words before realising how lame she sounded.

'Well, we have similar academic interests. I suppose that's it,' Douglas answered gruffly.

Taylor stood up suddenly to hide her embarrassment. His response clearly indicated he saw her as a student and nothing else. 'My goodness, that heater works well. I'm really warm now. Best get back, I suppose.'

They walked back to the hotel, having turned off the heater and closed the door behind them. They chatted once again, but it was a little forced. She cringed inwardly at making such a clumsy remark; he must think her a total idiot. He was a tenured professor at a presti-gious university and here she was making eyes at him like the silly little girl she was.

CHAPTER 22

*T*he blood-curdling scream could be heard throughout the hotel, Artie, Joe and Ryan were in the back office, enjoying a sandwich and a glass of milk, having 'worked' all morning for Artur. He had them loading and unloading the wheelbarrow with bark mulch for the new saplings, and then he'd given them two old radios to see if they could get them working.

The boys followed Artur in the direction of the noise to the small meeting room off the bar, used at the moment as the grooming station for Princess Bellachic. The groomer had come from Dublin and was much in demand up there, but apparently the demands of Ms O'Cleary were pushing her to the limits.

'What has happened?' Artur asked in dismay.

Shannon cradled one hand in the other, while the groomer cuddled a shaking dog.

'It bit me!' Shannon screeched.

Immediately Artur went to see the damage. The skin wasn't punctured, and while there was a red mark, it didn't look too bad.

'Miss O'Cleary, the dog's claws are not meant to be filed the way you want them – it's not right, it's not natural...' the groomer protested, cradling the shivering dog in her arms. 'She bit because you took the file from me and went too hard. You hit a nerve.'

'Just because you have no clue how to do your job!' Shannon hissed, examining her hand again and slapping Artur, who had brought some antiseptic spray, away.

'I do actually,' the groomer said, this time more forcefully. 'But this is ridiculous, polishing the dog's claws, insisting on using straightening irons on her fur, and now filing her nails down. You hurt her and the dog reacted – of course she did.'

Shannon O'Cleary turned then and gazed at Princess Bellachic, whose sparkly bow had come off in the melee but who glistened nonetheless as Shannon insisted the animal be bathed daily in glitter shampoo. 'No. My baby has gone wild. They all do in the end.' She sighed, resigned. 'I'll get another when I get home. For now, I'll have her put to sleep.'

'What?' Joe ran out from behind his grandfather. 'You can't do that! You can't kill the poor dog because she bit you! It was your own fault, and that's not right!' Artie stood stoically behind his twin, and Ryan cowered at the edge.

'Boys, please go back…' Artur began.

The filming was going well. It was a struggle managing all the personalities, but it was working, and the last thing they needed was something like this.

'But, *Didus*,' Artie began in rapid Ukrainian, 'she's nuts. Making the poor dog wear all that stupid stuff. It's not the dog's fault, and look how sad she is! No wonder, being owned by that horrible woman.'

The soprano puffed up in indignation. The woman didn't understand the words Artie had said, but his meaning was clear.

'Please, boys,' Artur said in English, 'please go and find your papa, all right? Now?'

'But, *Didus*…' Joe began.

'Now, Joe.' Artur's tone brooked no argument. 'Do it, please.'

With a mutinous glare at Shannon, the boys reluctantly left.

'Now, Ms O'Cleary, if you are sure you want no more the dog, I'm sure we can find other house. She's a lovely little –' Artur began.

'No.' She was firm. 'A dog that bites must be destroyed, it's as simple as that. You'd demand the same if it bit one of your grandchildren.'

Artur exchanged a glance with the groomer, who was close to tears. How could this woman, who seemed to dote on the dog to the point of obsession, turn against the poor animal so quickly?

'Can you at least do that?' Shannon turned to the groomer with disdain.

'Put the dog down?' the woman spluttered. 'Of course I can't, and even if I could, I wouldn't dream of it!'

'Fine.' Shannon sighed, as if this were further evidence of the woman's incompetence. 'Call a vet. I will want her cremated and the ashes delivered to me. I will bury her in my garden as I have the others.'

'We… I really don't think it's necessary to put the dog down… She –' the groomer began, cradling the animal protectively.

Shannon walked across the room and calmly took Princess Bellachic from the groomer by the scruff of the neck and dropped her into the pink cage, shooting the diamanté bolt. The animal curled up in her fluffy pink bed and looked miserable.

'Call the vet immediately,' she demanded of Artur as she swept past them without a backwards glance, leaving a shivering Bellachic in the cage.

Artur and the groomer stood, unsure what to do.

'This poor animal! She's such a cow.' The groomer was furious. 'What's wrong with her? She grabbed the file from me because I refused to sharpen the dog's claws any more. It was right down to the nerve. Of course she snapped, the poor thing.'

'I'd better get back to work. Please, do not worry,' Artur soothed. 'Maybe she can calm down and change her mind. The dog need some quiet now anyway – she shakes, see?' Artur reached into the cage and gave the pup a rub. He then closed the cage door and they left.

Joe, Artie and Ryan crept out from behind the stacked chairs.

'We can't let her kill that poor dog,' Joe whispered.

'What are we going to do?' Ryan's eyes were bright with excitement.

'Dognapping.' Artie grinned.

They released the bolt and gently extracted the little dog, stuffing her up Artie's jumper. She seemed none the worse for her ordeal, and so they crept out of the room via the window that led to the gardens.

'Stand in front of Artie,' Joe whispered as Ryan's mother and father appeared around the corner.

Artie stood behind Joe and Ryan as the couple approached.

'I'm just going to finish the new script now, Mom,' Ryan said as a pre-emptive strike. 'I read the first half this morning.'

Joel looked at his son, and then at his wife, who ruffled her son's hair with a smile.

'It's OK, sweetheart. Go have some fun with your friends. What are you guys up to anyway?' She smiled.

Artie tried to look relaxed as Princess Bellachic squirmed under his hoodie.

Ryan looked confusedly at his mother. 'What's going on?' he asked warily. He'd played with the twins every day but was getting good at sneaking off when his mother thought he was working.

Julie cast a glance at her husband, who gave her a nod. 'We realised – well, *I* realised, I guess – that you weren't happy, and seeing you playing with Joe and Artie the other day, and doing normal kid stuff, well, it's made me realise that you don't get much opportunity for that.'

'So...' Ryan spoke slowly, struggling to take this in, 'it's OK for me to play with them?'

'Yes, it's OK.' Julie smiled and ruffled his hair. She turned to the twins. 'Though please no scars to the face, all right?'

'Definitely not, nothing on his face, got it.' Joe grinned. 'Broken arms and legs are OK though, right?'

Ryan looked at his mother nervously, but she just put her hands over her ears. 'I didn't hear that.'

For the first time in his life, Ryan threw his arms around his mother's waist and gave her a hug. 'Thanks, Mom.'

The twins led Ryan around the back of the castle to the mainte-nance yard and to a new building that was faced in stone and land-scaped to look like it was an outbuilding. Inside, it housed a high-tech security system as well as was the nerve centre for the plumbing, heat-ing, internet and electric systems.

Joe let them in, and Artie extracted Princess Bellachic from under his hoodie. She blinked her bulging eyes.

'OK, I have an idea,' Joe said, his eyes gleaming.

Moments later, Ryan was using white spirits from the paint store to remove the nail polish from the dog's claws, and Artie filled a bucket with warm water. He found some sample bottles of human shampoo in a cupboard, and they washed the glitter out of Princess Bellachic's fur. The dog, used to being poked and prodded, didn't mind a bit.

'OK, we have to disguise her, and we'll take her home and hide her for a while. Then we can say we found a stray and our mam will let us keep her.' Joe was delighted with his idea.

Ryan gazed at the twins with a combination of excitement and horror. 'We're going to steal her?'

'Well, that horrible woman wants her put down, so we're not stealing her – we're saving her life.' Joe was adamant.

'OK, what about this?' Artie had found a small manicure set, complimentary for guests' use, and set about chopping clumps of the dog's wet fur.

'We need to change her stupid name too,' Joe muttered, soothing her as Artie chopped. 'What do you think, Ryan?'

'Are you sure this is a good idea, Joe?' Ryan was still unsure. 'If we get caught, we'll be in so much trouble. Like, my mom would go crazy.'

'She won't know,' Artie replied confidently. 'Besides, Joe's right, we're not doing anything wrong.'

'But what about when Miss Shannon comes back to find her gone?' Ryan had never done a naughty thing in his entire life.

'What about it?' Joe shrugged as Artie continued to butcher the fur of the normally immaculately groomed Princess Bellachic. 'Nothing to do with us. We were sent out.'

'OK, what you think?' Artie asked, gesturing to the comically shorn dog. All that was left of her straightened fur were a few clumps.

'Still too clean,' Joe decided. 'C'mon.'

He led the other two to the side of the castle while cradling the little dog, who was none the worse for wear from her grooming session. The waterfall was around a quarter of a mile away, and they headed there. There was a bracken- and moss-filled stream leading to the pool at the bottom of the waterfall, and it was muddy after all the rain.

They gently placed the dog at the water's edge, their feet sinking into the mud. Princess Bellachic sniffed around for a moment, unused to being free. The dog had spent her life in a cage or on a lead, and she looked up at the boys.

'Go on, doggie, go and have a roll in the mud,' Joe urged.

She sniffed about a bit more and gingerly approached the stream bank. It was only a few inches deep and hardly flowing, so there was no risk she would be swept away. The sunlight dappled off the green foliage all around and glinted on the surface of the stream. The noise of the waterfall behind them was deafening.

'We could get in, and she might follow?' Artie suggested. It was an unusually warm Saturday, and they often swam at the bottom of the waterfall with their dad in the summer. He'd ensured they could swim from the time they were babies.

'Into the water?' Ryan was appalled. 'Us? But it's freezing, and I don't have a bathing suit.' He swallowed.

'Go in your boxers.' Joe shrugged with a smile. 'I'd say it's not that cold once you get used to it. Loads of people swim in the sea every day of the year, how bad can it be?' He pulled off his tracksuit bottoms and jersey. Within seconds, he and Artie had dived head first into the pool, their blond heads popping up moments later, gasping at the cold. Ryan and Princess Bellachic stood watching.

'Come on, Ryan, the water's lovely,' Artie called, his teeth chattering. He dove underwater again.

Ryan stood for a moment and then, with determination, removed his jacket, shirt and trousers, shoes and socks. He shivered for a moment – the Irish boys' idea of warm and his were not the same thing – but then jumped in.

'Wayhey!' Joe and Artie grinned as Ryan came up, blue around his lips from the icy water.

To their delight, they watched as Princess Bellachic ran from the edge of the stream over to where it was much deeper, barked for a moment and jumped. Expertly, she doggy-paddled to where the boys cavorted in the water.

'OK.' Artie was treading water. 'Princess Bellachic is a stupid name, and anyway, we don't want her recognised, so what should we call her?'

'You pick, Ryan,' Joe said magnanimously. 'We got to name our dog Lionel Messi.'

'Is he?' Ryan asked.

'Is he what?' Joe and Artie were confused.

'Messy? Does he make a big mess?' Ryan asked innocently.

'No.' The boys laughed. 'He's named after Lionel Messi, the footballer?'

'Oh, I never heard of him,' Ryan mumbled.

Joe explained through chattering teeth. 'Well, he's Argentinian but he plays for Barca, so maybe he's not that famous in America.'

'Is Barca an Argentina football team?' Ryan asked.

'No,' Artie explained gently, hiding his incredulity that a boy of his age wouldn't know who Lionel Messi was. 'Barca is Barcelona, a Spanish team?'

Ryan shrugged sadly. 'I don't know about sports.'

'Don't you follow any sport?' Joe asked, astonished.

'I don't,' Ryan said as he treaded water, trying to get used to the cold. 'I have a tutor, then I read scripts, learn lines and do interviews, and that's it.'

'But you made a film with SilliB! That must have been amazing,' Artie said as the dog paddled around them, then went to the bank and shook herself. With her new haircut, she looked even more hilarious now, her oddly cut fur standing on end.

'Come on let's get out.' Joe swam to the bank and dragged himself out, followed by the other two boys. They pulled their clothes on over their wet skin and jumped and slapped their arms around their bodies to warm up.

'It was, but I wasn't allowed to hang out on set. SilliB is nice, she's funny, but her people kept her away in her trailer and I was in mine, so we didn't see each other that much.'

'Well, we loved it. Artie knows all the words of "Living it Highway". He's really good at the rap bit too, but I'm not good at remembering long things like that. Do it for him, Art.' Joe turned to Ryan and nodded at his twin. 'He's really good.'

'I will not.' Artie was embarrassed.

'Can you do it?' Ryan asked. 'I'd love to be able to rap.'

'No,' Artie protested. 'I'm only messing at doing it.'

'Please?'

'You're brilliant, you know you are,' Joe said.

'All right, but no laughing at me, right?' Artie warned.

The dog was sniffing about on the edge of the pool as the boys warmed up on the bank, turning their faces to the weak sunshine.

Artie began, his rhythm perfect as he rapped. 'Living in the fast lane, the main lane, the highway, make me feel like it's my way, the way to be flyway. When all I do is workin', flat out making money, and all the other kids is dreaming of that honey. What they don't know is crazy, lazy, two days drivin'. New city, new people, and they don't care who's cryin'. I wanna be a kid, yo, hang out with my crew yo, drivin' through McDonald's, goin' to the zoo yo. But like the critters in there, I'm in a cage too.'

'That was amazing,' Ryan gasped. 'You sound just like SilliB, except she's a girl. But you sounded so cool, Artie! You should really think about being a rapper.'

Artie laughed, colouring at the praise.

'Told you he was good.' Joe basked in his twin's reflected glory. 'Hey, look!'

Princess Bellachic, still on the bank, was unrecognisable. She was rolling in a puddle of muddy water she'd found, clearly loving her new-found freedom. The boys laughed as they ran to her.

'Nobody will recognise her now!' Artie announced as he watched the dog pulling at a bit of old rope nailed to a piece of timber that she'd found.

She turned to look at them. Her ears stood out sideways from her head, and her fur clung to her tiny body.

'She looks like Dobby, the house elf in Harry Potter.' Joe chuckled.

The twins looked at Ryan.

'I have heard of Harry Potter.' He grinned. 'I'm an actor, not a Martian.'

'I think we just found her new name. How do you feel about Dobby?'

He picked up the wet, dirty dog, a huge grin on his face. 'Welcome to your new life, Dobby.'

CHAPTER 23

*E*ddie placed a cup of strong tea and two chocolate biscuits from his secret stash in front of Fintan. He'd seen the man come out of Leonard's Pub just before closing time and knew from Conor that there were media elements recently arrived in the town that were just waiting for their chance to catch the celebrity a bit worse for wear. Eugene Rafferty had called during the week, knowing Eddie's history with helping addicts, and asked him to intervene. Fintan had showed up at his and Geraldine's place a few times absolutely plastered drunk, and he had frightened the children. Fintan's brothers were concerned, but they were all out of ideas. Nothing got through to Fintan; he was determined to self-destruct.

'Thanks, Father.'

'Eddie is fine.' The priest sat opposite him.

Fintan nodded.

'I arrived to the parish after you'd left for America, I think, that's how I never knew you. But I know your brother Eugene and Geraldine, and your other brother Derry too. He and Jo moved out to Cratloe a while back, didn't they? How are they getting on out there?'

'Fine,' Fintan replied, sipping the tea. 'Thanks for rescuing me out there.' He gave a half smile. 'The press don't give me a moment's peace.'

Eddie nodded. The man looked shattered. 'The spare room is made up. Why don't you drink your tea and have a rest. Nobody'll disturb you. I'll let Conor know that you're here.'

'Ah, thanks, Father – I mean Eddie. That's very kind of you, but I'll go back to the hotel.'

Eddie knew from Conor that the night porter spent most of every evening serving Fintan alcohol and that was what was pulling him back. 'I think a night's sleep would do you good. The press know you're staying up there, but they have no idea you're in here now. So it's up to you, but you could get a good night's sleep. And maybe in the morning, we could have a talk – if you wanted to, that is – about everything?' Eddie noted the look of scepticism on Fintan's face, but he was used to it and went on. 'Talking to a priest, who has never had a drink problem, never had a wife or children and never paid a mortgage in his life is often strangely restful for people, and whatever you say is strictly between us.' Eddie smiled and got a weak one in return.

'You think I've a drink problem?' Fintan asked enigmatically. Eddie had no idea if the man was spoiling for a fight or asking a genuine question.

'Well, this is a small place, as you know, and people talk. So I'd say you're hitting the bottle hard to try to find a way to deal with the last year, and few would blame you. But 'tisn't doing you any good, you know?'

Fintan nodded sadly. After a long silence, he said, 'I'm tired.'

'I bet you are. Come on down here and I'll show you your quarters.'

He led Fintan down a passageway and opened the door to a simple bedroom, with a single bed, a wardrobe and a locker. There was a picture of Saint Honoratus of Amiens on the wall, a gift from Declan and Lucia that was given half in jest, as he was the patron saint of bakers.

'The bathroom is the second door on the left. There's a towel on the bed and an old t-shirt to sleep in. I'll be upstairs. Martina is the housekeeper – she sleeps across the hall – in case you bump into her in the morning. I'll leave her a note to say you're here, so don't worry.'

'Thanks, Eddie,' Fintan said, swaying slightly. He looked wretched.

'You're welcome.' Eddie smiled. 'Do you play golf?'

'Er…not for a while. I used to play as a young fella around here, why?' Fintan asked, confused.

'Grand, we'll tee off tomorrow so, the two of us. Is that all right?' Eddie asked, as if picking a Hollywood celebrity off the street, putting him up for the night and then arranging to play golf with him was the most natural thing in the world.

'I suppose so,' Fintan agreed uncertainly.

'Great, see you in the morning. God bless.' Eddie closed the door and made his way up to bed.

The following morning dawned clear but chilly. Eddie heard stirring downstairs, and he turned over, relieved he'd hidden the chocolate biscuit evidence before Martina arrived in the kitchen. He didn't need a housekeeper, but she had also taken on a lot of parish administration work and he was glad to have her. Despite his frustration at the lack of anything good to eat in the house, he had to admit she was a nice woman.

Martina Dromey was foisted on him by the bishop; she was somehow connected to His Excellency's sister. She had fled an abusive marriage and was desperate. The whole story came out one night over a cup of tea. She told Eddie a horrific tale of a classic street angel, house devil. Her husband was a pillar of the community, and of the church too, but he made poor Martina's life a living hell. He actually tried to kill her and thankfully was thwarted by the intervention of a neighbour who heard screaming, and her now ex-husband was serving six years for attempted murder in Portlaoise Prison. She was a nice woman, in her late thirties, good-looking too, he supposed, with her curly dark hair and green eyes, but he was no judge of those things. She had no children, something that was a source of great sadness to her, he knew. They were fond of each other and rubbed along all right, despite her efforts to starve him to death.

He showered and dressed, and without even a cup of tea, went up to say nine o'clock Mass.

The weekday congregation was small as usual. With every passing year, the numbers dwindled. He couldn't blame anyone, he supposed. People were just moving away naturally from the Church anyway, and the scandals and how they were handled didn't help. He often thought he might be part of the problem. He was so vehemently opposed to how the Church he loved had behaved in the past that he worried maybe he was somehow complicit or forgiving of it, but it was more complicated than that. For so many of his congregation, the church provided comfort, both socially and spiritually, and if he were to stop preaching, it would hurt them so deeply, these people who had done no wrong. So he carried on. He was almost seventy-five years old and was tired, but there wasn't anyone else to do it.

Every day he had the chats after Mass with his flock, asked after their health and their families, listened to their worries and woes, shared their triumphs. He admired pictures of new babies on phone screens and commiserated with the bereaved. He arranged weddings for young couples who'd not darkened the door of the church since they got their confirmation from the bishop at twelve years old. Other priests, he knew, were annoyed at the audacity of it, claiming those people were just using the church as a beautiful venue, and maybe they were right. But who was he to judge? Maybe they had deep personal faith and being married before God meant something to them. He was not the owner of the house of the Lord; he was merely the caretaker. He married them with good humour and grace and made sure they knew they were always welcome.

He strolled back up the street, greeting this one and that, and texted Conor.

I have one of your celebrities in the parochial house. Found him outside Leonard's last night. Eugene asked me to keep an eye. Bit shook. So gave him a bed. Have a tee time at 11 if you want to join us? Btw, your man looks like the wreck of the Hesperus, so bring something to put on him, will you?

Seconds later Conor replied.

Love to. Thanks, Ed.

Eddie pocketed his phone. Life wasn't too bad. At least he got to play golf a few times a week with his friend. He and Conor snuck off, usually mid-week, to play a round, and had a sandwich afterwards in the clubhouse.

He heard voices as he let himself back in. Fintan and Martina were in the kitchen; she was cooking sausages and rashers as he sipped coffee. Their laughter met him as he came down the hallway.

'Ah, Fintan, you're up,' he said as he entered. 'That smells delicious, Martina.' He picked up a piece of bacon, intending to put it onto a plate.

'No, not for you.' Martina slapped his hand away. 'Yours is already done.'

She took a tray from the countertop. It contained a boiled egg and one slice of thin soda bread with such a tiny scrape of margarine, it was barely there. She placed it at one end of the table. At the other, Fintan was tucking into a full fry-up: sausages, rashers, black and white pudding, scrambled eggs, mushrooms and several slices of buttered toast. Fintan had the good grace to look embarrassed.

'It is his own fault,' Martina explained to Fintan, giving Eddie an admonishing look. 'Doctor Curtin said he needed to control his diabetes, but he's scurrying around the town, eating scones and apple tarts behind my back. Someone has to manage him.'

Fintan held her gaze for an extra second, and Martina blushed. Eddie noticed a frisson of something between them and hoped he was imagining it. Martina was fragile, despite all her laying down the law, and after everything she'd been through, a drunk was the last thing she needed.

'You're a hard woman, Martina Dromey, do you know that?' Eddie grumbled, eating his unappetising breakfast.

'I do.' She winked at Fintan. 'And while we're on the subject, I have Chris Kingston up at the golf course warned that vegetable soup, one slice of soda bread with no butter and salads are all you are allowed to order. I tried to get Conor on board, but he refused.'

'At least I have one friend left to me, you infernal woman,' Eddie muttered as Martina poured Fintan another cup of tea.

'We'll go around quarter to eleven, so will we?' Eddie said to Fintan as he finished his meagre meal. "Tis only out the road. Conor is joining us.'

Fintan looked down at his scruffy jeans and stained t-shirt. 'I'm not really dressed. Maybe I'll let you off –' he began, but Eddie cut across him.

Eddie knew Fintan was headed straight back to the high stool if left to his own devices, and Eddie wasn't having that. 'Conor is bringing you something to wear.' He smiled. 'Now, see you in a bit.' He left to change for golf and make a few telephone calls.

CHAPTER 24

*C*onor tried not to move too much as he slid Lily off his chest and onto the bed beside his sleeping wife. She was the most adorable baby, and he could spend hours just gazing at her, but she was a terrible sleeper. The twins were conked out at the end of each busy day, but Lily was like a gremlin, coming to life at midnight. She wasn't upset or even crying, but she howled with determined fury if she was put in her cot.

Ana had tried everything, but since neither of them could let her cry – and she knew it too, the little minx – she yelled blue murder whenever they tried to get her to sleep. He and Ana were both suffering the effects of sleep deprivation.

He was cranky, he knew it, and Kayla was absolutely wrecking his head. She wanted him to pretend to be amazed that Fintan Rafferty's ancestors were IRA men, and wanted him to call them bandits and rebels, which he absolutely refused to do. He tried to explain that most Irish people had IRA ancestors, and that whilst it was something to be proud of, it would be totally ridiculous to look stunned. And as for calling them bandits, well, she could forget that. He'd never be able to raise his head again if he referred to the men that freed his country from 800 years of oppression as bandits.

Fintan's grandfather and his brothers had all served with the West Clare Brigade and had played their part in driving the British out. His granduncle had been shot dead, and they'd had their house burned. Fintan's grandfather was imprisoned in 1920 and became famous in jail for writing satirical poetry, some of which Douglas had managed to unearth. It was an interesting story and fulfilled Fintan's obligation to the programme.

Fintan already knew everything – of course he did, it was the family story – but Kayla had needled him over and over, calling 'cut' far more often than she'd done in other interviews, and it took all Conor could do to keep his temper. Apparently neither he nor Fintan was amazed enough. She came up behind him at one stage and started to massage his shoulders, telling him he was coming across as tense on film. He'd shaken her off and walked out, but returned once he'd cooled down a few minutes later. Havie never said a word, which also frustrated him, but he just reminded himself it was almost over.

Poor old Fintan managed to remain sober at least until his story was shot, but he went straight to the pub once they'd finished. He was to be found in any one of the bars in Ennis each night. He'd finally arrived back in the small hours and was carried out of a taxi by the porter. He was a mess.

Lily stirred as he tried to get out of bed without waking her, her blue eyes fluttering open after only three hours of sleep. It was six a.m., and he'd walked the floor with her in his arms from midnight till just before three. Ana did the pre-midnight shift.

He groaned, lifting his daughter up before she woke her mother, and carried her downstairs. To his surprise, he met Joe coming in the back door, looking shifty.

'What has you out there this early in the morning?' he asked, instantly suspicious. His sons were always up to something.

'Er...nothing.' Joe turned his attention to his little sister. 'Hello, Lilyboo,' he said, taking her from his father. 'I'll hold her while you make your coffee.' He cuddled her, and she rewarded him with a gummy grin and a delighted scream as he tickled her tummy. 'And

Mammy hid the proper coffee in the flour tin 'cause she knew you'd never look there.' He winked.

'Thanks, Joe, you're a lifesaver, but I better not. I promised her I'd cut down.' Whatever about managing on three hours of sleep a night without caffeine in his system. Doing so without was a nonstarter, but his wife was adamant.

'Are you working today?' Joe asked as he placed Lily on the floor on her play mat and rolled her favourite duck over her tummy.

'Yes, filming the last one of the celebrities today, Shannon O'Cleary, and I'm not looking forward to it.' He sat down to drink his decaf coffee.

Joe left Lily where they could see her and made his father some toast and marmalade. He placed it in front of Conor. 'You have to eat.'

Conor ruffled Joe's carefully gelled hair.

'Get off! That took me twenty minutes!'

Conor grinned.

'So how's it all going?' Joe asked, filling a glass of orange juice for himself and sitting back down beside his sister.

Conor marvelled at them, the twins and Lily, and sometimes could hardly believe they were his. The twins were growing up so fast, and now they had real conversations with him, not just about dinosaurs or cartoons. Last week Artie had asked him to explain about the Paris climate agreement.

'It's going fine. The main thing is we got the money for the flood barrier, which is coming on really well. The engineer was worried about the soil composition on the sea bed for the foundation of the new wall, but it's all OK apparently. Don't ask me the details – I kind of tune out on poor John Gerrity when he's telling me the technical details – but it's all going fine anyway.'

'I know what you mean,' Joe agreed. 'He's such a great coach, like he really knows his stuff, but he's a bit boring all right.' Gerrity trained their hurling team and rated the boys highly but never gave them any special treatment. If anything, he was harder on his two young stars.

'So all we need to do is get Miss O'Cleary done and in the bag, and we're out the gap, cheque in pocket.' Conor sighed. 'It's funny, Joe. You know, this has taught me that no matter how bad things look, there's always hope.' He bit into his toast. 'The situation with the hotel was bad, like really dire, but then Katherine asked Eddie to talk to Fintan Rafferty's brother, and then it's all systems go.'

'He was holding Damien Dromey's auntie's hand in the Old Ground last week, did you know that?'

'Where did you hear that?' Conor asked. It was true that keeping a secret was impossible around here. He suspected that Fintan and Eddie's housekeeper had hit it off – she was a lovely woman and deserved a break after being married to a total monster by all accounts – but he was worried; Fintan was a complicated, troubled man.

'Damien Dromey told us at training that his auntie was friends with your man that won the Oscars.' Joe rolled the duck back and forth, to Lily's delight. 'But he was only saying it 'cause me and Artie are friends with Ryan and everyone knows him from *Virtuosilli*.'

'It's nice of you to be friends with him. His mam is happy too.' Conor ignored the childish gossip about the priest's housekeeper and Fintan. No mention was made of her when they played golf, so it was probably unfounded. Conor had won easily, Eddie was off his game, and Fintan very rusty.

'He's sound. A bit weird, like, 'cause he never went to school and he doesn't know anything about sport, like not one thing about any sport at all, but we like him.'

Joe looked up at his father, and Conor thought his heart would melt with love for him.

'Can we bring him over here to play? Would his mam allow that? She might if you asked her.'

'I thought you were happy up at the castle. Artur says you're forever following him around to look at the wiring and fixing things.'

'We are. Well, to be honest, Ryan is mad about all of that stuff, and he thinks *Didus* is some kind of magician. But we have all our toys here and Ryan's never played PlayStation or met Lionel, so we were going to show him.'

Conor stood and drained his coffee. 'I'll ask her. I suppose *Babusya* will be here minding this madam anyway.' He picked his daughter up, and she snuggled her face into his neck.

'You're lucky you're cute,' he said to her, and her face cracked into a huge grin. 'Could you watch her while I get ready for work, Joe?'

'Course.' Joe took her from him. 'We'll go watch telly, won't we, Lilyboo?' He blew a raspberry on her cheek. 'She loves *Friday Night SmackDown*, don't you, Lilyboo?'

'If your mammy catches you watching that nonsense, she'll murder you and make me get rid of the cable, so don't say you weren't warned.' Conor knew the stupid play-fighting that went on during wrestling shows was all acting, but Ana hated it and forbade the boys to watch it. He normally backed her in everything, and he upheld her law on that too, but he didn't necessarily agree with it. Boys liked that sort of thing; he'd loved to watch boxing as a kid himself. It didn't make him aggressive. But Ana hated it and that was that.

'I know, I know,' Joe said wearily, as if it were just one of the many millions of dictates of his mother. 'No wrestling, no climbing on the roof, no dive-bombing into the waterfall, no swords, no knives. That woman, your wife, is killing every bit of fun we have, you know that, don't you?'

Conor chuckled. 'I do. It's awful. I'd write to the government if I was you. She's totally unreasonable.' He looked around. 'Where's Lionel?'

'I put him out. It's fine, the gate's locked,' Joe reassured him.

* * *

CONOR STOOD IN THE SHOWER, allowing the steaming water to wake him up properly. Today's interview was going to be the hardest to do. Havie was unequivocal; Shannon could be given no clue and nothing was to be leaked. It was the kind of sensationalism he loved, though it didn't sit well with Conor at all. If it had been anyone else, any of the others, he would have argued more forcefully in their favour, but he disliked Ms O'Cleary intensely.

The hullabaloo she'd created when she discovered her dog missing two weeks ago was nobody's business, despite the fact that she intended to have the poor animal put down anyway. Conor suspected one of the staff overheard her and had taken the dog, or possibly it was the groomer who fled the scene after the dog bit her owner, but either way the dog was gone. The Celtic Colleen went mental, threatening all sorts, and Conor had had to soothe her, though that was the last thing he felt like doing.

She had an annoying querulous voice and swanned around the hotel, making demands of everyone. Kayla ensured it was all filmed, surreptitiously of course, and Conor had no doubt that Shannon O'Cleary would come across very badly in the editing.

As he allowed the water to drum on the top of his head, he thought about the whole process. Some of it was how the person presented themselves, that was true, but so much of it was how Havie and Kayla wanted them to appear to the audience.

Bob McCullough was a lovely man, and fame did nothing to dim the light of a warm and generous personality. He was a talented musician and singer and considered a national treasure in the US with good reason. His story was interesting and created a link between the music of Ireland and the country and bluegrass tradition, which Conor was sure people would find interesting. Bob often just picked up his guitar at night and played for everyone, totally unstaged, completely unplanned, and those sessions were magical.

Conor knew the episode featuring Bob would show him mastering, albeit hilariously, the Irish language and baking soda bread. He'd made a delicious Irish coffee and even managed to puc the sliotar when they were challenged to play hurling, the Irish national sport. Using Joe and Artie as coaches was Kayla's idea, and although Conor wasn't keen initially, not wanting his kids on TV, they overheard him discussing it with Ana and wore him down. They'd loved doing it, and he'd seen the footage – they were fabulous, so funny and cute. Explaining that the word puc meant not just to hit the ball or slitter, but to really wallop it as hard as you could. And the way they finished each other's sentences would undoubtedly have audiences in love with them.

Taylor Davis was a real feel-good story too. She was a sweet girl. She'd told him the story of her grandparents, and he could see how proud she was of them. Havie had plans for that episode apparently, but he'd not seen them.

Taylor and Douglas seemed to spend a lot of time together. He was a bit older than her but they were both academics, and Conor could see how Taylor would struggle to blend in with other girls her age. They were often seen eating together in the evenings, and it was lovely for both of them that they'd found a friend in this whole crazy scene.

Shelby took the news of her less-than-fancy relatives surprisingly well. She was a seasoned manipulator of audiences and knew that kicking up a fuss or being disappointed would damage her, so she was choosing to embrace it. The family she'd thought she had bore no resemblance to the reality, but hers was a story of intrigue and skulduggery and nobody could resist that. Kayla dropped a hint that she and Shelby were talking about making the story into a miniseries, so it was an ill wind that didn't blow some good.

Conor sighed. Kayla. He could not wait to see the back of her. She was still being incredibly rude to Ana and completely over the top with him. No admonishment from him seemed to have the slightest effect, and Havie was oblivious to her constant flirting or efforts to provoke him into reacting to her. She wafted around the hotel, stinking of that awful perfume, but every time he wanted to really have it out with her, he looked outside where large yellow machinery was working hard to protect his hotel from the wild Atlantic. Fintan, Katherine, Carlos and even Ana had warned him about not blowing it all at the last minute. If Kayla wanted something, they could all see that she got it. Havie was putty in her hands, though with time the dynamics of that relationship had not become any clearer. It was bizarre but none of his business.

Conor's heart sank each morning when she walked on set. He wondered how many women around the world had that experience daily. Probably far more than men, but for the first time, he knew what it was like to be sexually harassed. Women had often taken a

187

shine to him over the years, and before he met Ana, of course there were a few times when it was reciprocated – he wasn't a monk – but from the day he and Ana got together, he'd never looked at another woman, nor would he. He had all he needed at home. But Kayla had no respect for him. She looked at him as a cat saw a mouse, something to be used and abused, and he hated it.

She never lost an opportunity to touch him. She also discussed him with Havie as if he weren't in the room. It made his blood boil, but he knew they just had to get through this and hopefully he'd never have to lay eyes on that bizarre obnoxious woman again.

CHAPTER 25

'*P*roblem,' Katherine announced as Conor entered the hotel.
'Good morning, Katherine. How are you today?' He smiled but she didn't respond.

'Fintan Rafferty's been arrested, so Havie said for you to continue and shoot Shannon O'Cleary's bit today with Kayla while he goes to try to sort it out. Miss O'Cleary is still like a demon over that stupid dog, asking if we've managed to contact the groomer who she's convinced has stolen the dog that had a death sentence anyway. And this came.' She handed him a letter with the letterhead of a local wildlife action group.

He scanned it. The group seemed concerned about a local snail whose habitat was being disturbed by the building on the grounds, and they were going to seek a court order to stop the work.

Conor's heart sank. This would go nowhere, he knew, but they could delay things. He'd need to make contact with them and try to figure out what the problem was and see if there wasn't some way around it. But for now he needed to focus on finishing the last programme and getting Acorn Productions out of his hotel. Dealing with Kayla when Havie was there was bad enough, but without him to rein her in, it would be impossible. And then having to deal with that diva Shannon at the same time was a horrible prospect.

'All right.' He sighed. 'Ana won't be in until later as she's exhausted. Lily hasn't slept for more than two hours in…well…' – he paused – 'ever, it seems like.'

'You look done in as well. Make-up won't be happy,' Olga said as she passed.

'OK, before the mayhem starts, can we have a quick meeting – you, Carlos, Katherine, Artur and me in my office? Five minutes?' He passed through the reception area and opened his door. 'And would someone, without a lecture or a discussion about it, get me a proper coffee, *please?*'

Olga and Katherine exchanged a look. 'Coming up, I'll get it,' Olga responded.

'And I'll call the others.' Katherine picked up her mobile to call them.

Conor shut the door and sat at his desk. His mobile pinged. It was a message from Laoise.

Can't wait for the wrap party. We arrive Shannon on Thurs at 4:40. Can you or someone pick us up? Can't wait to see you all and meet Lily O'Shea. Hugs, L xx

He smiled. Laoise was a breath of fresh air, and she and Dylan would be as welcome as the flowers of May in Castle Dysert. Laoise had such raw and rare talent, but it was almost incidental. She was still as daft as when she was a kid, weaving her magic on Dylan, who was then, and was now, helpless in the face of her charms. She'd had dreadlocks the last time Conor saw her, interwoven with coloured silk ribbons. She had so many piercings and tattoos, it was impossible to count. Conor and his family loved her dearly. She was kind and brave and loyal to a fault. He would never forget how supportive she was when that Russian gardener fell for Ana and Conor nearly went out of his mind with jealousy and grief – it had been Laoise who spoke sense to him.

Laoise's family were coming too. Her father, Diarmuid, was himself a wonderful piper, and it was he who was Dylan's mentor.

Apparently Corlene and Colm would be there as well, so it would be lovely to see them all. Now if they could just get through the next week.

He sent her a quick thumbs-up text and then scrolled for a number, pressing the dial button.

'Conor, how are you?' Sergeant Mike McNamara answered.

'Grand, Mike. Listen, do you have Fintan Rafferty there?'

'We do. He's being charged with assault, drunk and disorderly. He hit one of our lads a right clatter – he needs stitches and he's supposed to be getting married next weekend. Your man Rafferty will need more than stitches if Chloe Redmond gets her hands on him, ruining the groom before the big day.' He chuckled.

'What happened?' Conor asked. Strictly speaking, Mike shouldn't say, but he and Conor had known each other for years and trusted each other.

'Yerra, some eejit, you know, one of the Deasys out the Kilkee Road? Well, one of them made some remark about Rafferty's ex – first I heard of it was last night. Anyway, he took it bad and drew a clatter on young Deasy. No more than he deserved, but the young one behind the bar got nervous so called us. My lads went in, tried to break it up, but in the mess anyhow, the Rafferty fella hit the guard a box and split his eye. He'd have done more damage if he wasn't plastered. He's gone very hard on the drink it seems?'

Conor thought for a moment. 'He is, God love him. He's OK, Mike. I know him a bit, and he's just not coping with it all. She went off with one of his oldest friends and is now doing the rounds on the telly over there making out like he was a monster to be married to.'

'Ah, that's desperate altogether,' Mike replied. 'Look, don't worry, we'll look after him. He'll be charged and have to face the court, but yerra, we won't push too hard in that case.'

'I'd appreciate that, Mike. There'll be a fella who'll turn up there called Xavier Gonzales. He's the guy making the TV show here, and he's a buddy of Fintan's going way back, so he's going to go down to see what's happening. But maybe it would be best if he didn't?'

'It would. I can do a certain amount, as you know, Conor, but the more of a circus it turns into, the worse it will be for your man. So if you can play it down on your end, I'll see what I can do, right?'

'Perfect. Thanks, Mike.' Conor hung up and quickly dialled Havie.

'Conor, I'm here in Ennis now. I need to bail Fintan out. Can't you just –'

'Havie, it doesn't work like that here. Trust me. I'll deal with this, OK, but you need to just come back and let me handle it.'

'He's in trouble. Apparently the cop was badly hurt, Conor. I don't know...' Havie sounded worried, unusual for the normally unflappable director.

'He's fine. I spoke to the sergeant there – I know him. Just come back and I'll explain, but whatever you do, don't go in there.' Conor exhaled, rubbing his temples to ease the beginning of a headache. 'We can sort this, but it has to be done quietly.'

'OK, Conor, if you say so.' Havie sighed. 'Stupid dumbass. I told him he was going off the rails, but he wouldn't listen. I don't know what to do with him. I thought this show might give him something to focus on, but it hasn't.'

'He's heartbroken, Havie, and he's an alcoholic. He needs medical treatment. OK, see you later.'

Before the others arrived, he rang Eddie and briefly explained everything.

'Right,' Eddie said. 'I'm just off the phone with his brother actually – he asked me to see what I could do. I'll go and get him, bring him here.'

'Thanks, Eddie.' Conor ended the call as his management team arrived.

'OK, folks, we have a few fires to fight today.' He grinned and saw the relief flood their faces. So long as Conor was joking, all would be well. 'So first things first. Princess Bellachic. Carlos, any luck tracking down the groomer?'

Carlos Manner looked distastefully at him. Conor knew he felt this whole stupid dog business was such a waste of time. 'I spoke to her yesterday. She says she left the hotel that day after the argument and didn't take the dog. I told Miss O'Cleary that, but Miss O'Cleary said that of course the groomer would say that and that she was still convinced that the woman stole the dog. She's saying this has gone on long enough and insisting that we call the Garda today. She also says she's instructing her lawyer, so there will be a case taken against the hotel. It's ludicrous, I know, but it could escalate, and I'm not sure what to do next.'

'All right.' Conor sat back, making an arch with his fingers as he thought about the problem. 'I think we just let this slide for a bit.'

'But, Conor, what if she does sue us?' Katherine was outraged. 'She's like a cut cat these days – you can't lead nor drive her – and she's hell-bent on making us pay.'

'I hear you, Katherine, and if she did sue, that would be bad all right, but I think she won't. Leave that one for a little while. She's doing her segment today, so let's get that over with and then we'll see, OK?'

'Are you sure?' Carlos looked doubtful. 'And the guards?'

'Mike McNamara has bigger problems than dealing with her and a missing dog, even if she does call him.'

Conor picked up the letter from his desk. 'Now, the environmentalists.' He looked at Olga, easily the most diplomatic of his team. Carlos would be terrible at dealing with them, dismissive and cold, and Katherine was too schoolmistress-like, so Olga might just manage to appease them somehow and avoid this turning into a big drama.

'Olga, could you meet with' – he checked to see who signed the letter – 'Felicity Worthington-Smythe, and see if there's some way we can solve this business of the snail or slug or whatever it is? I think actually she's an aunt of Harry in the bar, so she's probably fine. They might just need us to do something, I don't know, but you'll be able to figure that out anyway. We can make concessions up to a point, but we need to press on with the work. If it's still a problem, get back to me. And for God's sake, don't leave John Gerrity next to or near her – he'd definitely insult her.'

'No problem, Conor. I'll talk to her today,' Olga replied.

'Why don't you invite them here, the wildlife committee, give them lunch, whatever, charm them a bit?' He smiled.

'That's generally your area, getting people to do what you want through flattery and flowery words,' Katherine suggested, with a tone that suggested he was some kind of a con man.

'Well, I would meet them, and if it would be helpful, I'll certainly pop into the lunch to say hello, but I am kind of flat to the mat this week,' Conor said to Olga, ignoring Katherine.

'If I need you, I'll call you, but hopefully I can handle it,' Olga said confidently, and Conor felt a surge of gratitude for the young woman who was rapidly becoming an invaluable asset to the hotel.

'Right. Katherine, how's everything else?' he asked. He knew she was exhausted, and having the TV crew in the hotel was taking its toll on everyone.

'Fine, but I am going to suggest a full staff meeting this week. The crew are all installed in the staff quarters, as you know, and there has been a lot of cavorting and God knows what going on there at night. It's not appropriate, and I think you should say something.'

Conor suppressed a smile. 'About what?'

'About the carry on,' Katherine retorted. 'Drinking and all kinds of hook-ups. Honestly, Conor, it's not fitting for an establishment such as ours...' Two pink spots rose on her cheeks, and Conor refused to catch Olga's eye at the idea that the stern Miss O'Brien even knew what a hook-up was.

'And is this affecting their work in the hotel?' Conor asked gently, knowing the answer.

'Well, they do their jobs, but some of them are the worse for wear. Young James MacElroy had his tie undone on Wednesday, and Katie O'Connor had to be sent to polish her shoes yesterday.'

'Hardly anarchy though?' He smiled. 'Look, Katherine, I know, and I have heard about the shenanigans, but I can't tell people what to do on their time off now, can I? They're grown adults, and besides, the whole gang will be gone before we know it, thanks be to God. So if we can all just endure it for a little bit more, we'll be rid of them and have the money in the bank.'

'Fine,' Katherine snapped, but everybody in the room knew she felt it was anything but fine.

'Right. Artur, how's everything else?'

'All good. No problems. The lawns are reseeding very well, and the horses are due back today from the riding school. Havie wants that the celebrities ride on the beach, so the stables are being painted and refreshed, and Aoife Mullane has been in all week checking the tack and all of the things, so it is all good. Also, the decking area at the base of the waterfall for private picnics is almost ready – I just need one more coat of wood preserver and is good.' He gave a rare smile.

It had been Artur's idea to build a picnic deck beside the waterfall for guests who wanted to have something special. They added the option to the new brochure, and already there were only a few days left available to book it. The idea was that the hotel would supply a picnic, with champagne, and deliver it to the gazebo. Conor knew already that there would be several diamond rings produced there.

'Well, that was an inspired idea. The photos in the brochure look incredible. We would never have thought of it, but it's the perfect proposal spot. So that's a whole other business we can go after now, weddings, engagements and all, because you saw the potential, Artur. I could have looked at that for forty years and not come up with it.' Conor wanted Artur acknowledged for his hard work. 'Just ask your daughter how romantic I am.' He chuckled.

'You do OK.' Artur chuckled as well.

'Conor's right, Artur,' Olga said. 'It's incredibly beautiful. We took a walk up there yesterday. It looks amazing, the hanging baskets with all the winter flowering plants, the beautiful gazebo – it's like something from a storybook, isn't it, Carlos?'

'It is very impressive, and sure to be a huge hit with the guests,' Carlos confirmed. 'And excellent attention to health and safety, as there's no way to access the actual waterfall from there. The last thing we need is someone full of champagne trying to get into the water.' This was positively gushing praise from the normally dour Mr Manner.

'Well, I thought it was the loveliest place, Artur, and I know how hard you worked on it.' Olga patted Artur's hand; the pair had a very affectionate connection.

Olga's family were in Iceland, so she spent a lot of time with Danika and Artur, who adored her, not least because she spoke Russian. They often invited her for lunch to their house and had become kind of surrogate parents.

Conor sat back and smiled. 'You've all been so brilliant, honestly. I know between hosting the show and trying to manage the baby that never sleeps, I'm not exactly a hundred percent hands on, and some days I'm in terrible form, so I'm really grateful to you all for all you do, and for putting up with me.' He stood. 'Right, we better get this show on the road. Thanks, everyone.'

They gathered their papers and files and everyone but Katherine left.

'Conor, I was thinking...' She didn't sound her usual confident self. He hoped she wasn't going to say she wanted to retire, or was upset that he refused to give out to the staff for partying on their time off.

'Let's walk and talk. I'm late.' He grabbed his phone from the desk.

'It will only take a second. And say if it's a bad idea – I mean, it might be, it probably is, but we think we could do it...' Katherine was flustered.

Conor paused. 'Katherine, what's up?' He put his hands on her shoulders.

'Well, Jimmy and I – and please don't think we are being presumptuous – were going to buy a cot, and if it was all right with you and Ana, we were thinking of offering to have Lily overnight, the boys too if you like. We'd love to have them, and you two could get a night's sleep. I mean, she takes a bottle now, I know, so she might take it from us, and I know we've no idea about babies, but it looks manageable enough, and we could do it, I think. We got some books from the library as well. So we read up about it. And we thought maybe you two could go out for a meal or something, and we'd have the children...'

Conor felt a surge of love for her. She really was one in a million. 'We'd love it. Yes, please, when can you take her? We're absolutely knackered.' He chuckled.

'Are you sure? Hadn't you better check with Ana?' Katherine seemed alarmed now that he'd agreed.

'Nope, she'll be fine. We don't like to ask Artur and Danika as they do so much during the day, but we'd absolutely love a night off. I warn you though, she's a right little devil and won't sleep in a cot, so save your money. You'll end up with her in the bed with you, guaranteed.'

Katherine smiled, a broad beam. 'Saturday night?'

'Fantastic. Thank you. You're a lifesaver. And you'll take the other two as well?'

'We'd love it.' Katherine grinned.

'I'll text Ana and she'll see it when she wakes up. She'll probably murder me for not waking her this morning, but her mother arrived and she was still sleeping, so I left her and turned off the alarm. The boys are at school, so it's all under control for once.' He winked at her. 'Now I better go or your one O'Cleary will have yet another reason to lose the plot.'

CHAPTER 26

*E*ddie was sitting in Mike McNamara's office, helping himself to a chocolate-covered shortcake and a cup of tea, when Fintan was brought to him.

'Eddie, look, I'm sorry. I don't know why they called you. It's not your problem. I just –'

Eddie raised his hand, pulled out a chair and poured a second cup of tea. 'Shh… 'Tis all right.' He waved away Fintan's protests. 'Eugene rang me, then Conor. Your friend, the American, wanted to come, but they thought it might be better if it was just me. Milk?'

'Er…no…I don't want any tea, I just need to…' Fintan was distraught.

Eddie had thought he looked bad before, but he was a hundred times worse now. He had congealed blood on his knuckles, and his eye was swollen so much he could barely see out of it. 'Sit down like a good man, and we'll sort everything out.'

'Sorry, but I can't. I assaulted a police officer. I need to get my lawyer in the States, or maybe one here, I don't know.' Fintan ran his hands through his greasy hair.

'Fintan.' Eddie got up and led the other man to the chair. 'Listen to me. It's going to be fine.'

'It's not fine! I assaulted a guard, for God's sake!' Fintan shouted. 'And some other guy! I don't know –'

'Keep your voice down now for fear the lads outside think you're going to hit *me* a clatter next and they're in on top of us. Listen to me now and don't interrupt. The young guard you hit is a fella called Darren Kelly, and I'm due to marry him and his girl at the weekend. I baptised both of them, gave them communion and all the rest of it, so here's what's going to happen.' Eddie kept his voice calm and quiet, and Fintan sat with his head in his hands. 'You're going to give the young couple a nice cheque to help cover the costs of the wedding and a card saying you're sorry, and they'll say no more about it. 'Tis plenty of clatters he'll get as a guard around here, I can tell you. You weren't the first, and you won't be the last. As for the other eejit, Deasy, well he's an awful gom altogether and he's fine – you did no damage there.'

'Are you serious?' Fintan looked at him incredulously. 'You can make this go away just like that?'

'Well, yes. The sergeant here knows your situation and how this could blow up out of all proportion if we let it, and that wouldn't help anyone. But you need to do something for me too.' Eddie sipped his tea.

'What's that?' Fintan asked, suddenly dubious.

'There's a priest I know, an old friend from the seminary, and he's a decent skin, so he is. He's got a place below in County Waterford for men and women such as yourself.'

'What do you mean, such as myself?' Fintan sounded wary.

'Alcoholics,' Eddie said quietly. The word hung in the air between them.

'OK, look, I'll go back to the States, go to rehab, whatever. I don't need –'

Eddie shook his head. 'No, that won't do at all. It's Waterford or face charges. I'm sorry to do this, Fintan, and believe it or not, 'tis for your own good, but if you won't go – and it's entirely your choice, nobody will force you – then I'll have to let the law do as it should. They are only willing to turn a blind eye on my word that I'll straighten you out, so those are my terms, I'm afraid.'

199

'Look, there are clinics in the States, places that –'

'I don't doubt it, but this is the one I want you to go to. No press, nobody will know you, or if they do, they won't say it. Miah Linehan has great success. He uses the twelve steps, and so many people have got their lives back because of the work him and his team are doing.' Eddie placed his hand on Fintan's shoulder. 'You've had a terrible time, you poor man. I can't imagine the pain, and no wonder you tried to block it all out – nobody blames you – but you'll destroy yourself this way. The bottom of a bottle never holds the answers.' Eddie wished he could ease the man's suffering, but this was all he could do. He just hoped it would work.

'I can't...' Fintan's shoulders shook, and Eddie realised he was crying.

'You can, Fintan. It may not feel like it today, but this is day one. It's a long road, but you can do it. And I'll be there to help. I'll visit you if you like.' He smiled.

'Thanks, but I'm no good to anyone...' Fintan's breath came in ragged rasps.

'Indeed, it's true. In this state you're no use to yourself or anyone else, but get yourself better and who knows what might happen.'

Fintan turned and locked eyes with the small priest. 'I know you say I can do it, but I can't, Eddie, I just can't. I see her face every night before I sleep. I see her, and him, and them lying to me... I loved them both. And the lies she said about me... I never hurt a hair on her head. I love her.'

Eddie gently placed his hand on Fintan's shoulder. The man's breath was sour and his stubble rough. He wouldn't look out of place begging under a bridge. 'Do you want to live again, Fintan? Be happy again?'

The pain in Fintan's eyes was there for anyone to see. He was a broken man, and Eddie's heart went out to him.

Slowly he nodded.

'Right, I'll drive you to Waterford now so. Conor has had them pack your bag at the hotel, and we'll pick it up on the way.' Eddie stood up, and like a five-year-old child, Fintan followed him out.

* * *

'No, that's wrong! Can you people not do hair either? I would have thought hairdressers in Ireland could manage naturally auburn hair, but it seems not!' Shannon O'Cleary snapped at the hairdresser who was trying to arrange her copper curls.

'She's no more a redhead than I am,' muttered the raven-haired stylist as she swept past Conor in high dudgeon as he took his place at the mirror for his daily gussying up.

They'd already filmed a piece by the beach where the Celtic Colleen's flowing tresses were swept by the wind and she looked every inch the part. She wanted to sing, but Kayla refused. For once Conor agreed with her.

Her audience was very much Irish America, and her promo videos featured audience members wiping their tears as she sang 'Danny Boy' or 'Toora Loora'. Today's garment was an emerald-green velvet floor-length dress with a gold silk scarf over her shoulders.

One of the many things that annoyed Conor about her was how she considered herself more Irish than the others. She claimed she could speak Irish fluently, though of course she couldn't. She parroted a few phrases she learned, and to a non-speaker it probably sounded impressive, but it wasn't. While Taylor and Bob knew very little about their family background, they were anxious to learn. Even Shelby had become fascinated with her nefarious ancestors and had embraced the whole tale, and the Farrells, who were altogether happier now that Ryan seemed like a normal kid for once, were trying to find out more. They'd even taken a road trip to County Longford to try to find the old family homestead. They had no luck – either they looked in the wrong place or the place was knocked – but they had a great day and Ryan showed the twins pictures of him with his parents enjoying an ice cream in the sun. But Shannon O'Cleary was so superior and acted like she knew it all; it drove Conor mad.

He was used to the prodding and poking that went on by now so succumbed to the make-up and hairstylist, Niamh, without complaint.

'How women put this muck on every day is a mystery to me. It feels horrible,' he joked as Niamh fixed his hair with spray.

'You'll have a new respect for your wife after this.' She smiled.

'Oh, my wife hardly ever wears make-up,' he said proudly. 'She doesn't need it.'

'It's more a trowel and a shovel than brushes is needed there,' Niamh murmured as she jerked her head in Shannon's direction and then leaned in close to Conor to check everything was perfect. The Celtic Colleen was under a hairdryer so oblivious to them all.

'Now, now!' he admonished quietly, giving her a surreptitious wink. 'She's the talent after all.'

Niamh giggled. Shannon O'Cleary actually referred to herself in the third person as 'the talent' regularly.

'OK, let's get on set!' Kayla ordered.

As Conor began his spiel, she called, 'Cut!' and murmured something to the wardrobe assistant, who ran over to Conor. His heart sank; Kayla was doing it again, just like with the scenes with Fintan.

'OK, we're just going to open these buttons a little…' The assistant began unbuttoning his shirt.

'What?' Conor pulled back, buttoning them back up again. 'No, it's fine as it is.'

The wardrobe woman looked uncertain.

Kayla called from behind the camera, 'We just need to see a bit more flesh, Conor, nothing to worry about. Just open the first three buttons, and can you pull the collar out a little so we can see your chest? Maybe if we can get some oil on him as well?' Her tone suggested she was asking him to shut the door.

He stood up; he'd had enough. She had insisted that wardrobe alter his trousers so they were so tight he was afraid they would split when he sat down, and he'd refused point-blank to cutting his hair in a ridiculously trendy style for someone his age. She never lost an opportunity to touch him or to make a remark about his appearance, and she was so rude to Ana. He was sick of all of it. Walking towards her, he asked, 'Could we have a word, please, in private?'

'We're in the middle of filming. We can talk later.' She shooed him away with a wave of her hand.

'You won't be filming me again until we talk,' he said firmly. 'We can do it here, in front of everyone, or we can do it in my office. Up to you.'

She sighed theatrically. 'Fine.' Then she yelled, 'Take five, everyone!'

Shannon O'Cleary was carping like a chicken at the delay, but Conor ignored her and strode to his office. His made-up face elicited a few smiles from the staff and they would normally have teased him, but the look on his face told them today was not the day.

He pulled a packet of wipes from his desk and cleaned the make-up off his face.

'Don't do that! We'll need to do it again!' Kayla protested.

'Please sit down, Kayla.' He sat, for once, behind his desk. 'Listen carefully.' He inhaled, steadying the pulsing fury that coursed through him. 'I am sick of your sexual harassment of me. And it ends now. As a man, if I treated any of my female colleagues the way you treat me, I would find myself in court, and rightly so. You constantly refer to me as sexy and draw attention to my physique, which is embarrassing for me and everyone around me. You touch me without my consent, the way you want me to dress and be made up is ridiculous, and I've had enough.' He was livid, and the frustration of dealing with her for weeks all came out. 'That business with the shirt and the oil, for goodness sake! Your behaviour is so inappropriate, it would be laughable if it weren't so annoying. On top of that, you are rude to my staff and in particular to my wife, and I have put up with it for the sake of the project, but no more.'

Kayla stood up and moved quickly around the desk to stand beside him, the smell of her perfume making him wince.

'Get away from me.' He enunciated each word. He stood up and as he did she ran her hands down his chest and knelt down which meant Kayla's face was level with his groin. Shocked, he tried to take a step back but the filing cabinet was in his way. The door opened. Ana stood there, Havie behind her, and they both took in the scene of

Conor standing behind his desk with Kayla on her knees in front of him.

'Oops.' Kayla grinned and stood up. 'Looks like we're in trouble, Conor.' She winked and patted his cheek, then she swept out past him, leaving a startled Ana in her wake. Havie, his face inscrutable, followed her out.

'Ana, I swear…' Conor began.

'You don't need to,' she reassured him, shutting the door. 'I know you didn't do anything. I went to look for you on the set and Niamh told me what she wanted with the shirt and the oil and all of that and that you were cross. I was coming to try and talk you out of losing the show.'

Conor ran his hands through his hair, exhaling raggedly. He shoved his office chair out of the way and came out from behind his desk. 'I have *never* wanted to slap a woman in my life, and I never would, but she is testing me, Ana. I swear, it's like a game for her. I tried to talk to Havie about her, but he has no control over her.'

Ana moved across the room and put her arms around his waist. 'It's OK. She'll be gone soon and you'll never have to see her again.'

He sighed into her hair, holding her close. 'It's so embarrassing, and then complaining about it as a man is so hard. I feel ridiculous. If we didn't need the money so much, I swear I'd have turfed her out on her ear long ago. Apart from anything else, if she was the last woman on earth, I wouldn't touch her with a ten-foot pole. The stink off her, and all that muck she puts on her face, and the outfits she wears – she's repulsive.'

'She's something unusual, that's for sure, but let's just keep everything going. There's only one more show to do and then we're finished.' Ana sounded drained. 'Can you do it? The horse riding is tomorrow, and you don't need to be there for that, so it's over for you once you do Shannon's interview.'

'I can.' He nodded. He had to. There was no choice. Hopefully today's admonishment would buy him enough time to get through this last one. 'Hey, in better news, guess what?' He kissed her gently.

'What?' she asked.

'Katherine and Jimmy are having all the kids on Saturday night. They have books on baby management and a cot and everything – not that our little micro-queen would deign to sleep in it – but for one full night, we can do whatever we want, for as long as we want, wherever we want.' He kissed her neck.

'Oh wow, really? That's amazing.' Ana ran her hands up his back as he nibbled her ear. 'And you know what I really want, husband?'

'I do.' He kissed her again.

'A full night's sleep,' they said together and laughed.

CHAPTER 27

'So, Shannon,' Conor began, this time with Havie behind the camera. Of the horror Kayla, there was no sign thankfully.

Kayla had explained that morning that this one was going to be interesting. She assured everyone it was going to be a huge surprise. Conor feared she meant a shock, but he was too weary of the whole thing to argue. So far Douglas had found interesting and often inspirational people for all the other celebrities, so there was no reason to think Shannon would be any different. Kayla was going to hand Conor the envelope with the details of Shannon's ancestor while the cameras were running to see the reaction for real.

In the meantime, he began as he always did, with some background on the family name generally. This time they were filming in the relaxation room off the spa, the glass backdrop of the Atlantic providing a dramatic setting. It was blowing a gale now. The sky was an angry grey, and the crashing surf looked ferocious. A table and some chairs had been added, and despite his initial reservations, he had to admit it looked impressive.

'So, Shannon, the surname O'Cleary is a Gaelic one, and in fact is probably the oldest recorded surname in Europe. There's evidence of variations of that name as far back as 916 AD, and as far as we can gather, they were a branch of the Uí Fiachrach dynasty, the kings of Connaught.'

Shannon looked like the cat that got the cream. The royal connection was always what she was after. Kayla wanted him to play it up as much as he could. Shannon's identity as an Irish woman was at the epicentre of her career, and her haunting Celtic lyrics and melodies had placed her in the cannon of all things wonderful and Irish in the eyes of America. She was up there with *Riverdance*, 'Danny Boy', corned beef and cabbage and St Patrick's Day parades. To America, Shannon O'Cleary was Ireland, and her sold-out concerts were performed all over the country in front of a gigantic screen showing impossibly dreamy but accurate scenes of Ireland. Rocky outcrops, green fields, atmospheric castles reminiscent of a romantic and dramatic past –Shannon O'Cleary was the personification of all of it. She looked Irish, she even had a slight lilt to her accent, and her speech was peppered with Irishisms.

The disdain with which she spoke to everyone in the hotel, including the other celebrities, was completely at odds with her image. She felt she was the most Irish of them all, even out-greening Fintan, who was born and raised there. She was dismissive of Taylor, and had been very cutting to the girl when she didn't know about some aspect of Irish life. She told everyone over a bonding dinner about her recent visit to Australia and about how in the past, nobody there wanted to claim convict heritage but now people were proud of it. The same was true, according to Ms O'Cleary at least, with Irish Americans. They had been for a long time ashamed of their heritage, being associated with alcoholism, crime and corruption, but since she and people like her had popularised Ireland, everyone was on the Irish bandwagon. She seemed to take all the credit for the popularity of the country in the US.

To everyone gathered, the entire premise of the show being they had Irish roots, it was such an arrogant statement. Conor had seen it often before – people thinking they had more of a claim to the history and culture of the country than someone else – and it irritated him. Apparently her Irish ancestor was far more important and significant than anyone the others could dredge from their pasts. She waxed lyrical whenever anyone would listen to her going on about Charles O'Cleary, a gentleman who went on to achieve great things in America.

Charles was a very successful businessman and was well regarded by the movers and shakers of the day, she explained to anyone who would listen. She stated that she could have followed in the family tradition of a life in business, were it not for her exceptional talent that she felt she had a moral duty to share with the world. No matter who she was talking to, Conor noticed they had an identical glaze in their eyes. She was anti everything. She was a devout Catholic and disliked other religions. She was anti-gay and very vocal on that subject, demanding of Carlos that he reprimand two women staff members – a couple – who she'd observed arrive to work together and give each other a brief kiss in the car park before starting their day. Carlos explained to her, citing the equality act again, his favourite piece of legislation, that even if he wanted to, which he definitely did not, he was in no position legally to do so. People were entitled to love whomever they wished, and their employers needed to respect that.

On that first night over dinner, Shannon also went on to explain why Ireland was better than America in so many ways because they didn't allow immigrants in.

At that point Conor had to intervene. 'I'll have to correct you there, Shannon.' He'd had everyone's attention. 'The Irish have emigrated all over the globe for centuries and for the most part were welcomed and thrived, but now, and admittedly it's a relatively recent phenomenon, we have people from all over the world coming here. We are a fast-growing economy because of the new Irish. They have been a wonderful addition to our country on so many levels, and we are delighted so many people born elsewhere have decided to call Ireland home.'

'But you don't understand, Conor. You're being naïve. Immigrants will not contribute to your economy the way the Irish would – they just won't. Whatever they earn returns to wherever they came from, and they don't want to assimilate to your culture. I think it would be a terrible thing to see the culture that is the birthright of people like us polluted by less-evolved people. I mean, jungle drums and dancing naked around a fire is all right if that's what you're into, I suppose, but take for example my music, my songs – it's all just on a higher level.'

To Conor's astonishment, Havie said nothing but gave Kayla the tiniest nod. Conor realised she was filming the entire exchange on her phone. Everything was an opportunity for sensationalism for them, nothing more.

'Well, we'll have to agree to differ,' Conor said firmly. He wasn't going to sit and listen to this racist woman and do nothing. 'This hotel would not operate at all were it not for its staff, over half of whom were not born in Ireland. Carlos Manner, the deputy manager, is from South Africa, the maintenance manager is from Ukraine, as is the receptionist, the other deputy manager is from Iceland, and if I was to start on housekeeping, the kitchens, the gardens, we'd be here all day.'

'Well, they sure are doing a mighty job, Conor. This is some hotel you've got.' Bob held his glass up in a toast. 'I've stayed in all sorts of places all around the world, and there's nowhere like here, I can tell you that.'

Everyone agreed, and Conor realised that, apart from Bob, the rest of the contestants were boxing very clever around Shannon. She was a bully, and they were either afraid of her or didn't want to take her on.

Conor had no idea what this Charles O'Cleary did and he couldn't have cared less, but he nailed a smile on his face and went on.

'So that family can be traced back to Fiachrae, what we call Fiachra today, who was the son of the high king of all Ireland and brother to the famous Niall of the Nine Hostages. Now – and we are straying from documented history here and into the realm of legend – they say that family are descended from Na Fir Bolg, the third wave of immigrants to come to Ireland and who famously did battle with the Tuatha Dé Danann, the pagan gods, for supremacy of the island.'

Shannon was beaming. 'I guess you can't look like I do and not have Celtic queens in your blood,' she tittered.

Conor smiled but was noncommittal. 'So during the Norman invasion of the twelfth century then, they were thrown off their land by their cousins the O'Shaughnessys and had to go north to Tir Chonaill, Donegal, where they became the scholars and scribes, poets and historians to the mighty O'Donnell clan that ruled there.'

'I'm sure there were one or two singers there too.' She smiled smugly.

'Very possibly, but it's hard to know without written records.'

'So my father died when I was little, but his name was Charles O'Cleary and he told me that his great-grandfather – for whom he was named – came into the US on a ship from Ireland. I have his birth certificate here.' She pulled an envelope from her voluminous bag.

She showed Conor the certificate, and he examined it. He knew of its existence already since she'd taken great pains to show it to Douglas previously.

'Yes, this is certainly the birth certificate for a man born here in Ireland, and he sailed to the United States in 1847.'

Shannon's face was a mask of polite interest as Conor spoke.

'So we found details of him here also. He was educated at Trinity College, and that would suggest the family were Protestant as opposed to Catholic, because though Trinity admitted Catholics from 1793, it was very much frowned upon and was seen very much as the university of the Protestant Ascendancy.'

'Oh no. My family has always been Catholic. He must have been the exception. He was probably gifted, so they would have been pleased to have him.' Shannon dismissed Conor with a wave of her bejewelled hand.

Conor didn't respond to that but went on. 'So we know that he was a man of about forty-seven years of age when he emigrated. He was a land owner, and we see here some mention of him in the land registry as owning the estate known as Derrycourt. But what is interesting is we couldn't find a listing for him on any ship's manifest. He was clearly wealthy, so would have travelled first class, but we searched all of the ships in and around the dates in question and found no trace of him.'

Shannon again made no gesture other than to look complacently superior. 'Perhaps he travelled by private ship? He would have known people.'

'It's possible, I suppose, but we unearthed another interesting piece of information.' Conor slid a document across the table.

Shannon scanned a list of names on a ship's manifest and read the one highlighted. 'James Kennelly, aged 24, of Derrycourt, County Galway.' She furrowed her brow. 'Who is he?'

There was a flurry of movement, and Conor saw Kayla arrive, brandishing an envelope. He took it and extracted a file. The first page said 'Read this aloud'. The cameras were still rolling, and Conor did as instructed. 'So this entry for a man called James Kennelly is strange because we also have a death certificate for James Kennelly, same age, same address, citing date of death three days before the ship's manifest.'

'So some man from my ancestor's estate died? But is listed on a ship's manifest?' Shannon raised a haughty eyebrow. 'So what?'

Havie, from behind the camera, instructed him to turn the page, and there was an envelope, clearly marked with 'Get Shannon to read this article aloud' printed on it.

Conor felt uneasy. What was going on? He glanced at Havie, who just nodded. Kayla was leaning on Havie's shoulder, clearly loving every second.

'So if you could just read this aloud.' Conor extracted a piece of paper that looked like one of those old posters that used to be put up denouncing people for excessive greed and cruelty during the famine. The famous Captain Boycott, from which the word 'boycott' in English was derived, was a victim of such a campaign. Whatever this contained, it probably wasn't good news for Shannon. Without reading it, he handed it to the Celtic Colleen.

She took it from him and began reading as the cameras closed in. 'Rack-rent landlord Charles O'Cleary has appeared to have fled the country after the altercation on his estate, Derrycourt, in which a young man, James Kennelly, was executed by forces in O'Cleary's employ for resisting them as they attempted to take a battering ram to his home as punishment for failure to pay rent.'

She paused, the enormity of the words dawning on her, but from behind the camera, Havie, using hand gestures, urged her on. Unsure of what to do, and conscious that the camera were still rolling, she had no choice but continue reading. . 'O'Cleary has evicted seventy families from his estate for failure to pay in the past year, forcing them into workhouses, while he still profits from his ill-gotten estate. This is the land of Ireland, and his victims are the natural owners of this land, reduced to the status of beggars.

She swallowed nervously. 'O'Cleary is a notorious tyrant and is the third landlord to go missing from the region in as many months. There is blood on his hands and he will pay. Our campaign will succeed. Please report sightings, should he reappear.

'Signed on this day, the 15th of April, 1847, by Captain Rock.'

Shannon's voice trailed off. 'I...I don't understand.'

Conor exhaled. So that was their game. Let her think her ancestor was a great man, and then give her evidence to the contrary, with no warning. Despite the fact that he disliked the soprano, it was a very underhanded thing to do and Conor hated being part of it. There was nothing for it, he would have to explain. He'd just have to try to be gentle. 'English landlords and their agents operated very profitable farms here during the famine of the middle 1800s, Shannon. Thousands of tonnes of produce left these shores every day. It's not true to say that the entire country starved – they didn't. The Protestant land-owning class did very well, while the tenant farmers starved to death.' Conor tried to ignore the cameras closing in on both him and Shannon.

'Tenants had to sell what they grew, you see, to pay the rent, and all that was left to them were potatoes. That's why when the blight came on the crop, people starved. The Irish Potato Famine wasn't caused by the crop failure as such – it was caused by greedy landlords. Resistance came in many forms, but one group were called the Whiteboys and their leader was a shadowy figure called Captain Rock. The likelihood is that there were several Captain Rocks, or it was a concept rather than a person, but landlords who showed disregard for the welfare of their tenants usually were the subject of attacks under the name of Captain Rock.'

'So my ancestor was such a landlord?'

Conor was surprised to hear the vulnerability in her voice; he was so used to her barking and rudeness. 'It would seem so,' he confirmed, taking no joy in it.

'And he used the identity of someone he had killed to get to the US undetected?'

She didn't need a response. She'd worked it out for herself. Conor felt a wave of pity for her. Her entire identity was as an Irish woman, a Celtic Colleen, and it turned out her relative was an enemy of the people she claimed as her own. It was a hard blow to take.

'Wow.' She exhaled. 'I didn't expect that.'

Conor saw the tears gather unshed in her eyes. 'Shannon' – he laid his hand on hers – 'we are only responsible for ourselves, you know. This is a great country for people living the past glories of their ancestors vicariously, but that's nonsense. Nobody can take the credit for the actions of those that went before them, nor should we take the blame either.'

Shannon swallowed and nodded, self-consciously wiping a tear from the corner of her eye. 'Thank you, Conor,' she managed.

'Cut!' yelled Kayla. 'And that, folks, is a wrap!'

CHAPTER 28

Taylor listened as her father ranted on FaceTime. Apparently someone had leaked tapes to the press of her explaining to Douglas how the senator was not Irish at all and was just using his daughter to manipulate the electorate. She'd had that conversation but assumed it was private, and to her surprise, the worst hurt she felt was due to Douglas's betrayal.

He was the one who had encouraged her to be honest, to tell her story. He got it all out of her. She was so foolish that she thought it was because he cared, that he might even like her a bit, but it was just so he could get a few bucks from the gutter press. She felt sick.

They'd enjoyed many meals together and had taken a few walks around the grounds. She enjoyed his company immensely and found in him an acceptance and understanding she'd never experienced before. She'd never known any men except her father. There were the boys at college, but she never really mixed with them. She had no interest in sororities or fashion or boys, and she found herself alone a lot. It was fine – she enjoyed reading and studying – but it got a little lonely sometimes. She and Douglas talked about literature and history and things that she found fascinating. He was so learned and patient, explaining things and taking her opinion seriously. He hardly ever stammered when they spoke in private, but when he addressed the group or when Havie asked him a question, he struggled to get the words out. Her heart ached for him in such circumstances. He never came across as remotely duplicitous, but he was the only one who knew the truth; she'd told him the whole sorry tale on the plane. She'd never confided in anyone else, so it had to have been him.

Reluctantly, she tuned back into her father.

'You said I was *Slovenian*, and that it was your mother's family that's Irish! And then' – he was fuming and she heard the familiar slur in his words, so he was probably drunk now as well – 'as if that wasn't bad enough, you start talking about the state of our marriage. And claiming I'm an alcoholic to put the tin hat on it! Taylor, you have let me down so badly. I'm so ashamed of you. How could you?'

She gazed at her father's face, distorted as the internet buffered. He looked not handsome to her as he always had been but instead weak and spoiled and vain. She had spoken plainly to him the last time she was wracked with guilt, but she was wrong to apologise, she knew that now.

She'd tried to please him all her life, but it was never enough. He never once chose her over his work, or increasingly over his drinking. She was right when she said that he treated her like everything else, a commodity to be used. The realisation was depressing, but she was sure for the first time that he had no redeeming qualities. The excuses she made for him, the allowances for his behaviour – he didn't deserve them.

The screen unfroze and she waited as he continued ranting.

'What do you have to say for yourself? For God's sake, Taylor, I gave you one simple job to do and you couldn't even get that right. Incredibly, you've managed to make a bad situation even worse!' He reached for a glass, not caring if she saw the amber liquid he downed in one gulp. He wasn't even pretending any more.

Taylor felt unusually calm. The deferential, almost wheedling tone she used with him was gone. 'Daddy, like I said, you got yourself into this mess, so don't blame me. I didn't know I was being recorded, but every single thing I said was true. You were the one who cheated on your wife, you are the one addicted to alcohol, you're the one who said those things about your constituents, and you have to be the one to take the consequences. I didn't want to come here and do this – it's interrupting my studies and besides, I hate the limelight – but it never occurred to you that I would hate it because you never think about anyone but yourself.'

He didn't respond, so she went on, the frustration and hurt of years finally being vented. 'So you'll have to sort your own mess out, Daddy. And I hope you do, for your own sake, but count me out.'

She pressed the red 'end' button in the middle of the screen, feeling sad but calm. This time she meant it.

The last episode with Shannon O'Cleary had been shot and all the challenges had been done. All that was left to do was ride a horse on the beach. She could bail out of that surely, considering the circumstances? She needed to get away; the press would be there soon.

She thought about what she'd said to her father. It was true she had dreaded the prospect of coming to Ireland and participating in the programme, but now that she had, she was glad. She'd spent most of her free time researching Ned and Cecilia O'Hara, and the more she uncovered about them, the prouder she was. They led community action groups, set up soup kitchens and did all manner of public service, all in an atmosphere of fear and distrust on the part of the authorities. They were agitators and unafraid to call things out as wrong.

She had another call to make. She had to look up the number, so infrequently had she called it. She made a voice call rather than a video call; this was going to be difficult enough without being face-to-face. It was answered on the second ring.

'Taylor. Are you all right?' Her mother's clipped tones grated on her as usual.

'Yes, Mom, I'm fine. Do you have a moment to talk? There's something I need to say to you.' The rehearsed lines sounded ridiculous to her own ears now.

'Sure. One minute.'

Taylor heard her mother's muffled voice; she'd placed her hand over the phone and moved someplace else.

'OK, what's up?' her mother asked.

'Nothing. Well, Daddy just called...'

'What did he want?' Marcia's voice sounded tired.

'Nothing. Well, to yell at me actually, because I told the researcher for the show the truth and somehow it was leaked to the press – it must have been him.' Taylor could hear the hurt in her voice as she said it. 'Anyway, they have me on tape saying that it was you who had the Irish connection, not Daddy, and how he'd said some things to that woman he was with, and how you and he were not really in a good marriage, the whole thing really. I didn't know they were going to record it, but now there are reporters at the house asking him for a comment and it's going to be public knowledge by tonight. I just wanted you to know first.'

Taylor caught a glimpse of herself in the mirror of the wardrobe opposite the bed. She was actually wincing, waiting for the impact. Whatever about her father and bad publicity; her mother hated scandal.

The silence went on so long Taylor wondered if her mother had been cut off. 'Mom?' she asked. 'Are you there?'

'Yes.' There was a long pause. 'Can I FaceTime you? I need to see you.'

'Sure.'

Seconds later her phone notified her of the incoming video call. With trembling fingers, she pressed 'accept'.

Her mother's face was there on the screen, but she didn't look like herself. Taylor had never seen her mother without make-up, or without her hair blow-dried perfectly. But now her hair was wet from the shower, her face lined and tired, and she appeared to be wearing sweats.

'Mom? Are you OK?' Taylor asked.

Her mother sighed. 'Yeah, I'm fine. I'm in Virginia, at Estelle's.'

'What are you doing there?' Taylor had never heard of her mother visiting her sister before.

'I... I...' Marcia swallowed. 'I had a breakdown, Taylor. I just freaked out, I guess, dealing with it all, making such a mess of everything. I...' A large fat tear slid down her mother's face. 'I lost it in a restaurant, started screaming at people. They called the cops, and well...your father wasn't available, you were in Ireland, so Estelle was the next person.'

'Oh, Mom, I'm so sorry –'

Her mother held up her hand. 'It's OK. It was a few weeks ago. That's why I wasn't speaking to you – I was in a centre, trying to get my head around how my life turned into such a shambles. I'm doing better now.'

'Oh, I didn't know. I thought...'

'Taylor, I should apologise. This wasn't right, and it wasn't fair to you. Your father and I should have divorced years ago, and dragging you through this mess was unforgivable. I should have stopped him making you do it. I'm sorry.'

Taylor looked at her mother's face and felt deep compassion and connection, possibly for the first time ever. It had been kind of an awful childhood, lonely and fraught with the need to please two people who refused to be happy, but she didn't blame her mother.

'I failed you. I guess I thought I only had one identity and that was as Ted's wife. Everything – my business, everything – pivoted on that. But that was built on sand and I couldn't see it.' She sipped a cup of something placed in front of her by someone; Taylor assumed it was her aunt Estelle.

'We were terrible parents, Taylor. You deserved so much better. I... I know we haven't really gotten along in the past, and I guess I resented how you always went to Ted over me, but I'd like to try to rebuild it now, if you'd let me?'

Taylor saw an openness and a decency in her mother that she'd never seen before. Throughout her life, Marcia Davis was a cold beautiful statue, to be admired but never touched. For the first time, she saw her mother as a woman, a mother and a wife, struggling to be married to a chronic alcoholic, living life in the public eye and trying to maintain the veneer of impossible perfection.

Suddenly Taylor had an idea. She dismissed it quickly as her mother would never agree. But then maybe…

'Mom, I was just thinking. Maybe you don't want to or can't and that's OK, but after this show finishes, I was going to stay for a week or two and research our ancestor Ned O'Hara. He was a really fascinating guy, and I think you'll be interested to learn about him.' She paused and swallowed. 'Would you like to come over here, to Ireland, and we could find out about him together?'

Marcia stared at the screen, her face inscrutable. Then she took another sip of the drink before saying, in a voice Taylor didn't recognise, 'I'd love to, but I'm not sure I can travel right now. I just have so much to deal with.'

Taylor fought to not have the disappointment show on her face. Things were better with her mother, but she shouldn't expect miracles. Marcia had never put Taylor first – she didn't even know how to – so it would be weird for her to start now.

'That's OK. It was probably a dumb idea.'

To ease the tension, Taylor gave her mother a brief outline of Ned and Cecilia and all they achieved, and it was all news to her mother.

'My father was a very conservative man. I doubt he would have approved of people like that. Probably thought they were communists.' She smiled. 'I guess that's why Estelle and I never knew about our grandparents growing up.'

'Well, they were wonderful. I'm going to go and find the family house if I can. Who knows – we might even have relatives here.' Taylor smiled.

'That sounds like an interesting quest. And Taylor' – Marcia smiled and it was a beautiful thing, as a genuine smile was so rare from her – 'your father has problems and he's got to be the one to fix them. I won't tell you what to do, and I've got my own issues with him, but for as long as you prop him up, he'll never take responsibility. I filed for divorce. You should know that.'

Taylor nodded. 'I'm glad. I love you both, and I think you're right. Daddy needs help, and I'll help him as soon as he wants to help himself, but I can't fix him.'

'Exactly.' Marcia wiped a tear. 'I'm so proud of you, Taylor. I never told you that, but so many kids of people like us are entitled, vacuous people with no purpose beyond how they look or where they're seen. We set you up perfectly for that pointless life, but here you are, a scholar and now an international traveller. You're amazing. And I'll never regret marrying Ted because I got you.'

Taylor laughed. 'I thought I was an embarrassment to you. Everyone around you always looked so glamorous, and I couldn't be.'

'I'll be honest – there was a long time when I did wish you were different. I wanted a daughter to go to the hair salon with, or who cared about the new Balenciaga collection. But you were never that, and I was the shallow one, not you.'

It was as if a knot in her chest had finally come undone. All the years of feeling like such a disappointment, such an oddity, were melting away. Discovering Ned and Cecilia and learning about all they achieved, and now reconnecting with her mother, was so good. She'd never even thought it was something she wanted. She'd been in therapy for years to help her disconnect, to not care what her mother thought of her, because she'd given up long ago the idea of ever having a real relationship with her. But now, tentatively at least, there was hope. 'We've got some catching up to do,' she said.

'We sure do. See you when you get home.' Marcia wiped another tear, and Taylor realised she'd never once seen her mother cry before.

'Bye, Mom.' Taylor ended the video call.

As she did, the tablet buzzed with an incoming call from a number she didn't recognise. Perhaps her mother was calling back from Estelle's. She hit 'accept'.

A man she didn't recognise popped on her screen. 'Hi, Taylor. Just wondering if you have any further comment on the –'

She pressed the red 'end call' button.

Immediately her tablet buzzed again, as did her phone. Then the phone in the room. She frantically turned everything off and left her bedroom to rush downstairs. What if more press were at the hotel? She swallowed the bile that rose up in her throat.

Conor was in conversation with his wife when she ran to the desk.

'Don't let any calls go through to my room, and I'm not available if anyone –' she said, breathless.

'Woah, woah! Taylor, calm down. What's wrong?' Conor asked kindly. 'Come to my office and tell me what's up. I'm sure we can sort it out.'

Taylor followed Conor into his office and sat down, but then she realised he may have been the one who leaked the tape. It was impossible to know who to trust. She couldn't call her father or her mother; neither of them would be of any use. And Douglas was definitely in on it. For all she knew, Conor could have tipped them off to get more publicity for the hotel or the show or something.

'I'm going. Sorry, I…' She stood to leave. 'Please, just get out of my way. I need a cab.'

'Taylor,' Conor said calmly, 'I'm going to call my wife, OK? You might feel more comfortable if she was here?'

He opened the door and Ana came in. She led Taylor back to the sofa. 'What is the matter, Taylor? Please tell me. I can help.' She cast a glance at her husband, who shrugged.

Taylor searched Ana's face for signs of threat; it was impossible to know. 'The press have got a tape – someone leaked it – of me talking about my father and my mother, and now they won't stop calling and…' She struggled to stay calm.

'Do you know about this, Conor?' Ana asked.

'No idea, what tape? What are you talking about, Taylor? A tape of a conversation or something?'

'Did you leak it?' Taylor asked him straight.

'Me?' Conor was nonplussed. 'I don't even know what you're talking about…'

Katherine appeared at the door of the office and interrupted them. She took in the scene and knowingly said, 'Conor, a word please.'

'OK, just wait here.' Conor went down on his hunkers so that he and Taylor were level. 'I swear to you, I never leaked anything, nor do I know anything about a tape. But I promise you, we'll get to the bottom of it. And you are safe here.'

Ana took Taylor's hand.

'I'm going to figure out what's going on, and then I'll be back to you. I'll have some drinks sent in.'

* * *

CONOR LEFT and once out in the reception area, drew Katherine to one side. 'What the hell is going on?'

'The phones are hopping with reporters looking for a story, and I'm sure it's just a matter of time until they get here in person. I'm not sure exactly, but…'

Olga appeared, holding an iPad. She led Conor and Katherine to a spare meeting room and closed the door. She held the screen up and pressed 'play' on a video clip in which Taylor Davis was talking to Douglas Wilson on the plane. Taylor's voice filled the small room.

'I'm sure you know the story, but for the record, my father is the sitting democrat for South Boston, and being Irish and having Irish roots is very important. He married my mother – Marcia O'Hara – for her Irishness, I think. Anyway they've never been close, but they stick together because it suits them. Or at least it did until recent events.'

'Taylor…' Douglas paused. *'May I call you Taylor?'*

'Of course.' She nodded.

'I know this is difficult for you, but you don't have to go into it if you don't want to…' Douglas glanced around.

'I don't really. In fact, if there was a parachute available, I just might take my chances down there.' She sighed and nodded at the ocean below. *'But if you're doing the research, you need to know. I'm doing this to try to regain some position politically for my dad. I think it's a stupid idea, but he really wants me to try. There were taped conversations and video of him with a woman, and in the tape he's talking about how dumb his Irish constituents are, how ugly Irish women are, how Ireland and the Irish are just a bunch of morons, all sorts of horrible stuff. He didn't mean it. He's an alcoholic. He'd been sober for nine years, but he had an affair with this woman and started drinking again. A journalist got a tip, suffice to say, and the whole thing exploded. It's been horrific. My mother has effectively left him, and so she's not keen on helping him to regain anything. But she's not stupid and likes*

her life and the money, so a divorce will be more profitable if he can get back in the good books. So she told me that there was some Irish relative but that she had no idea who or when.'

'Right. This was recorded on the plane on the way over obviously?' Conor was confused. The set was completely sealed, security everywhere, so nobody but the contestants, Conor, Douglas Wilson and the small crew knew what was happening. Everyone had been briefed on the legal demand for privacy, so whoever leaked it would be in serious trouble.

'I suppose so,' Olga said.

Conor took his phone from his pocket. 'Havie, it's me. Can you meet me in the meeting room off reception, please? Right now. There's a problem.'

Katherine and Olga listened to the video clip again.

'That poor girl,' Olga said. 'This is going to blow up all over the place now.'

'Havie will go mad. There's going to be American lawyers crawling all over this.' Katherine sounded horrified at such a prospect.

Within seconds, Havie and Kayla arrived. Briefly Conor filled them in and showed them the tape. Havie remained stoic as he always did, but Conor thought he detected a hint of a smirk on Kayla's face.

Suddenly it dawned on him. 'It was you, wasn't it?' he asked, glaring at Kayla.

She shrugged, entirely without remorse. 'Don't stress, Conor, you'll get wrinkles.'

'Don't stress?' Conor exploded. 'You're drawing all the press of the world down on our heads and you're telling me not to stress? Not to mention that there is a distraught young woman in my office who is already coping with enough without adding this to it! Did you know about this?' he demanded of Havie.

Havie shrugged noncommittally. 'No, but you gotta admit, it's a good idea.'

'What?' Conor couldn't believe what he was hearing. The whole thing was so close to completion, but the final tranche of the money was yet to be paid.

Neither Havie nor Kayla seemed remotely put out by the leak. 'This show is actually good, something to be proud of,' Havie explained. 'And if you knew anything about it, which you clearly don't, you'd know that this is the best thing that could have happened to poor little Taylor Davis. She'll be loved as the kid with the nasty parents, and she's so girl next door, with her dowdy clothes and mousy look, they'll love her. She'll be doing Oprah before you know it, so don't worry about her.'

Havie smiled, but it was impossible to know if it was real or fake. He was a complete enigma. His relationship with Kayla was a mystery. He seemed to genuinely care about Fintan, and he was undoubtedly brilliant at what he did, but you could never really understand him.

'So let's get this in the can. A few more scenes to shoot with just you, and a chat between you and Douglas, and we'll wrap it up. Party tomorrow night, and Sunday we're out of your hair for good.'

'And the press that are going to turn up and harass us all?' Conor asked wearily. 'What am I meant to do about that?'

'You've got security, right?' Havie asked, as if it were the simplest thing in the world.

'Not the kind that you're talking about.'

'Well, I suggest you get some.' Havie walked out, trailed by Kayla, who was smirking like the cat that got the cream.

CHAPTER 29

*C*onor was exhausted. He lay in bed, staring at the ceiling. He figured he might as well get up; the alarm would go off in ten minutes anyway. Ana was already downstairs with Lily. Shooting the TV show had been more stressful than he could ever have imagined, and between that and Lily's nocturnal shenanigans, he wasn't sleeping well. They were both looking forward to Katherine and Jimmy babysitting.

The boys would be spoiled rotten over there of course. Pizza and fizzy drinks, normally contraband, were allowed at Katherine's.

When Conor had dropped Katherine home last week, her car was in the garage, he was so touched to see not just a brand new cot for Lily but that they'd got a new TV with a subscription service to some expensive sports package for the boys, as well as lots of Lego sets and books. They'd even set up a soft play area in their living room for Lily to roll around on. Their house had always been neat but a bit bland, Conor thought, and having all the colourful children's stuff around was an incredible transformation.

Katherine was a little embarrassed and tried to downplay it, but he told her how much her help meant to him and Ana. Though she brushed him away, he could tell she was pleased.

Jamsie had to go to London to tie up some deals – he still kept a finger in the property market there – Conor had asked him to consider moving to Clare. They'd gone for a pint together the night before he left.

At first Conor thought he'd made a mistake in asking. Jamsie was silent and his face inscrutable. Conor worried that he wanted to say no, that maybe he felt used or that they were over-relying on him for care of the boys, but when his father spoke, it was in a voice Conor barely recognised.

'I'd love nothing more than that, Conor, but I would never have done it except that you asked.' He swallowed. 'Did the boys put you up to it?'

Conor shook his head. 'No, they never said a word. Why?'

Jamsie nodded. 'They saw a house for sale beside the hurling pitch– you know, the white bungalow?'

Conor nodded. 'Yeah, old Mrs Tynan's place. She's gone into a nursing home, so her daughter Yvonne has put it on the market. What about it?'

'Well, Joe and Artie wanted me to buy it and live permanently down here. I...I got choked up, Conor, because they are such smashing little lads and they don't see me for the failure I was. They just want me around.' He paused. 'But I asked them not to say anything to you about it. I didn't want you to feel pressured. You need not have opened your door to me – God knows nobody would blame you if you gave me the high road. I know it's been complicated for you, remembering your mam and how hard life was for her because of me.'

'Look, that's all water under the bridge now –'

'No, it's not. Nor should it be. Ana and the lads, and little Lily now too, have no idea how selfish I was. I mean, they know what I did, but to actually do it, to walk out the door and leave your wife and kids with nothing, not a word, well, there's few men who are that selfish. But I was.' There was no self-pity, no looking for absolution. It was the truth as he saw it.

On another day, Conor would have brushed his father's protestations of guilt aside. He'd said he forgave him and so that was that, but he was tired and fed up with humouring people. 'Well, you're right. Even before I had my own children, it bewildered me how you did it. And you didn't just leave once. Every day you were gone, you could have come back. You could have picked up the phone, written a letter, a card, anything. So every day, for decades, you left us. Mam died alone. Did you know that? She was in the hospital, cancer everywhere, and I used to visit her every day. Gerry was only a kid, so I usually went on my own to see her after work. Towards the end, I don't know if she even knew I was there. She was in pain, you know? She had a horrific death, and in the very end, I wasn't even there. I arrived after work as normal – I was only sixteen, six years older than Joe and Artie – but they said I was too late, that she was gone.'

Jamsie said nothing, just let him talk.

'They made her pay, every day, the whispering neighbours, like somehow it was her fault that you didn't give enough of a damn about any of us to even make contact. And sometimes when I look at Lily, I think how much Mam would have loved to know her and the boys.' He fixed his father with a gaze and said what had been there inside for so long. 'She shouldn't be dead, Jamsie. She should have had a better life, an easier life, better care than I could afford. She deserved better. Gerry deserved better and so did I.'

Jamsie sat there and took it all. 'You did. And somehow, despite everything, you've turned out to be such a wonderful husband and father. You didn't learn it from me, that's for sure. I'm so proud of you, Son.'

'But it's the past. It's over, and no amount of bearing grudges or holding onto bitterness will change it. I've let it go. And you're making up for it by being a great granda to my kids. So I'll ask you again, will you move down?'

'I'd love that.'

Conor and his father finished their drinks and walked home companionably together in the cold night air.

Laoise and Dylan, and Corlene and Colm, were on their way from Dublin for the party and had promised to call in for coffee to his office at the hotel so they could have a proper chat. Once the party started in Castle Dysert, he knew it would be bedlam.

As he lay there, Conor mentally went through everything that he needed to do that day.

All of the scenes had been shot now, and Havie was happy. The final payment was lodged yesterday, and there was a huge sigh of relief all round.

Security had been arranged for the party; they'd been necessary to protect poor Taylor as well. Several TV networks and reporters had tried to get in, and one gang of them actually managed to get as far as the grounds; some local was undoubtedly paid to show them a way in by a small side road only used occasionally for deliveries. Conor knew who it was and would ensure the entire place did too. Everyone's livelihood was on the line if the hotel was in trouble, so the man would be an unpopular person in the area once word got out.

Taylor had been accosted as she was admiring the horses in the stables. The reporters with cameras had popped out of an unused stall, and she was caught unawares. They just got a bit of footage, but in her effort to get away, she tripped and fell. It was all over the news. Conor's heart went out to the poor girl. Ana and she had struck up a good relationship. Ana had provided tea and a bandage for her cut knee, and they'd had a long talk about everything. Conor felt a surge of admiration for his wife; she really was remarkable. She still volunteered on the phone for a helpline for women from former Soviet countries who found themselves in Ireland, effectively trafficked into prostitution or arranged marriages, and that ability to connect with women was useful when helping Taylor. The poor girl had been raised it seemed by two selfish people, and she had never known love.

Ana had confided to him that Taylor was so hurt when she thought Douglas Wilson had leaked the conversation, and though there was an age gap – he was in his early forties and she was only twenty-two – she had deep feelings for the professor. Conor doubted Douglas had any idea, or if he did, Conor was certain the man wouldn't have the faintest notion how to go about doing anything about it.

The wrap party was arranged, and Katherine had the genius idea of inviting all the locals. The thinking was that if they were at the party, they wouldn't need the staff and they wouldn't complain about the noise. Everyone seemed happy about the complimentary buffet, the free bar and the opportunity to rub shoulders with the celebrities, so it looked like everything was on track.

Martin Lowry had finally wound his neck in and wasn't so cranky – it seemed it had worked when Conor called his bluff – so everything in the kitchen was going fine when Conor had popped in last night. It was Martin's idea to have a buffet, as so much of it could be prepared in advance, and he was right. It felt good to be able to give local businesses big orders to supply the event.

The staff were relieved that the work rebuilding the wall was saving the hotel, and so was he. It was a miracle really. And although he was grateful for the money the show generated – the alternative was unthinkable – he would be relieved when it was all over.

His phone buzzed on the locker. He picked it up. It was Eddie.

'Hi, Conor, how's things?' The priest sounded cheerful.

'Grand out, thanks. The whole thing is over as of tonight, and I'll tell you, I won't be sorry to see the back of them.' Conor chuckled. 'But the money is in the bank, the wall is almost complete and nobody was murdered. We'll call that a win.'

'Indeed,' Eddie agreed. 'The Lord works in mysterious ways, my friend. Aren't I always telling you that?'

'You are.' Conor smiled. 'I assume you're coming tonight? The dessert platters are incredible.'

'Wild horses wouldn't stop me. But some busybody invited Martina the Hun too, so her beady eyes will be everywhere no doubt,' Eddie grumbled.

'Well, that's not very ecclesiastical now, Father,' Conor admonished him jokingly. 'She's only looking out for you.'

'I suppose so. Come here till I tell you a funny turn up for the books though.' Eddie's tone was light.

'Go on.' Conor sat up.

'Well, as you know, a certain Irish American actor is currently below in Waterford at the Dominican friary, availing of the services of

Father Miah Linehan – Curly, we always called him, though he's bald as a coot now – and he's doing very well by all accounts. Curly won't talk about any of the people who go there, but Fintan rang me and just wanted to say thanks for sorting out that mess he got himself into.'

'Well, that he might. That could have been very tricky had you not intervened.'

'Yerra, he more or less paid for the young guard's wedding. They're happy as Larry, so all's well that ends well.' Eddie paused for dramatic effect. 'But you'll never guess who has been invited to see him and who he's been texting?'

'Who?' Conor asked.

'Only Martina the Hun!' Eddie revealed. 'Now, I had my reservations – she's had enough to put up with from our gender – but she's not thick and says he's changed, so we'll see.'

'Go on! Your housekeeper and Fintan Rafferty? Well, who'd have thought it? Joe did say something ages ago, but I thought it was just the rumour mill, you know how it is. I suppose she's a fine-looking woman and a decent person too by all accounts, and he's probably had enough of Hollywood.'

'Well, he rang the other night and asked me if I thought it would be all right to invite her down – I check in with him every few days – like I was her father or something. She's the one telling me what to do, not the other way round! But he assured me he was on the road to recovery, and though he wasn't really able to commit to anything long term, he is serious about her and really likes her. She's been flapping around like a teenager, dyeing her hair and everything, so as I said, the Lord works in mysterious ways.'

'Well, it would be great for both of them if it worked out. She's not had it easy, and he's a nice man, genuine, you know. Poor devil just got dealt an awful hand. If anyone deserves a shot at happiness, it's the pair of them.' Conor was pleased to hear that there might be some happiness for Fintan after such a horrible experience.

'It might cheer her up and she might let the odd biscuit into the house too, so everyone's a winner.' Eddie chuckled.

'I doubt that, my friend. She's determined to turn you into a holy Adonis,' Conor teased.

'A holy show more like. Anyway, see you later. I just thought you'd like to hear that.'

'See you, Eddie.' Conor hung up as Ana entered the room with a sleeping Lily in her arms. He told her the news about Fintan and Martina in a whisper.

'Ah, that's so good news,' Ana said, settling their daughter into her crib, where she would now sleep by day but still not by night. 'He always looked so sad, that man. He is kind, you know, a good heart, but that must have been so bad for him. A good woman is what he needs.'

Conor admired her. She was dressed in a beautifully simple red dress that showed off her lovely figure. 'It's the making of us all,' he said.

'Correct, Mr O'Shea.' She blew him a kiss. 'So are we all set for tonight?' she asked.

'I think so. Bob is going to do a bit of a set with Laoise and Dylan. They've met already at a concert in Nashville, so they're looking forward to meeting up again. The press will love it, I'm sure, so it will be good publicity. Bob McCullough is such a nice man. I'm glad he was first to do his genealogy. He's secure in his own talent and skin. He had nothing to prove and was happy to just be.' Conor got up and walked to the shower. Ana chatted with him, settling herself on the side of the bath.

'He is. All the staff love him too, and he poses for selfies with the locals. He's got no diva in him at all, though he's the most famous of them all. Now, did you speak to Douglas yet about Taylor?'

Conor groaned. 'Ah, Ana, I don't know. He's great, but he's kind of from another planet with the tweed suits and the glasses and all of that. He's such an academic, I'm not sure matters of the heart even enter his radar. And anyway, he's a bit old for her, don't you think?'

Ana shrugged. 'She loves him. Besides, you're old and I love you.' She threw a towel at him and he laughed. 'Anyway, of course he likes her – they had lots of meals and walks and all of that. He just needs a little nudge.'

'But why me?' Conor protested. 'I'm not a flippin' matchmaker. If you're so keen on this romance, why don't you speak to him?'

'Because he is afraid of women, and he stammers every time I ask him anything. He is more relaxed with you, and you're a man and he's a man, and you'll be fine. Just do it.'

'I love it when you get all Soviet, issuing orders.' He grinned and turned on the water.

'OK.' She ticked each thing off on her fingers. 'So food, OK, music, OK, the ballroom is being staged today, a company are doing it in an Irish American theme, whatever that is. Anyway, Kayla is in charge of that.' Ana rolled her eyes at the mention of the other woman. 'The contestants are going to do a piece to camera alone, tonight, just reflecting on the whole thing, and they've all but one said they are going to say great things about the hotel. Taylor loves us, and Bob says he'd stay forever and will definitely be bringing his wife back to visit. The Farrells are going to have to tear Ryan away from our two – they've been glued together for weeks. For some reason, they spend hours down in my father's shed. No idea what they're doing, but he says they're fine. Anyway, Ryan is such a happy boy now, it's lovely to see.'

'What about Fintan's bit?' Conor asked, rinsing his hair and turning off the shower.

'Havie is going to see him today before he flies out, and if he wants to, he'll shoot him then or else he said he can do it when they're back in the States. Though from what Eddie said, maybe Fintan will be sticking around for some time now, eh?' Ana handed him a towel, and they continued chatting as he shaved.

'Could be. So many people used to say that to me over the years, that there was something else here in Ireland. You know, not just the scenery and the music and food and all of that, but there's something deeper here, a kind of soothing for the soul. I think it's true, maybe because the land is so old and has seen so much – it's wise or something.'

'I think so too,' Ana agreed. 'Sometimes when the cancer treatment was hard and I was worried about the future, I walk by the sea and I understand. It is a peaceful place, all of this land. This cliffs and ocean and fields have been here for so long, so many people, so many life-times, and it makes you realise your problems are small.'

'You're amazing, you know that?' Conor wiped his face and took her hand, leading her to their bed and wrapping his arms around her.

'Yes, I am.' She kissed his nose but pushed him back playfully. 'And maybe later you can tell me how much I am wonderful, but for now, Mr Big Shot, let's get going. They need us up at the castle. Olga and Carlos are all sorted with everything, but Katherine looks like that thing you say – a bull chewing a spider?'

Conor chuckled. 'A bulldog chewing a wasp.'

'Yes, this.' Ana grinned. 'There is going to be the wrap party in the castle, which will be very nice, all the important people, politicians and all of this, but there are plans for the real party back at the staff quarters after.'

'Best I know nothing about it,' Conor said wryly.

'Exactly. But Katherine is making herself crazy thinking about what will happen.' Ana giggled.

'Look, that's not our business. Just making sure Havie and that Kayla and all the celebs are happy and leaving is all I care about now.' Conor dressed in a charcoal suit with an ivory linen shirt and his favourite aquamarine tie. 'Shelby is fine too, isn't she? I thought discovering her ancestors were all criminals of one kind or another would have been a blow, but she's loving it.' He laughed. 'Kayla is talking about a miniseries of her family, and she and Havie are going to do a new makeover show where the history of a person's life and family are reflected in the décor. She explained it to me. Like they take a couple where he's of Mexican descent and she's of German heritage and they fuse those two styles and then take items from their families or whatever to create this really unique house, or "space", as she calls it. It's actually not a bad idea.'

'Imagine if we did that here.' Ana sighed. 'Ireland and Ukraine, with a million toys and a dog and hurleys and footballs and baby stuff everywhere. It's not exactly a style, is it? I see those houses, you know, on TV, everything so neat and tidy, and I wonder how do they do it?'

Conor turned to her and placed his hands on her shoulders. 'They spend all day tidying, and their kids are terrified to play. Our "space" is chaotic and mad and noisy, and I absolutely love it. We don't need to answer to anyone, Ana. This is our home.'

She smiled. 'OK. We don't have time to tidy now anyway. I often think, though, if anyone saw how we look so perfect in the hotel, and the place doesn't have one speck of the dust, they would not recognise us here.'

'And that's a good thing,' he replied as she fastened his cufflinks.

'OK, so the only fly in the custard is Shannon,' Ana mused, and she caught Conor's smile. 'What?' she asked.

'Nothing.' He tied his tie, suppressing a grin.

'What did I say? Always you have this smile when I say the wrong thing.'

'Tell me!' she demanded. 'Otherwise I say it to other people and they laugh at me.'

'OK, it's a fly in the ointment, not custard.' Conor chuckled.

'What is ointment?' she asked, bewildered.

'It's an old word for cream, like medical cream for your skin or something. It used to be called ointment years ago.'

'Ah, yes, I think like cream you put on dessert, and then I mixed it up with custard. Stupid language, this English. You know that, don't you?'

'I do, darling, incredibly stupid,' he agreed as he tied his shoelaces. 'Anyway, talk to me about Shannon. I've been ducking her.'

'I know,' Ana replied darkly as they went downstairs. 'She's been quiet. She forgot about calling the police about that dog. But she does think the groomer did take it. Maybe she's right. She wants it back now because she's afraid the woman will go to the press or something.'

Conor handed her a cup of coffee. 'Is Danika bringing the kids back here or keeping them at your parents' place today?'

'The twins wanted to go to my father, so they are at my parents' house. Ryan is going too – they are doing some jobs or something – and we have a babysitter for the micro-queen. Mama said just to call her when it is time to bring them to the party, and she will have them ready.' Ana sipped the coffee. 'This is not decaf!' she exclaimed. He'd accidentally used the secret stash of proper coffee Joe had revealed to him.

'I'll go back on it once this is over, I promise.' He held his hands up.

'Between you and the coffee, and Eddie and the cakes,' she said, exasperated, 'it's like you want to be dead.'

'I'll go back on the decaf, I promise, love, just not today, OK?' he begged.

'Fine.' She sighed. 'OK, so Shannon, she is still fuming. And she's got her lawyers all over Havie because she is saying that the show set her up and it would ruin her reputation if it got out that her ancestor was a horrible man.'

Conor shrugged. 'It was an ambush, she's right, and I feel bad for my part in it, but I didn't know. And from what I've seen of Havie's lawyers in the contract negotiations, she'll have her work cut out getting him to retract that episode. It's reality TV gold, so he's going to milk it for all it's worth.'

'Well, I will be glad for her to go. They can fight about it in America.'

'You and me both. Between her and that Kayla, I don't know how some people become so impossible.'

Ana drained her coffee just as her friend Valentina arrived to babysit. Ana quickly ran through all of Lily's needs in rapid Russian and then turned to Conor. 'Let's go.'

'*Dasvidaniya*, Valentina,' Conor said, kissing Lily's head. '*Spasiba*.'

Valentina waved Lily's hand. '*Dasvidaniya*, Papa.'

Ana grabbed his keys and they went out to the car.

CHAPTER 30

'When this is all over, let's go on holidays,' Conor suggested as they pulled in to the driveway of Castle Dysert.

'Well, the last holiday we took, I came home pregnant, so maybe we need to think about that.' Ana grinned.

'The result of that carry on is in our bed every night and never sleeps, so I think she's the best contraceptive known to mankind,' Conor replied.

As they got out of the car, Ana's phone rang. She answered and spoke in rapid Ukrainian. Conor had learned a rudimentary amount of his wife's language and could communicate with his mother-in-law, who found English too bewildering and had decided at her age she was too old to learn. It was definitely Danika on the line.

'All OK?' Conor mouthed.

Ana nodded and then gestured to Douglas, who was sitting having a coffee outside the castle, admiring the architecture and grounds as was his habit. She put her hand over the receiver. 'Go and talk to him, Conor,' she commanded.

Conor wasn't inclined, but Ana seemed adamant it was a good

idea. He raised his hands in submission and crossed the car park to where the professor sat.

'Morning, Douglas,' he said cheerfully.

'Good morning, Conor.' Douglas looked like he had the weight of the world on his shoulders.

Conor decided to cut to the chase. Everyone had seen the clips on TV of Taylor. 'Taylor thinks it was you who leaked the story.' Conor didn't care if he was unprofessional any more; they had their wall.

'I know.' Douglas sighed. 'But it wasn't me, and Taylor hasn't spoken to me since it all blew up.'

He might have a brain the size of a planet, Conor thought, but his interpersonal skills were abysmal. He was like someone who existed only in the dusty halls of a university library and had no clue about real life. The kind of person who could write a book on the bloodlines of the Hanoverian royal family – he'd actually done that, much to Conor's amazement – but if he had to buy a pint of milk, he would be absolutely stumped. Conor wasn't at all sure he was a good match for Taylor, or anyone actually, but Ana had insisted.

'Did you try to tell her it wasn't you?' he asked, knowing the answer.

'No. She wouldn't believe me, and anyway, it's too late now. It's out there, and the poor girl has been dragged through the media.'

'Why is it too late?' Conor asked, exasperated.

'Well, because it's the last day. We all leave tomorrow, and I wouldn't see her again anyway,' Douglas replied miserably.

'Douglas,' Conor said, feeling like he was prying, 'are you happy with that, or would you like to see Taylor again?'

The other man sighed. 'I...I've never... um... Well, I... Look, girls, women, all of that, always seemed...well, a bit of a mystery actually, and I...I don't think...'

For a very articulate, erudite man, he really was making a dog's dinner of this.

'OK, listen to me.' Conor felt like a schoolteacher, but he went on. 'Taylor is very upset because she thinks you were the one who leaked the story, and according to my wife, she likes you, very much, so it's particularly hurtful. If you have feelings for her, Douglas, then you need to convince her it wasn't you. And you need to make a move. Tell her you'd like to see her when you get back to the US, tell her you like her too and would like to have a relationship, if it's what you want.'

Douglas looked nothing short of horrified at such a prospect. 'I couldn't, I mean...it would be too... No, I couldn't...'

'You can,' Conor said gently, 'and you should. You and she get along and you seem to get each other in ways that maybe others don't, so you should definitely say something.'

'Screw my courage to the sticking place and I'll not fail?' Douglas smiled ruefully. 'It's from *Macbeth*.'

Conor nodded. 'I know.'

* * *

THE HOTEL WAS a hive of activity. The electrical wires and lights that were everywhere had been removed, and it was returned to its former glory. Conor was delighted to see it. He made for his office, passing Katherine, who was supervising the removal of the residual glue of the electrical tape from the floor. The poor lad doing the scrubbing looked like he was headed to the gallows.

A taxi pulled up and a woman got out. The castle was not open for guests yet, but Conor figured she might have been someone to do with Acorn Productions. He ducked into his office; Katherine could deal with her.

He'd call them all in in a bit – Carlos, Olga, Katherine, Ana and Artur – to update them on progress with the work.

'Yes, of course we can do that.' He could hear Katherine talking to the lone female guest.

He opened his email and read a message from the insurance company. They'd come out to inspect the work done and were satisfied everything was fine and would be happy to insure the castle for the coming year. It was a huge relief, and though Gerrity had been hopeful the flood measures would pass their inspection, one could never be sure.

He looked up when there was a knock on the door and called, 'Come in.'

His heart sank; it was Kayla. 'What can I do for you, Kayla?' Things were frosty between them, to say the least.

She was carrying a wooden box, and he recognised the stampings of Midleton Very Rare whiskey. At around 200 Euro a bottle, it was a very rare indulgence of his, but he did enjoy an odd glass on special occasions. His father had bought him a bottle for Christmas and it was halfway gone, the joke being it would take him a year to drink it. He'd mentioned it to Havie one day in a general conversation about whiskey as he'd explained the difference between Irish whiskey, scotch and bourbon. Irish whiskey was distilled three times over wood chips, whereas scotch was distilled twice over peat, giving it that smoky flavour, and American bourbon was distilled just once. The process accounted for the smoothness of Irish whiskey, and in his humble opinion, its superiority.

'This is for you.' Kayla handed him the box, and as she did, he noticed she seemed different. She was dressed in jeans and a black t-shirt, and while she still had the fright mask make-up, she looked less threatening somehow in normal clothes.

'Er...thanks.' He took the proffered box, unsure of what was going on.

'I just wanted to say thanks, and that I'm sorry for bugging you. It was deliberate.' She shrugged.

'What do you mean?'

Kayla smiled, and not her cat-like smirk, but an actual genuine smile. 'Well, it's kinda what I do. I googled you before we came and you seemed like a nice guy, but a bit...I dunno, wholesome. I needed to rile you up a bit to see some other side of you, not just the unflappable Irish dude that everyone loves. So I wound you up on purpose, pressed your buttons.' She smiled. 'Believe me, you'll come out as much more attractive in the show because there's that broody temper under the sunny smile. You seem too good to be true, Conor. Most people wear a mask, and I needed to get behind yours – that's what reality TV is all about, a kind of voyeurism, if you like. But I didn't think you were really that squeaky-clean guy, that genuinely kind and caring kind of person, so I needed to rattle your cage to see what came up.'

'So all of that was just to wind me up?' Conor struggled to get his head around it.

She shrugged. 'Sure. You're a one-woman guy, anyone could see that, so a combination of flirting with you and ignoring your wife was surely going to get you mad, and it did. I do that. It's kinda the secret of our success, and that's why Havie lets me. He knows it works and that there's nothing to worry about. I figure out people's spot, y'know? The thing they want to conceal, or the thing they care most about, and work on that.'

Conor had to smile; she'd played him like a fiddle. 'And the perfume? You don't seriously wear that on purpose, do you? It absolutely stinks.'

'Oh, I do. It drives Havie wild.' She winked. 'So this is from me to you. No hard feelings?'

'Join me.' He offered her a seat and took two glasses from his sideboard. He opened the lovely bottle and poured them each a glass. Picking up his phone, he got through to Katherine. 'Hold my calls, please, and give me a few minutes.'

'Thanks.' She sat down on the sofa opposite him and took the glass. She didn't try to touch his hand, and even her body language wasn't the predatory thing he was used to.

'And that works, annoying people?' he asked, intrigued. He was fairly emotionally intelligent – years of driving tours and meeting all sorts of people from all over the world had made him so – but he had never been manipulated so successfully before.

'Well, it's more than annoying people, a bit more subtle, I like to think. It's finding their thing, as I said. It's not necessarily the same for everyone. Some people do a great job of showing us the whole person without even realising it, but my job is to get them to open up, show us the bits they don't want to share. Shannon is a self-centred narcissist, so she's simple. Bob is plain and open – there's nothing lurking there. He's what you see is what you get, so no point in looking for what's not there. Shelby is all about the look, the appearance. Her whole life is a performance, so I'd make sure her make-up and clothes were almost right but not exactly what she wanted, have her a little on edge. Taylor is too sweet, the girl next door. Nobody's that nice, so getting that footage of her telling the truth about her old man was gold. I know you think it's immoral, but it isn't, not really.' She sipped the amber liquid. 'Mmm, that's so good.'

'And Ryan and Fintan?' he asked, fascinated.

'Well, Ryan's just a kid, but the mom there was a bit of a weapon. That was an unexpected feel-good thing actually, your kids befriending him, the mom realising he might be a movie star but he's just a little boy too. That's gonna be a huge hit, and she's given us some great footage admitting that.' Kayla looked at him. 'This show is not going to look how you think it will look, but it will be great, I promise you. Havie is a genius. Trust him. As for Fintan, they go back a long way, so he'll be very gentle with him. We all will. He's got good friends, Conor.'

It seemed like it was important to her that he knew that. He nodded, sipped the warming whiskey and exhaled deeply. 'Rarely, if ever, in my life have I had such a visceral reaction to anyone. It surprised even me how much you got under my skin.' He held her eye. 'Not in a good way.'

'Mission accomplished.' She winked. 'Look, don't get me wrong, you're a good-looking old guy, but not my type. It was just business – I wouldn't have ever done anything. Besides, if I did make a move, your wife would probably make sure nobody ever found my body.'

Conor laughed out loud. 'You're not wrong there.'

Kayla drained her whiskey and handed him the glass. He finished his and placed both glasses on the desk.

She extended her hand. 'You told me you'd rather shake hands than hug – more professional.'

He took her hand and shook it, then planted a kiss on her cheek. 'You're a pain in the ass, but OK, no hard feelings.' He paused. 'But for us to be totally square, I need you to do something for me.'

'If I can.' She shrugged.

He explained the Taylor and Douglas situation. 'Can you fix that?' he asked.

'I can try.'

He saw her out and asked Katherine to gather everyone, then went to the bar and quietly asked Harry to arrange a bottle of champagne and six glasses to be sent to his office. This was a red-letter day.

They were all there when he returned.

'OK, everyone, today is a big day for us. The wrap party is all arranged, the TV crew and the celebrities are out of here in the morning, and we are back to normal.'

There were a few housekeeping issues regarding parking and access with the new security measures, as well as some issue with the electric for the sound system in the ballroom, but he was assured all was under control.

Conor looked towards the door where Harry was coming in with a bottle of Moët and six flutes. He let the barman place everything on the desk and let himself out before speaking again. 'So I have some news.'

Ana looked at him quizzically, and he winked at her.

He paused, and Katherine snapped, 'Well, get on with it. We have a lot to do today.'

'It's called a dramatic pause.' He smiled. 'Castle Dysert has just been awarded a certificate of compliance with every single one of the terms and conditions of the insurance. They did the inspection the other day, and they are happy for us to go ahead, business as usual. We did it, lads!'

The room exploded in a hub of excited chatter. Artur looked pleased as punch and hugged Ana tightly. Two bright-pink spots of pleasure appeared on Katherine's cheeks as Conor poured her a glass of champagne.

To everyone's astonishment, Carlos lost his perpetual aloof professional veneer and yelled with delight, catching Olga up in a hug and spinning her around.

Ana stood beside Conor, her arm around his waist.

'Did you know?' her father asked her.

'No idea,' she said. 'A dark donkey, this husband of mine.' She saw them all suppress a smile. 'I know it's a horse, I know, OK? And I know you all laugh at me too! It's not fly in the custard!' She giggled.

The rest of the day was a blur. The preparations for the big party were underway and everyone was rushing about. Conor did his usual tour of the hotel, calling to the kitchens first where a young waitress was crying in the corner, Chef beside her. Conor needed Martin acting up again today like a hole in the head, so he went in prepared to have it out with him and threaten to fire him on the spot. Martin had recently bought a new car, so Conor was banking on him not being able to afford to be out of work with no notice.

'What's going on?' Conor demanded. 'Is everything all right, Riona?' He'd read her name badge; he didn't know her.

'Oh, yes, I'm sorry, Mr O'Shea,' she began.

'Conor, everyone just calls me Conor. What's up?' He cast a glance at Martin.

'Oh, I'm fine. I just got a call from my mam to say my dog was knocked down. They had to put him down and I was upset, and Chef was just telling me to take a break. He made me a hot chocolate.' She pointed to the frothy drink covered in marshmallows.

Conor realised he'd got it wrong. 'Ah, you poor thing. I'm really sorry about your dog – that's an awful thing to happen. We have a dog, and if anything happened to him, the whole family would be devastated, so I know how you feel.' Conor put his hand on her shoulder. 'Now, Chef is right. Off you go, take a break, and if you need to go home, then that's all right. We'll manage, OK?'

She wiped her face with her sleeve. She was only seventeen, he guessed, doing a bit of summer work. 'Thanks, Conor, and thanks, Chef.' She took her drink and went in the direction of the staff room.

'Nice work, Martin,' Conor said. 'I appreciate you looking out for her.'

'Can't have them crying into my carefully executed dishes,' Martin replied.

Chef turned back to his kitchen, but Conor saw a hint of a smile. There was a bit of good in even the grumpiest of people.

CHAPTER 31

$\mathcal{T}$aylor pressed 'refresh' for the thousandth time. She watched herself tumble in front of reporters, cutting her leg like a child. They could see her underwear as they continued filming and shouting questions even as she was lying in an undignified heap on the stones. She was mortified.

She should stop looking at it, she knew. It was done now. It had been aired as part of the story of her calling out her father for what he was. The whole thing was a nightmare, and she'd never felt so alone. Ana O'Shea, Conor's wife, was really nice, but now Taylor regretted confiding in her about her feelings for Douglas Wilson. What if Ana said something to him? She'd said she wouldn't, but oh, the idea of him realising she had a stupid schoolgirl crush on him was just horrific. He would never see her like that – of course not. He was a tenured professor and she was an undergraduate. It was yet another chapter in the embarrassment that was her life.

He'd tried to waylay her on her way upstairs this morning, but Douglas seemed not to know what to say, mumbling and stuttering. He was awkward and kind of cold, and she burned with shame and needed to get away.

She tried to read her book, *Susan B Anthony: A Biography of a*

Singular Feminist, but she couldn't focus on the text. The words swam before her eyes.

There was a knock on her door. Conor had assured her that the hotel was safe for her, that no reporters could get in, but they had, so she sat on the bed, frozen. What if it was more of them, and they'd managed to get in again somehow?

Then she heard a woman's voice calling her name. It was muffled through the door, and she remained where she was. If it was house-keeping, they could come back another time; she didn't need anything.

Then her phone rang. It was her mother.

'Hi, Mom,' she said.

'I'm outside your door. Are you going to let me in?'

Taylor ran to the door and there, incredibly, was her mother.

'What? I thought you said you couldn't come!'

Marcia just stood there. 'May I come in?' she asked.

'Of course.' Taylor stood aside and allowed her mother to enter.

Marcia looked better than she had the last time Taylor FaceTimed with her, but she looked nothing like her usual self. She wore blue jeans and a tailored jacket, with a round-necked t-shirt underneath. On her feet were sneakers. Her hair was longer than Taylor remembered it, and less perfect, and her face only had a light covering of make-up. She looked older, but somehow it was comforting.

'Estelle and I watched the news, and I saw how they hounded you and made you fall...' Marcia's voice was choked. 'And I realised I need to be here with you, to protect you. I should have done it before now, and for that, I'm sorry, Taylor. I saw you and your father as a unit that I could never break into, so I stopped trying. To be honest, I wanted to get away from him, and you were part of that package. But that was so wrong of me, and I'm so sorry.'

'It's OK,' Taylor said. 'I'm OK.'

'I know you are, sweetheart, because you have more courage and integrity in your little finger than I or your father do in our whole bodies. But I'm going to be better, be a proper mother to you...if you'll let me?'

Tears that had gone unshed on her birthdays when nobody got her a cake, during the school concerts where two empty seats were so obvious in a hall of people proudly waving cameras to catch their darling's big moment, when taking the graduation picture of her and the school principal when everyone else had a family photo found their way down her cheeks.

'Oh, Taylor, I'm sorry.' Marcia stepped forward tentatively, not sure if her daughter could forgive her. 'I've been so hopeless. I'll try to make it up to you, I promise. I'll spend my life doing it.'

'Well, coming here is a start.' Taylor smiled.

* * *

ANA DRAGGED Conor onto the dance floor as their sons made dramatic gestures like they were going to be sick. She playfully put her hands on his bum, causing them to shout in horror.

Laoise and Dylan had the entire place under their spell and had been joined for several songs by Bob McCullough, much to everyone's delight.

Conor and Ana passed Havie and Kayla on the dance floor, and Kayla laid her head on Havie's chest as he gently guided her around the floor. It was the first time Conor had seen any affection between them, and it made him wonder about people who could compartmentalise their lives so distinctly.

'She's sorry.' Havie winked as they danced past.

'Sorry about what?' Ana asked.

'Oh, I'll tell you later. She's not what she seems and I was being played, but it's all fine now.' Conor kissed her. Out of the corner of his eye, he spotted the twins sneaking out, Ryan behind them.

'I'm just going to check on the boys, OK?' He released her as her father and mother waltzed beautifully by. When Conor and Ana got married, to everyone's astonishment except Ana's, they'd danced a series of ballroom dances together and were amazing. Now, on any special occasion, people stood back when Artur and Danika took the floor.

'Sure.' Ana went to the bar to get a drink and spotted Taylor alone. 'How are you doing, Taylor?' she asked.

'Oh, hi, Ana. I'm OK.' Taylor smiled, and Ana noticed she looked happy for the first time in ages. 'My mom turned up today. She's just gone to the ladies' room. I had no idea, but she saw me on TV and realised I needed some help. Having the entire country see your underwear is a low point for anyone.' She gave a rueful chuckle.

Ana put her hand on Taylor's shoulder. 'If anybody is a decent person, they felt bad when they saw that. It was mean and horrible and you shouldn't let it bother you – you're better than that.'

Ana registered a change on Taylor's face, and as her eyes followed to where the young woman was watching, she could see why. Kayla was taking a very reluctant and frankly terrified Douglas Wilson onto the dance floor. Normal women alarmed him, so Kayla was a whole other level of terror. He was too polite to refuse so tried to shuffle around after her, looking like he would rather die than be there. Once they got to where Taylor stood, Kayla stopped abruptly, grabbing Taylor's hand and not releasing Douglas's.

'OK, you two. I did a bad thing and I'm sorry...well, kind of sorry...oh, not really, if I'm to be truthful, but that's TV for you. It was me. I recorded you two on the plane and leaked it to the press. But I'm going to say this – I think you two might thank me someday. You clearly like each other and neither one of you can get up the guts to do anything about it. So how about you guys have a dance and finally admit you have the hots for each other, huh?'

Taylor flushed bright red and tried to pull away from Kayla, but she wasn't letting go.

'OK, so it's going to take a bit more. This is a bit grade school for me, but I can see we need to take some drastic measures here. So boys first – that's how it was long ago, right, Professor?'

Douglas looked mortified but stood his ground.

'Professor Douglas Wilson, do you like Taylor? Would you like to take her on a date?'

Douglas swallowed. 'Well, I...' was all he managed in a strangled voice.

'It's a yes or no, Prof. Do you like her, as in girlfriend like her, or not?'

Ana felt terrible for the poor man, but while Kayla's tactic was brutal, maybe it was what was needed. She smiled and nodded encouragingly.

'I'd very much like that.' He exhaled.

Taylor's face registered shock initially, but then she beamed.

'OK, so, Taylor, how about you? You want to date this guy, see where it goes?'

'I'd love to,' she said quietly.

'OK.' Kayla chuckled. 'Let's play ball.' She placed Taylor's hand in Douglas's and gently pushed them away so that they moved onto the dance floor. Douglas put his arm around Taylor, and she smiled up at him.

'I think that might actually work. Crazy what does, eh?' Kayla said to Ana, then took a long gulp from a beer bottle.

'I suppose so,' Ana replied, still not a fan of Havie's pushy girlfriend.

'Ana, look,' Kayla said, 'I apologised to Conor and I wanted to say sorry to you too. He'll explain what I was doing, I'm sure. You know this anyway, but ten supermodels could lie naked in front of him and he'd only have eyes for you.'

'I know,' Ana said with certainty. 'And what about you and Havie? What does he think about how you go on?'

Kayla drained her bottle and placed it on the ledge beside Ana. 'Havie gets me. We're as solid as you guys. The rest of it is just a game.'

Kayla sauntered off, and Ana watched as Douglas Wilson nervously and self-consciously dipped his head and kissed Taylor Davis.

She went in search of Conor and found Shannon O'Cleary in the lobby, surrounded by her belongings, a taxi at the door.

'Are you leaving us, Miss O'Cleary?' Ana asked.

'Not a moment too soon,' Shannon said haughtily. 'This place, this entire operation, including that trashy television show, is a fraud. You purport to be one thing, a luxury castle, and that production was supposed to be tastefully done. You have no idea whatsoever about how to treat people of my –'

The taxi driver beeped his horn and called out the window, 'I've another fare, so if you're coming, let's be having you.'

'Urgh. The sooner I get out of this horrid little country, the better. It really is such a backwards, depressing place, populated by incompetent imbeciles.' Shannon dragged her bags down the steps, as no porter seemed to be available. Fuming, she threw her luggage in the boot of the taxi; the driver had not deigned to help. As the car pulled away, Ana heard a sound at her shoulder. Kayla had filmed the entire exchange from behind the suit of armour.

'That should make a nice piece to finish her episode. Her Irish audiences will love her even more now, right?' Kayla laughed and popped her phone in her pocket. 'See you, Ana!' And Kayla was gone.

Ana sighed. The vast majority of the people who came loved the hotel, loved Ireland and had a wonderful holiday, so one cranky old singer wasn't going to hurt them.

She had just returned to the ballroom when two dogs came bounding onto the dance floor, scattering dancers, with three small boys behind them, looking stricken.

Lionel, the twins' huge white Samoyed, bounded up to Ana and jumped up on her, putting his muddy paws all over her dress. Behind him stood a tiny scruffy dog, with matted fur and a yappy bark, delighted with all of the excitement.

Joe, Artie and Ryan tried to rescue the situation. The twins managed to grab Lionel's collar and they pulled him off their mother, while Ryan picked up the little dog that was barking its head off now.

Carlos was first on the scene and managed to quietly and quickly escort boys and dogs off the dance floor and out into the lobby, followed by Conor, Ana and Julie and Joel Farrell.

'Someone better have a very good explanation why there were two dogs in the ballroom,' Conor said sternly as Carlos tactfully withdrew.

Artie looked at Joe, always the braver twin. Ryan looked like a rabbit in the headlights.

'Ryan, what's going on here?' Joel asked.

Joe burst out, 'This is Lionel, our dog, and that's Dobby. We found him – he's a stray. We knew you all were so busy with the hotel and the television and everything, we decided to mind him.' He stopped and Artie took it up.

'He's been in *Didus's* shed behind the castle, and Ryan was taking care of Dobby 'cause he was here all the time, but we thought it wasn't fair that we got to go to a party and poor old Lionel and Dobby didn't.' He stopped and Joe resumed exactly where he left off without even a breath.

'So we put Lionel in *Didus's* jeep where he couldn't see him and brought him up here only for the evening, and we were going to just let them play in the shed for a while together, just as a treat.'

Both twins chorused, ''Cause they're best mates!'

Then Artie continued. 'But when we went to check on them, we accidentally left the door open, and Lionel smelled the food, you know what he's like, so he just took off and then Dobby followed him.'

Ryan waited for the twins to finish before adding miserably, 'It was my fault. I left the shed door open.'

All eyes went to Conor.

'And that little dog was a stray, was he?' Conor asked Ryan.

The boy couldn't speak but nodded.

'Nothing to do with a small dog called Princess Bellachic that went missing?' Conor asked his two sons, who both flushed red. Neither of them was capable of telling their father a direct lie.

'That horrible woman was going to kill her and she didn't do anything wrong,' Joe muttered.

Ryan had tears in his eyes now, and his father put his hand on his shoulder.

'OK, well, we'll have to tell Miss O'Cleary about this,' Joel said gently. 'This is her dog.'

'But she'll kill Dobby, Dad, and she's my pet now! I love her! Joe and Artie said she could be mine 'cause they already have Lionel.'

Joel bent down in front of his son and took the tiny dog from his arms. 'Maybe we can talk to her and see, but I don't want to make any promises. She's called the police and everything, remember?'

Artur and Danika appeared and everyone turned. Artur rarely spoke in groups of people, but he said, 'I think it is all right because she is gone and maybe this dog is a stray? I think I see a dog just like this around the place weeks and weeks ago. Yes, very like this one.'

Danika nodded enthusiastically. 'Yes. This dog, long time.'

The twins shot their grandparents an adoring glance.

'Papa is right. She's gone to the airport, took her bags and everything. She left ten minutes ago.' Ana put her arms around her sons. 'And it could be a stray?'

'So?' Conor asked the Farrells.

'Please, Mom, I swear I'll still do my lines and everything, but I'll have to leave Joe and Artie, and if I had to leave Dobby too, I…' His voice was muffled in a sob.

Julie and Joel exchanged a look, then Julie leaned down so she was eye level with her son. 'I guess we need to get a passport for Dobby the stray then, don't we?'

'I can keep her?' Ryan asked, incredulous.

'You can.' Julie wiped a tear from his cheek. 'And guess what?'

'What?' Ryan asked, as his father handed Dobby to him. He cuddled the tiny dog, who was happy to be in her master's loving arms again.

'It takes some time to get a dog's paperwork in order, so I guess we have to stay for a little vacation here once the crew leave, if that's OK?' Julie looked at Conor.

'Of course it's OK.' He nodded.

Joe and Artie cheered at this news and high-fived Ryan. Things were working out better than they could ever have imagined.

'OK, I think we have this sorted,' Conor said with a sigh. 'Dobby the stray is a new member of the Farrell family. And I think I'd better take my wife and the rest of the madhouse home since her dress is covered in mud.' He made a face at the boys, who grinned guiltily. 'You two stay and enjoy the party,' he said to Artur and Danika. 'And tell Carlos and Olga we've gone. We'll see everyone tomorrow.'

The boys both held Lionel's collar as they led him out of the lobby towards Conor's car.

'Let's get you home and out of that dress,' Conor murmured to his wife as he opened the car door for her, but the boys overheard him.

'Urgh, Dad, you two are *so* gross,' they chorused.

Conor and Ana laughed as they drove down the floodlit, tree-lined avenue of their castle, the wild Atlantic pounding the now sturdy sea wall.

* * *

THE END

I VERY MUCH hope that you enjoyed this book, if so, you might consider writing a review on Amazon here mybook.to/KaylasTrick.

If you would like to avail of a free download of one of my full length novels, please go to my website: www.jeangrainger.com and join my readers club. It is 100% free and always will be. I keep in touch with my readers through that, and let them know about new releases, special offers and even the odd freebie!

ABOUT THE AUTHOR

Jean Grainger is a USA Today bestselling Irish novelist living in a stone cottage in rural County Cork, Ireland. She writes a combination of contemporary and historical Irish fiction. She lives with her very nice and patient husband, and the youngest two of their four children. The older two come home occasionally to raid the fridge and moan about the cost of living now that they are paying for the toothpaste themselves! She also has two very cute but utterly clueless dogs called Scrappy and Scoobi.

f

ALSO BY JEAN GRAINGER

To get a free novel and to join my readers club (100% free and always will be)

Go to www.jeangrainger.com

The Tour Series

The Tour

Safe at the Edge of the World

The Story of Grenville King

The Homecoming of Bubbles O'Leary

Finding Billie Romano

Kayla's Trick

The Carmel Sheehan Story

Letters of Freedom

The Future's Not Ours To See

What Will Be

The Robinswood Story

What Once Was True

Return To Robinswood

Trials and Tribulations

The Star and the Shamrock Series

The Star and the Shamrock

The Emerald Horizon

The Hard Way Home

The World Starts Anew

The Queenstown Series

Last Port of Call

The West's Awake

The Harp and the Rose

Roaring Liberty

Standalone Books

So Much Owed

Shadow of a Century

Under Heaven's Shining Stars

Catriona's War

Sisters of the Southern Cross

Made in United States
North Haven, CT
03 May 2022

18828782R00155